TEARS FROM THE SUN

A Cretan Journey

JANE SHARP

authorHOUSE

AuthorHouse™ UK Ltd.
500 Avebury Boulevard
Central Milton Keynes, MK9 2BE
www.authorhouse.co.uk
Phone: 08001974150

This book is a work of fiction. People, places, events, and situations are the product of the author's imagination. Any resemblance to actual persons, living or dead, or historical events, is purely coincidental.

© 2010 Jane Sharp. All rights reserved.

No part of this book may be reproduced, stored in a retrieval system, or transmitted by any means without the written permission of the author.

First published by AuthorHouse 4/19/2010

ISBN: 978-1-4490-7397-8 (sc)

This book is printed on acid-free paper.

Acknowledgements

I would like to thank David, my wonderful husband, for his never ending support, Mrs. Isabel Warren, my college lecturer in English, for encouraging me to keep writing, Mrs. Gillian Ruddick, for all her hard work in preparing the manuscript, and Mrs. Lydia Flynn, for her constructive criticism.

For David

When the lid of my box outside the door
Stands sentinel to my journeying soul
And sunlight throws a prismic-cross across
The name plate of my chest, think then of the
Day we scrambled up the knoll through thicket
Only fit for a girded Prince to brave
In attempt to raise his Sleeping Beauty
And remember the apex of rock which
Gave us solitude; It was a place to
Sense parameters wider than the world
We were drip-fed by threads of lurex-light
Until so large had we become and yet
So small, so much a part of the strata
That all below seemed, as from a magic
Carpet, to flow upstream and we remained
Unseen observers perched on a warm rock
Go there now or top some other apogee
And say 'Goodbye' for I am already
Out of reach on Charon's ferry and can
See your words unfurl like almond blossom
In the ether: soft whispered curls of sound
That becomes the hush dance of the ocean
And when you light a candle think of me
Put a kiss on your fingertips and blow
It to the winds of Africa, for I
Am in each spec of the Sahara, my
Life but a memory that is flashing
Across the universe, a shooting star
Death a mirror fractured by blinding light.

Do you believe in the existence of spirit as a metaphysical form independent of flesh? Do you believe in fairies at the bottom of the garden? In writing my story I have written that which had to be written - that which was written. Know that beyond your focus there exists a world of consciousness, and know that I have seen the fairies.

When your head is someone else's
And your toes are not your own
When life's something you invented
And you're far away from home
When the sound you hear is muffled
And the thud is in your chest
When wild desires are buzzing wires
And fear's your only guest
Make a paper aeroplane
To fly away your mind
Take a journey into blue
And pocket what you find.

1

My story begins in the half light of a stormy October evening. The sea and the mountains are infused with an intense darkness. The sky is bound to the land with a black shroud of threaded jet, and a melancholy is reaching out over the water to catch the great ferryboat *Festos* in an invisible time-tunnel of mystery. We enter Heraklion harbour on a swell of the deep - a swell which rises inside me like those sad sobs of sorrow that break a lover's heart. I have travelled over two thousand miles, yet I have not escaped the rain - the rain and the memories that it brings with it - memories of a life in the Cumbrian mountains, a life of damp and drizzle and so much agony. Will I ever be rid of the water in my bones?

Crete is awash. Roads are rivers. Cars have been abandoned and look like chariots swamped in the Red Sea. Houses are swilling in a flow of filth which rises from split drains. A soup of debris curdles and bogs the coastal plain of Malia and it all swirls and swashes in my head as I travel by taxi to the mountain village of Vrahassi. I watch contaminated life force race from the top of Selena as her veins pour forth rust-red silt.

It gushes through a thousand fissures of scarred granite in a great bleeding of the mountain.

It is exactly fifteen years to the day that Stuart and Annie fell into that soft, cold, suffocating ice. I had told them so many times not to go near the lake. Why hadn't they listened? Why didn't God protect them? No, it wasn't God's fault, it was mine. What sort of a mother was I not to have kept them near me? My hands grab the door handle as the taxi rounds a sharp bend, a white grip of fear and determination - determination to start a new life. But my tears this moment are real and I cannot escape them. I cannot help thinking about what I have left behind. Have I made the right decision? It is so black outside, so wild. What am I doing in this foreign place? Jack, where are you my love? Oh Jack, hold me, please hold me, I need you so much.

'*Kala, Kiria*, you OK?' My taxi driver is concerned.

'Yes, sure, it's just a woman thing… I am so happy to be here.' My reply is flippant. I must sound crazy. If he only knew, my tears are uncontrollable sadness; a tap of tears filling an empty bowl, so that I can be washed clean, my sins washed away. There are so many guilt ghosts. I stare into the night and my reflection is staring back, a portrait of a prisoner. More bends in the road. The taxi skids slightly. I hold on even tighter thinking about the pale zombie that I have become - an automaton, nothing but an automaton. I reach into my handbag and take out the miniature bottle of brandy that I bought on the boat, my medicine. It sooths me like babies' milk and I calm, my eyes fixed on the outline of *Mount Doom* as it gets closer and closer.

Jack, you were so cold up on that mountain, so cold yet so warm - and alone. Or were you alone at the end? Did our babies come for you? Were they waiting for you? Did you walk into the light to meet them, like in the movies? Did you know, Jack? Or did you just go to sleep to wait out the storm in that bower of snow crystal? Where have you taken him, Ferryman? Where is my Jack now?

Don't lose it Kate - try not to lose it. Have you followed me, GUILT? Have you bloody followed me in the rain? My anger hardens at my thoughts. I know that I have to break out of this depression; it is consuming me, but how? I gulp another slug of brandy. It helps.

We are slowing down. There are houses on each side, tall with balconies cascading waterfalls; street lights like beacons illuminating arrow-shower lines of rain. The street narrows then widens into a square full of parked cars. I am here, Vrahassi. This is where I will begin life as it should be lived. This is where I will find peace - a mountain village in Crete, a step back in time. An adventure in the world beyond: beyond the boundaries of a child bride, beyond the Victorian restrictions, the condemning smiles of step-scrubbing neighbours - beyond the limitations in my own head.

My driver keeps the car engine running and the wipers working, as he lifts the boot and heaves out my luggage, slinging it under a deserted verandah to keep dry.

'*Posso kani?*' I have done my homework, and can at least ask how much the fare is. Putting enough thousands of drachmas into his hand to cover the cost, I mumble something about how sorry I am for the tears. He gets into his flash, silver Mercedes and heads off into the blackness with the feeble sound of my 'thank you,' disappearing in the wind and rain. But as I turn to gather my bags into one spot, I see him returning, jumping across puddles in the road.

'Manolis,' he says, holding out a hand, 'Coffee? *Ela*… come on.'

I blow my nose and dry my eyes, holding back a little, but he links his arm in mine and pulls me into the *kafeneo*, the male domain of Vrahassi man. They all stare at me. I am being stared at by a bunch of inquisitive orangutans, and no sooner am I inside, than I want to be outside. I am in no state to be scrutinized by my new neighbours, I know that. I am not smiling, and they are not smiling. I can't change my mood so easily.

'Sorry Manolis, it's not what I want.' I say. All I want is to find my house and be alone. I return to my bags. Manolis is on my heels.

'*Ela moray*, where house?' I show him the piece of paper with the address. It says: *The house of Leekos*. Manolis smiles as though he knows something that I don't. He picks up my two cases and tilts his head to indicate up.

'I take you.' His voice is kind. Even though the rain is still pelting down my very considerate taxi driver leads me up and over slippery cobbles, till we reach the place that I will make my home. An old rusty gate screeks and scraks open over gravelly debris. Manolis takes the key from me; it is not a Yale it is a hand sized iron one that should be winding up a grandfather clock. He yanks open the old, wooden stable door, disturbing bugs and beasties. As we enter spores of wet fungi crumble off the walls in a powdery dust. I had not really looked at Manolis, but now the electric light goes on, and I see him

'A little work,' he says, and the expression behind the beard of his soft Cretan face tells me that he senses my unhappiness. His head drops, he is obviously embarrassed, and doesn't want to hang around. 'I go now,' he says, and backs off into the night.

I look around, shocked at what I see. It is horrible, it is so horrible. This is not a house, it is a hovel built into the rock, almost a cave, barely habitable.

Can you imagine a room with a concrete block partition about four feet high at one end. Behind this slab of disintegrating masonry there is a grimy shower tray full of algal water which will not drain away. A filthy rubber hose is dangling over broken tiles, like a dead eel. Matching floor tiles are covered in black slime. 'God, where have I come to?' The house would be condemned in England, but this is not England, this is rural Crete. Welcome to the outer limits of twentieth century Europe. Comfort is an old iron hospital bed that looks like it came from the leper colony on Spinalonga. I can't stand it! No - Kate, be strong, try not to think of those hospital beds. White marble statues draped under dust sheets. This one is covered in a layer of cobwebs that are heavy with half-eaten bluebottles. Death - beds with death on them. Is that what beds have come to mean to me? Hold back those tears Kate. Did I run away from one bed of death to discover another? The mattress is rotten, stinking of rats that have plundered it for nesting material. Oh Jack, have

I done the right thing? We didn't have much when we were first married, but it was better than this.

My lover, my best friend, my soul-mate, the one person who shared the intimacy of my life is gone. He is gone - they are all gone - lost in the sea of time. And now, I too am losing myself in this pothole of misery. The memory of that soul-splitting day haunts me; a single red rose on cold granite, the chiselled stone, it is in my eyes, it is under my finger tips, and it is on my breath. "HE CLIMBED THE DARK BROW OF THE MIGHTY HELVELLYN." The hell of that day comes rushing back.

I knew then that I would have to leave Jack's empty body under the great Yew tree beside Annie and Stuart, and continue my life alone. Now the reality of alone is crushing me. My mute scream of - *I love you* - empties from the cavern of my stomach and tears through the confines of my heart. It rushes every pore disturbing the night and sending a thousand ripples through the ether, until finally I cry myself to I sleep.

• •

–Rain smashes the summer- brown foliage in the yard outside, and splashes through my open window. I seem to be in the middle of some Frankenstein experiment, as though the turmoil of this electric, primordial night is giving birth to my new life. I can hear the sound of waves and I imagine a sea of greenness, like a meadow of watercolour awash with white flowers which toss in the wind. The sky is angry, yet the sea is like a fresh spring field of sapling corn blowing shoreward with the incoming tide. And in

my head I am weightless as dust in the air, gently settling in a ray of sunlight; as if I have entered through a portal to a land where people pass me by without interest. In front of me is a huge courtyard, paved with stone, and behind me a columned building. I am at the bottom of a wide staircase. I can feel the rough surface of rock beneath me - but how? - I have no body. I am moving like an amoeba in a microscope - slowly entering undiscovered space. And I know that I am floating on the ripples of time, with only awareness to carry me forward. Yet, I am not alone. In the comfort of blue that surrounds me someone takes hold of my hand and pulls me close, so close that I can feel a strong embrace. I am being cradled in a celestial purity of love that comforts and confuses me. Slowly, slowly, I begin to ascend, and, as a bubble rises to the surface, I rise to the surface, still in the grip of my strong companion, his hands tight on mine, safely returning me to my bed.-

· ·

The first light of morning is wet and camphoric. Fear chills me. My hair is dripping in the cloud-drizzle of dawn. Whose hands had I felt? What strange space had I slipped into and been drawn out of? For a few seconds I glare, disorientated, at the knots in the beams above me. I can still hear a voice calling me. Is it you Jack? I can still feel the touch of those strong hands.

Reality kicks in with the sound of, '*Kalosti Kalosti.*' Words of welcome are pouring out of the old woman who is battling her way through my stubborn gate. She is not a very old woman, and her dress is grey rather than black, but her style is something between a 1950s twinset granny and a be-wellied goat-herder. In one hand she is carrying a dish of oil-sloppy greens and in the other a bag of pomegranates. 'Maria, Maria, *Kalosti, Kalosti,*' she introduces herself, as she pushes her way in and clears a space on the table for her gifts. And without ceremony she pulls a chair into position and slides her dripping coat onto the back of it. I take the bowl of hot greens from her, gratefully warming my hands around it. '*Fa-ee, fa-ee* - eat,' I am commanded, and I do just that, instantly, like some child being told to sit at the table and eat. The taste is bitter and unfamiliar, but I eat. How the warm oil slides down my throat. I feel its heat keeping the light inside me from going out. '*Avrio* - tomorrow,' she points to the dish, capes her coat over her head, and disappears into the torrent of rain, merging with the greyness of the day.

I want to call after her to come back, to keep me company. Don't you know that I want someone near me? I want someone to hold me. I want to be close enough to snuggle up and smell maternal breath. To nuzzle into a soft bosom and know I am loved. But no, she is gone and I am alone - alone with my thoughts. You should be here with me Jack. But there is only me.

Anger begins to take over from grief, and I stomp around looking at all the repairs that need doing. A small window in the kitchen is broken and needs boarding up. Kitchen, that's a joke. There are no cupboards; old dusty bottles sit on a concrete shelf over a concrete sink. A two-ring gas hob is attached to a bomb-like cylinder by a tube of rubber pipe, and the old fridge looks ready for the tip. I am cold, and I need my medicine. There is none. The bottle is empty. Shit! Why didn't you buy more Kate? Now I am really mad. I squeeze the broom handle tight, wanting to destroy something with it. My throttling grip isn't enough. I kick over an old three legged stool and wield my weapon like some manic warrior. My battle cry sets up a resonance between the old iron door and the old iron bed, and I shout to the wind. 'What the hell are you doing here Kate? You can't run away from your own head. Just who do you think you are anyway? Agatha bloody Christie. Well you're not. You're a 40 year old, husbandless, childless, woman, that's who you are. What makes you think you can write anyway?' My rage ends in a smashing of glass as I thrust the sweeping brush through the already broken window pane. The sound of the breaking glass is a climax in my head as I cry out, 'Jack... Annie... Stuart...' and crease to the floor holding my stomach. It's here. It's come for me - the gloom, the blackness.

• •

–I am inside a familiar shadow. It is washing over me and through me and around me. It is seeping into my existence like osmotic phlegm, and I am saturated with its consciousness. I stand alone by the edge of the sea. Ice fingers are needling my face. My knuckles are tight fisted. I am on the brink of vomit, and I am gut to gut with a grieving spirit. The despair and the affliction of bitterness that he is suffering produce images that begin to stab and rip my flesh in Promethean-like torment. I am lashed and torn apart. Screaming mouths of hungry chicks push out towards me. They melt into wailing ghosts that become an accusing mob

of stone-throwing judges. My body is racked with searing pains that make me scream. I scream into the waves. I scream into the storm-blast of crashing sea-spit. I scream into the banshee wind. I am on the breath of oblivion.

. . . .

Cluck-clacking voices are muffling about me, inside me, outside me. I am somewhere in the blackness, a lead weight descending the depths, descending into soft - just soft. The ground is moving from under me. I am being lifted up, carried to safety.

A warm sweet scent of mother's apple pie comforts me in the cradle. I hear and see and feel the flames of a hissing log fire. A black-clad granny stoops over her charcoaled hearth and takes away a sooty pot. Her face is weather-wizen. Her top lip mushes up to her nose and her cheeks hang in flaps, like the contour lines of a map. The sound she is making is an archetypal cackle. She raises a crack across the brown moonscape of her face, which splits into a wide, gummy smile. Minute fireballs of light appear from deep behind her smoke-yellow eyes. She is *Yaya*, she is the old hag. She is the future.

My throat and chest burn as I sip clear spirit. I sleep. I dream. My dream is about a time long ago - a very long time ago. There is turmoil, there is destruction. People are crying out for help. I am crying out for help.

Sweet fetid breath and white spirit fill my nostrils. There is chatter. There is silence. There is night. There is day. I open my eyes to find myself swaddled in a thick, brown blanket. My hair is a greasy mop and my stomach rises to my throat. Above me, skew-wiff on an old rusty nail, hangs an equally rusty icon of Saint George slaying the dragon. Is he the knight that has come to save me? I notice a roughly-carved crucifix on a small lace-covered table beside me. God, give me strength, I ask, and lever myself onto my elbows croaking pathetically, 'Hello.' My dry vocal chords are echoed by the almost pubertal effort of the family cockerel.

Stone walls around me are half boulder, half rock - a semi-domestic cave of flickering shadows. Shadowy rock-creatures grow and distort. Primitive oil light projects primitive life. Then the familiar face of Manolis comes out of the blurriness. He drags a chair to my bedside. The *Yaya*, lace in hand, is watching from the fireside while her daughter shuffles about between the hearth and the bare split-wood table.

'Maria,' commands the *Yaya*, and then croaks a flow of sounds that rise and fall in some alien-like garble. Something is about to happen. I don't know what. I am weak and I cannot argue. Manolis is leaving. Strangely I don't want him to go. No... I don't think I want this. No... Please. "*Vendoozers*" - it is the only word that I can make out. What the hell are they doing? I am being rolled onto my tummy, my blouse is lifted up to my shoulders and I close my eyes tight, gripping the pillow under my face. Meanwhile Maria sets to work. Her little glass jars clink as she takes them off the tray and one by one inverts them onto my back. There is a heavy smell of methylated spirit and burning cotton wool as each jar is placed onto my cold skin, and a loud 'popping' noise, as one by one they are removed. I want to die. I am being tortured and I want to die. I pretend to sleep. Then arrive the herbal teas and horrible tasting remedies, but the good Manolis is back. He quietly smiles and puts his warm hand, reassuringly on mine.

Maria and her family have brought me out of the blackness, and for that I will be eternally grateful, but I know that I have to get back to my hovel and do my best. It was very good of my neighbours to nurse me back to health, but most of all I have to thank Manolis, my kind taxi driver. He had been visiting his mother, Maria, that day and decided to check on me. Finding me on the floor, in my state of desperation, he had picked me up and taken me next door to be cared for.

2

My cases are still just as they were three days ago, in the middle of the room, unpacked. Where am I going to put my clothes? There is no wardrobe and the drawers stink of mothballs. At least it has stopped raining. The day is bright and little sparrows are fluttering around the telegraph pole outside. Leave the cases Kate. You need fresh air. Go and explore a little.

I am getting some funny looks as I walk through the main square - stranger in town. Somewhere in the back of my mind is Clint in his poncho - a little music-box fob, the good, the bad and the ugly. Curtains move. Old men shuffle on their *kafeneo* seats. A dog barks, but even though the streets are deserted I can sense the powerhouse that Vrahassi once was: the rattle of weaving looms, the clopping of donkeys, the butchering of meat, the tapping of cobblers, the vendors, the shepherds, the sheep, goats, pigs. Breathe Kate. Smell the animals. Listen. Hear the bartering, the gossiping, and the arguments. See the spirits of all those people who hewed the rock to build Vrahassi, stone by stone. They are calling out with every clang of the church bell.

I have learned that the Greek word for rock is *Vrakos*, and Vrahassi is a village built into the rock. It is clinging to the mountainside in a very Mediterranean way, all higgledy-piggledy and neglected. I wander through its narrow streets, which lead either up or down from the main square in a maze of uneven terraces. Some houses have been left to fall down, unwanted hovels abandoned in favour of new property by the coast. Alongside them are pristine, be-flowered balconies, perfectly paved yards, and houses with modern shutters. No two properties are the same shape; no piece of ground is uniform.

As I reach a rude-stone water fountain I see a peasant woman leading her donkey up the track, its saddle baskets are laden with branches of olive wood. Fountains that were once the only source of water are now only visited by the occasional peasant-farmer. It is easy to imagine a time not so long ago, when all the women would have had to make several trips to the springs each day. Their earthenware pitchers would have been confidently rested on muscular shoulders, as they climbed the narrow cobbled streets, shoulders which would have been covered with a brightly coloured piece of hand-woven cloth. They would all have congregated around the old stone troughs to do their washing. The whole day would have been taken in fetching and carrying while their men were working in the olive groves, the family donkey grazing the day away, before being laden with sacks of greasy black and green olives. Now, the abundance of fresh tap water to every house has made the fountains redundant.

Tap water or not, the village is still quite medieval. In between the houses, or under the houses, or on the rooves of the houses are smelly chicken coops and rabbit pens. The occasional goat or lamb peeps out from behind its stony manger. I know that rats are a problem, and wild cats are almost as bad.

Every nook and cranny is decorated with beautiful terracotta pots and pithoi from which bloom geraniums, fuchsias, hydrangea, cacti, palms and plants of every kind. They are unceremoniously jumbled together with old tins, holed buckets and any suitable container in which it is possible to grow flowers or food.

Vrahassi is another world - a world that my grandmother possibly touched on. I suppose in rural Cumbria, where there was no electricity and no plumbing, daily life would have been the same - once upon a time. Shepherds will always be shepherds, sheep will always be sheep.

Kate, you have got to break free and be who you are. So, who am I? I am Kate Sutcliff, 40 year old widow, independent, as in, have enough money to survive without a man, and strong, yes strong enough to take a journey into the unknown. I want solitude to work through my grief, and to begin a new life, make new friends, and write my novel. Breathe Kate. Breathe. Breathe in this wakening morning; it belongs to you, thank you God for allowing me to be part of this wonderful world. As the first rays of the sun wash over me I breathe in all that being alive really means. I listen to the twittering of birds. The smell of wild herbs and wood smoke infuse my nostrils, and beyond the village a collage of emerald trees and grass appear, as through a kaleidoscope, in the spotlight of a new day.

• •

The stormy weather has passed and I am much stronger. I have settled into the house but have a list of repairs ready for the landlord when he visits. I know he will, because the Agency in England said that he would collect the rent every month. The tea in my Lake District mug is *Tetley's*, but my surroundings are far from anything I was brought up with. Wind song and bird song are *sound track* to my neighbour's daily script, "Good morning. How are you? What are you cooking today?" I can't escape, even from up here on my roof. Maria knows where I am. She hears my footsteps and glances up on her way to visit her daughter.

'*Yasou Katy, ti kanis, ti magerepsis?*'

'*Yasou* Maria,' I answer, and that satisfies her. I can hear her asking the same questions of every neighbour as she passes their door. It's her routine. '*Yasou Sofia, ti kanis simera? Ti magerepsis Yasou Aspasia*, how today? What are you cooking? *Yasou Aristaia*, how today? What are you cooking?' And so on, until she is out of earshot. I don't have a routine yet, but I am going to have to settle into one if I am to be serious about my writing. I'll finish my tea and get to work. How lucky you are Kate, to be able to breathe in this warm sun-soaked air.

I have got this idea for a story. It's not the one I had thought of writing before I left England. I did intend to write a family history, but my dreams have led me into another story, and I think it will be good to divert my mind a little. I don't want to forget my past, though it would be a release just for a while. This idea is growing inside me and I am getting quite excited about it. I will have to do some research though, lots of research.

My story will be about a Minoan prince and princess and their part in the destruction of the great Minoan Civilization. I have read that the Minoan people were wiped out after a catastrophic tidal wave hit the northern shores of Crete in about 1540 B.C. It was a direct result of an earthquake which erupted on the island of Thira, (Santorini), but my theory of the destruction is much more magical. Why not? Who really knows the truth?

I am so enthusiastic that I want to start right away. Where's your notepad Kate? Oh no, not Maria again, I really don't want to be disturbed right now. Hang on; it's a male voice that is booming through my gate.

'*Kalimera, Kalimera Kiria Katerina. Kalos irthatai.* House good, eh?'

Beware of Greeks with gold teeth, Kate. It is my landlord. His Captain Hook smile is worthy of a Walt Disney flashing star. He thrusts his hand forward to take mine. A lifetime of a million cigarettes has given him a bulbous nose and a gravelly voice, which would be very sexy if he wasn't so, um… ugly.

'*Hero Polee*,' I return, trying to pull my hand out of his. The owner of this, *exquisite cottage-type residence* is clearly used to exaggeration. His brochure description should have read "hovel". He has obviously waited until I got over the initial shock of the place, before coming to see me; a thousand summers of female pleasure have made him into a well practiced charmer with just a hint of eau d' hashish lingering around the bristles of his dark moustache.

'My name is Aleko,' he smolders, as he pulls out a chair and sits down. He looks around. Is it surprise on his face? Shock, maybe?

'I live *Heraklio*,' he says, seeming to mean that he didn't realize the place was in such a state. '*Po, po*, I mend broken window tomorrow.' He shakes his head in sympathy with my complaint. 'Yes, yes, and maybe a new boiler.'

'And a new mattress for the bed,' I insist, lifting the plastic cover that I have spread under the sheets, to show him the disgusting state of my bed.

'Yes, yes, *Kyria Katerina*, tomorrow, tomorrow.'

He seems genuine enough and I regret not having anything better to offer him than tea.

'Here is the rent, *Kyrie Aleko*.' I count out the notes into his hand and he pushes the money into his pocket.

'Tomorrow, *Kyria Katerina*,' he says, quickly taking my hand in both of his and patting it reassuringly before he leaves.

Something causes me to shiver as he disappears down the street, a shadow of a vampire perhaps? I shake the thought away.

So, what was I doing? Where is that notepad? I need to find the history books that I brought with me. The house is such a jumble. Ah! Here they are; Pre-Hellenic Crete, this one I think. It will give me the information I need about the Minoan Civilization, the history book version anyway. Let's see what it says:

"'In the year 1400 B.C. Megalonissos had many cities. Its people were of an advanced culture. They not only excelled in physical capabilities such as building and farming but they possibly had intuitive powers. They were a great seafaring people who traded with other lands such as Egypt and Sicily and they were skilled artists and craftsmen, taking for inspiration the plethora of nature which was all about them. The land had flowers and trees and crops of fruit and corn. There were birds and butterflies and bees. The sea was a harvest of fish, mollusks, vegetation, dolphins and umpteen living creatures, and the people appear to have been contented workers with busy minds; minds which were attuned to nature and at one with it.'"

And that is what you should aim for Kate, a mind that is attuned to nature and at one with it. So, get out there and attune.

• •

It is a warm November day. I am standing in the middle of Malia with the hills behind me and the sea somewhere in front, and I am finding it difficult to believe the scene. Gone is the scintillating summer sugar-rush of pink flesh and pina coladas. Malia is now a ghost town of faded yellows and rusting reds. It is nothing but a spaghetti-western, no-horse, dustville, rattling with advertisement hoardings. *Exchange, Quick Film, Rent a Car* - all scarred with seasonal grime. Ripped funeral posters hang from electricity poles; soggy and out of date. Threads of thick black wires join roof to roof. Television aerials stand beside naked clothes lines on empty terraces. As I walk down the main street I come across an old wooden table, a rickety rush bottom chair, a hanging pan for weighing bananas, and a man in black standing in a puddle of tab ends. A little further up the road there is an old woman on a donkey which has a nanny goat tethered alongside. The donkey is a four legged trailer loaded with straw. About to overtake the donkey is a gypsy truck, laden with roll upon roll of carpeting. '*Elatai na theetai!* Come and see! - Blasts the megaphone announcement to an accompaniment of dithering bouzouki music. I carry on, passing closed shop after closed shop, until I come to a butcher hacking meat on an old, deep-grooved chopping table. His round hacking-block is on the pavement. This half crippled old-boy is talking to himself like a tramp around Kings Cross: wizen, smoke-dried, pickled - *raki* and baccy - baccy and *raki*.

Young *Rambos* rort down the white line on little motorbikes, but there is no-one to impress. Young tarts putter around on scooters, wearing black leggings and black leather jackets. Where are the high street career women? Not in Malia. Where are all those people with money, land, fine houses and big cars? They are in *villa-world* - the world of plenty. Where are the poor? They are out in the olive groves, working for a pittance to keep their families in hovels. Life, love, song, dance – where is the music?

'*Yasou Katy*… Vrahassi?'

'Oh! Yes please.' I gratefully accept. It is Manolis Taxi, what luck! Malia is so depressing and I have had enough of that.

'We drink coffee first?' he asks. How can I refuse?

'OK, Manolis - this time I promise I won't be so miserable.' I get into the car feeling very relieved not to have to wait around for a bus in Malia ghost town.

'We go Sissi,' says Manolis. I nod in agreement as I fix my seat belt. As we speed along, lightness enters my head. I know that the adventure is beginning.

• •

The heartbeat of Sissi, a little fishing village, has been reduced to that of a hibernating tortoise. It is like a disused film set. Small blue and white caiques laden with bright yellow fishing nets and hooked buckets are moored to heavy iron rings on the quayside, but the hubbub of a small tourist resort is gone. Jack brought me here to try to mend my spirit after Annie and Stuart… no, don't go there Kate, think something good. The sweet Manolis Taxi comes to save me from my thoughts.

'Look at the sea, Katy, is beautiful, no?'

'Is very beautiful, Manolis, and very blue.' I gaze far out into the ocean and inhale the sea that brought me; the sea that protects Crete, like womb-fluid, the apocryphal sea. What secrets are you going to share with me, sea that has lulled and tormented this island? I breathe deeply and share the outward breath of the sea.

I am a bit uncertain, entering the men's coffee shop, but I follow Manolis who very quickly finds a cronky wooden, rush-bottom chair for me to sit on. Being the only woman in here except for the owner is very disconcerting.

'You will drink coffee?' asks Manolis.

'Yes, but Nescafe today please,' I reply.

The place is full of old men; it is a tiny room, full of smoke and full of the smell of olive oil. The olive harvest has begun and I am sitting in the middle of a heavy-sweet smell of crushed olives and a haze of tobacco smoke. Dirty work-wear hums of sweat and olive oil. Dirty teeth grin from dirty faces. Dirty fingers poke dirty noses and dirty minds, no doubt, are thinking dirty thoughts.

'Two coffees - e*liniko metrio*?' Manolis shouts across the room to the owner of the shop, he has obviously forgotten that I asked for Nescafe. Never mind, I'll let it ride. The old men slurp their thick Greek coffee. The owner, possibly the only woman to be respected in the *kafeneo*, is busy but acknowledges the request. I am getting the *stare* again. Today I don't mind - I am happy. This is a totally new experience for me. It is a little unnerving, I admit. My coffee arrives, it is thick, sweet and just enough of it to give me a zip. Maybe I will get used to it.

It seems as though the *kafeneo* is not just a coffee shop but a community hall, a rest centre, a place to hold meetings or simply to watch television. Not all, but most eyes, after registering my presence, have turned back to that - mesmerizer - the box on the wall.

'Do you know anything about the palace, at Malia, Manolis?' I attempt conversation.

'I take visitors there in summer,' he replies.

'I'd like to go there.'

'No open winter, wait summer.'

'Oh, that's a shame. Maybe I could take photos from the road side?'

'OK tomorrow I take you there,' says Manolis.

'OK, you're on, thanks.' I have every intention of paying Manolis the taxi fare tomorrow, so I feel good about arranging a time. '10 o'clock, in the square, OK?'

I am really interested in the history of the palace at Malia, but Manolis doesn't seem too clued up on it. Anyway, a guy on the next table has his ear in our conversation and is quick to jump in.

'My uncle to working there two years,' he says in broken English, but I have more chance of understanding him then the heavy Cretan dialect that is being spoken by the others.

'My uncle is to looking seals - many seals. My uncle knows everything about...' and mid flow he holds his hand out and introduces himself: 'Gregory...' and he sidles up a bit closer.

'Kate, *Hero Polee*, Gregory,' I say moving away a little. He immediately turns my name into Katy, as have done most people here. Actually, this guy is not that old, but it is hard to tell his age because of his hairy face and hunched shoulders. I notice his habit of picking the dirt out of his fingernails as he speaks, and I wish he wouldn't get so close to me. My nose tells me that he must not have had a bath for quite some time.

An alcoholic reek of *raki* is hanging about him, getting in the way of our conversation.

'I'd better get back to Vrahassi, Manolis.' I butt in politely at the earliest opportunity.

'OK, we go now.'

Our coffee has been paid for by Gregory, so we thank him and leave.

• •

Back in Vrahassi I feel safer some how. The evening is closing in and there is just a tiny bite of cold on the wind. I return to my hovel eagerly, where I know that Maria's daily food will be waiting for me.

There is something about an open fire. It is the living flame that dances and throws shadows. Fire-music cheers the silence and fire fairies dart from log to log. Well, that is how it should be. At the moment I would settle for a tiny spark, but my wood is sodden, and slimy with wet bark that won't catch alight, and I am on my knees trying to coax it to life. It's like when I blew into the beak of Annie's budgie, and it was only the warm of my hand that I could feel as I massaged its heart. How did I know where the heart of a budgie was anyway? I've got an idea; stuff from the bed, mouse nest stuff. It's sort of grey cotton-wool-y. I can just pull it out of the hole. It reminds me of my Teddy bear when its leg came off, and my mum had to stick her finger in, right into its tummy, to push the stuffing back. And every time the stitching came loose I would tug at the tiny strands of kapok till a great swathe of Teddy innards was pouring out. Teddy innards under the kindling - that should do it. It does, but a plother of smoke fills the room.

I have vacated the house, coughing all the way up the stone steps, onto my flat roof, where remnants of a tattered chicken coop are flopping and creaking in a fresh funnel of wind that is softly blowing in from the sea. There are no chickens, thank God! However, from up here I have a view over the rooftops of the village, down the V of the gorge to the sea, and to the world beyond. Like an express train shuddering to a stop at the sight of something on the line, I stand perfectly still and watch the shivering, dragon-hump mountains silhouette in the falling sable of night. It is a moment of magic. Crete, Kate, you are home.

This slum dwelling which you have rented is horrendous, but its flat roof is definitely a bonus. And, with the light disappearing into the west, leaving a fizzing after-glow over the hills of Lassithi, I take out my laptop and begin to write the story of Rhamu; a youth who is in love with the Princess Sisi. I have called my Princess, Sisi, because I imagine the tiny resort of Sissi was named after her. Both Rhamu and Sisi were people from the Minoan Palace at Malia.

3

Rhamu chases through the narrow streets like a young whippet after his first hare. He takes a shortcut through the busy agora, scuttling a pen of ducks and almost overturning a cartload of oranges. The momentary chaos causes an old woman to drop her pitcher, and Rhamu disappears in a hail of abuse from one of the hill-men. He races on through the columned courtyard, between elegant ladies of the Palace as they set out to the temple of Demeter, and finally up to the top of the great steps.

There, his lithe body enables him to slip down a side passage away from the gaze of the guard, where he calls excitedly. 'Come, come, the boats have arrived. Come we must see them beach. Sisi, Sisi, let's find out what they have brought.' A slight girl child appears through a small light opening on the wall of her chamber, making sure that no-one has seen her escape. She is dressed in a short white shift that is gathered at each shoulder with a gold flower-head pin, and she wears leather sandals which are tied, criss-crossed, up her bare legs. At twelve years old she has grown almost too big for her secret childhood exit, but she has no trouble leaping her own height to the ground, which she does with the nimbleness of the goat-herder's finest kri-kri.

Together with her friend Rhamu, she heads down the labyrinth of passageways which will eventually bring them to the sea. They squeeze past earthenware casks and fat clay pots into the large kitchen hall, where they furtively creep around the edge of one of the blazing furnaces, avoiding the crackle-spat of olive logs and the hissing spray of boiling cauldrons. They finally leave the aroma of warm spices and baking corn to burst out into the dazzle of the life-giving sun. Feeling like unleashed hounds, they speed to the perimeter wall and beyond to the edge of the sea.

From their secret crevice on the cliff top they watch the coming and going of boats in the wide sandy bay. The Palace of Sarpedon rises behind them, half hidden in a natural dip of the land. Towering high at its centre, the royal chambers are clearly visible in the midst of the olive groves and vineyards. Tall trees and gardens reach almost to the sea and spread across the great plain. Safely cupping the expanse of fertile land is a backdrop of forested mountain slopes, and the high peak of Selena rises into the sky like a finger pointing to heaven.

Two ships sweep towards them. Each one has a giant square sail which billows blue-white from a single mast. Dark-skinned sailors, glistening with sweat, cling to the long oars with which they weigh and force the vessels through the swell of a spring tide. Rhamu and Sisi are like children unwrapping a present at the sight of the two high prows dipping and rocking between the crested waves. Behind the boats, teeming and singing and leaping and playing, is an escort of dolphins, racing their long monster-friends of the water.

The sea is not always so wild. It usually bathes the shore gently like embryonic fluid, which provides protection and subsistence for the people of the land, but today the wind is high and the manoeuver is not so simple. Rhamu and Sisi look on as the sea-people battle with the waves Once they have caught the inward tide their streamlined boats chase the surf, and suddenly, with a loud creaking and banging and the thrashing of men in the water pulling on thick oxhide rope, they beach. When the tall hulls have been hauled up the soft sand and tightly secured to stone capstans, the hatches are forced open to reveal a cargo of banks of cotton cloth. Some are plain white, some are patterned and some are of the most bright cerulean blue that Rhamu and Sisi have every seen. When the cargo has been safely loaded onto several carts a group of men gather around a fire on the beach. One man steps forward. He is dressed in an emerald-green cloak which sweeps down to the ground in a huge fishtail behind him. Sprinkling the fire to make it flash and splutter, he speaks:

'O messenger of the invisible world, take our thanks to the Angel of Fire in our brother's land where he awaits news of the safe passage of his vessels. To the great Talus who protects our shores, we bow low and give praise.'

'It is for the festival of Demeter,' whispers Sisi. But Rhamu does not hear her words. As he looks at Sisi he sees how beautiful she has become, and he realizes that she is no longer a child. Her thick golden hair is like a flag fraying in the wind, and her blue-blue eyes match the intensity of the new Egyptian cloth. She is a fragile, virgin princess. She is no longer his playmate, no longer his daily companion. She is the Princess Sisi, the next Queen of the Hive, the most precious of the family Sarpedon. As Rhamu awakes to the magic beyond her eyes, Sisi takes hold of his look, and, in that very instant, they fall in love. The safe sure grip of

Rhamu's hands draws her close. His heavy breath warms her face, and she waits to receive the tenderness of his lips.

Stopped by the discovery of their passion they fall silent. Then, with sudden alarm, Sisi faces the palace. 'We must go,' she says, 'I am missed.'

• •

That is enough writing for now. My young prince has realized that he is in love. And his princess, how does she feel? I remember my first kiss. It was like living love being softly whispered onto my lips. That was a long time ago Kate. Still the thought is warming. Better than my pathetic log fire which has gone out - time for bed. I need to find out more about the tiny seals that the Minoan people used as identification stamps. Tomorrow, Kate. Make it your mission for tomorrow, and don't forget to write to Daddy and let him know how you are.

4

Clang, clang, clang, clang... What on earth is that? It's not Sunday. Why are the bells ringing? They are not stopping either. I am bleary eyed after working late last night. Clang, clang, clang, clang... there are people hurrying past my gate. What is going on? Clang, clang, clang, clang... It is a gathering sure enough: the young, the old, variations of greys and blacks all jostling together in the main square.

Centre point outside the *kafeneo* is a group of men one of whom is standing forward to speak. He begins to tap on the microphone to check whether it is working or not, his cigarette is balanced between his lips. Oh, slow down please. I can't understand a word of what he is saying. The crowd seems to be with him. They cheer at his words, fists raised in solidarity. Now they are chanting, "VRA-HA-SSI, VRA-HA-SSI" What on earth is going on? I spot a police car and a big, red box-van. It's the fire brigade. From my viewpoint up the hill a little, together with a couple of grannies, I watch them point out a building just across from us. It is the village Council office - what is left of it. There has been a fire. How did that happen? Was it an accident?

The crowd is shouting again. This time one of them has taken hold of the microphone. He is pretty good at inciting them further. Wait a minute, I know him. It is Gregory, the hairy one from Sissi. Well he obviously knows what is going on. He looks a bit tidier today too. Get a bit closer Kate. Ah, there is Manolis Taxi; I wave to him over the crowd. Gregory spots me as he leaves the podium for the next speaker. He obviously thinks I am waving at him and he waves back. He is busy organizing the rally so it doesn't matter. I seem to be intruding. The village women are making a meal of eyeing me up and down, but Maria comes to my rescue. 'Maria - *kalimera.*' I say shaking my head to indicate that I don't know the reason for the commotion. 'What's going on?' I ask. 'Neapolis,' she says, 'Problem Neapolis.' Neapolis is a small town a few kilometres away. 'Oh,' I say, but Maria is already gossiping with her neighbours. I know that they are asking her who I am - those who don't know already - that is.

Well, there is one place where I can find out what the problem is - inside the *kafeneo*. Wait until things have settled down, Kate, and when all the speeches are over, go for it. I see Manolis Taxi going inside so I know that there will be at least one friendly face.

The *kafeneo* is full, like there is a holiday. It is very noisy. Gregory is with a crowd, all men, but Manolis is sitting alone. It is only 9 o'clock; we have time before our trip to the archaeological site. I am about to sit at the table with Manolis when I hear, 'Yasou Katy.'

'*Yasou*, Gregory.'

'Katy… *Ela*…sit.' He doesn't hesitate to pull a chair round the table for me.

'Sit, Sit,' I am ordered, and I sit at the small round blue *kafeneo* table together with his mates. Manolis looks across and shrugs his shoulders. Gregory's mates introduce themselves one by one, thrusting forward a hand. 'Nikos.' He is a round guy, his dark striped t-shirt hugs his belly looking like it has shrunk in the wash. 'Petros,' says the next in an almost frightened mumble, his handshake dripping into my palm. He smiles but seems too afraid to speak, and then he grins nervously, a wide tooth-gappy grin that tells me he is not quite a whole jig-saw. And finally, the guy who is dressed in black from the tip of his knee length boots to the traditional Cretan '*mantilla*' bobbing around his forehead. 'Vassillis,' he says proudly, taking my hand and crushing it in his like he's clipping a sheep's ear with a pair of pincers.

Raki begins to appear on the table. Tot glasses are banged in front of us and I begin to feel very warm. They are a jolly crowd, happy to have a woman in their midst, and, for my part, I love the attention. Gregory might be hairy and a bit on the unwashed side, but at least he can speak English - well, sort of.

'Vrahassi, Katy, 'rebels', '*andartes*', '*communistria*', we to making war Neapolis.' Outside a couple of gun shots blast over the valley; I jump - the men laugh.

'More *raki* Katy,' - it's an order. I protest, but the *raki* is poured anyway. I take one sip and then, conscious of the time, make to leave. The music in the background is revolution music, bold and stirring. An old black and white war film is on the TV, chieftains in traditional dress, knives in their cummerbunds, and magazines of bullets around their chests.

'Where to going Katy?' asks Gregory.
'Malia,' I say.
'Stay, make company, we eat.'
'Sorry,' I say, 'but I have an appointment, some other time maybe.' Pity I have to leave really, because I could have learned more about Gregory's uncle, the one that is supposed to be an expert on Minoan seals. Never mind Kate, go and do your research then party.

• •

I had no idea that the site would be so impressive. I have read about it, but to actually see it and to be able to locate the nearby church of Prophet Elias, where once a Minoan temple stood, is remarkable. OK the place is closed but the gate is not locked, and I have easy access to the site.

'Leave me here Manolis. One hour, OK?' I shout back to the taxi. He disappears; probably to the first *kafeneo* he can find, to debate what is going on in Vrahassi. I am just so excited to be here. I can feel the past in every piece of stone that is standing firm; foundations that are just as strong as the day they were laid. OK, the place has been reduced to a ground plan, but these foundations were put here by the Minoan people over two thousand years ago. It is not a reconstruction, not a "maybe it looked like this" site, the Palace is coming out of the ground just as it was put in. The past echoes from chamber to chamber. It echoes across the great courtyard, through the storehouses, the granaries, and the workshops where all those seals were so intricately made: tiny thumb-nail sized stones engraved with pictures of flowers, animals, trees, and goddesses. I take a breath. I hear those people; I see ghost-shadows in the sunlight - children running. From the top of the great staircase I can see the *road of the sea* tracking its way to the perimeter wall, to the empty graveyard of Kings, *Chrysolakkos*. This is where the amazing gold pendant of two bees was found. I have a fizzing inside my head as though I were standing under an electricity pylon, high pitched resonances of the past bombard the space between my eyes. I know you were here Rhamu, and Sisi, I know you were here.

Toot! Toot! Heavens! The hour has gone so very quickly.

'I'm coming, Manolis, I'm coming.' I glance around one more time, taking in the layout, putting walls to the foundations, seeing people pass through doorways, hearing the joy of life; hearing the screams of death.

'I'll be back, Rhamu. Don't you worry, I'll be back,' I whisper to my spirit friend before making a dash for the taxi to avoid a sudden shower. I make it just in time.

'Where on earth did that come from, the weather seemed settled today.' I say, shaking the raindrops out of my hair. 'Thanks, Manolis, it was well worth the visit.'

On the way back up the mountain we talk about Neapolis and Vrahassi.

'So, what is all this trouble about Neapolis?' I ask. 'I think I understood what Gregory said, but his English isn't all that good.'

'Political,' is all Manolis will say. From what I gather it is to do with the restructure of Local Government - I think. Something about Neapolis being the administrative centre. It's a bit beyond me but the villagers are angry. Short of pitch forks and scythes, the scene this morning could have been one from the days of the Bastille. Ooh! Scary!

Anyway, I am so full of palace-madness that all I want to do is get to my hovel and write down a few ideas while they are all so fresh in my mind. It's raining again as we approach Vrahassi. I should be used to it by now. Trudging up the hill from the square I meet Maria, her arms full of shopping.

'Let me help you,' I say, taking one of her bags. I go right up to her front door and put the bag down in her little courtyard.

'Thank you Katy,' she says digging into her bag and pulling out a couple of oranges - leaves and stalk still attached. I return the thanks.

'Ela – Avrio.'

Come where tomorrow? It is an invitation to join the family in the olive groves, to lend a hand with the olive harvest. Ah! - A picnic with the workers in the warm sunshine, it sounds idyllic.

• •

Scrambling into the back of an old battered pickup is the last thing that I feel like doing at 7.30 in the morning. What sort of crazy woman would make a promise to go olive picking when she might have known that she would be a little hung-over? I returned to the *kafeneo* last night to see if my seal man was there. He wasn't, but Gregory was - Gregory and *raki*. Lack of sleep, abused guts and a mouth like the inside of a dusty vacuum bag, I silently accompany my neighbours out of the village along a stony, donkey road, bouncing our way to the family olive grove.

Katsounas, which are tennis racket sized sticks with three rubber prongs - a bit like Poseidon's trident only shorter - are thrust into my arms the minute the truck stops. I find out soon enough what they are used for. The others carry huge ground nets, hessian sacks and food, water and *raki* to see us through the day, and we set off on foot along a mountain goat track in the general direction of up. A hundred meters or so further on we reach the plot of land, which has been passed down the generations of Maria's family to ensure that there is enough olive oil for all. There is a constant sound of thrash, thrash, thrash, as the work begins. It is so hard. The trees have been planted on a slope and the ground is slippery. I have a job to stand upright. Catapulting olives keep scratching my face, and I have insect bites in places that insects should never reach, let alone bite. This is no picnic, and neither is there a picnic, well not yet anyway. We strike at the boughs of fruit with the katsounas as though we are beating dust from a carpet, and the olives shower down onto the nets below.

When one tree has been harvested we tip the olives from one net into another, and while I sit with the other women, separating leaves from black olive-bullets, the men spread sail-sized nets on the ground around the next tree. God, how many more? Thrash, thrash, thrash. The sound of *katsounas* whipping through the branches echoes around the hillside as other families work their own grounds, and finally, we stop for lunch. Never was bread and cheese so very welcome. Remind yourself never to do this again, Kate.

• •

I enter the *kafeneo* in Vrahassi, stinking of body odour and olive oil, with hands ingrained with an agricultural dye of earthen colours, I collapse onto a hard chair and quench my thirst with cold beer. I think about the Princess Sisi and her life of luxury at Malia Palace. There would have been no olive picking for her. She would have been waited on by handmaidens, bathed, sweetly perfumed, and dressed, taught how to dance - how to play music. She would have been treated as a precious vessel that would one day give birth to the next Protector of the Hive. I think the Palace would have been a sort of hive with a Queen Bee and workers. Everyone would have had his or her part in maintaining harmonious surroundings and community life. There would have been sun worship, sacrifices, magic ceremonies, games, and festivals as well as planting and harvesting, fishing and commerce. It would have been a true community, every person dependent on every other person. They may even have been telepathic because they lived so close to nature, and they would have enjoyed being alive.

O-oh! Sometimes fate is just fate - or am I being stalked? Gregory is at the door of the *kafeneo* about to come inside. He looks like he has been working in the olive groves, and for once I don't feel out of place. In fact I suddenly realize, the old clothes that I am wearing (now greasy and olive-smelling), make me fit company to be in the *kafeneo* with the other labourers. I can sense a sort of respect for a fellow worker; a one of the boys type attitude towards me that seems to go down very well with Gregory and his crowd.

'*Kalispera* Katy. You work?' They all laugh as they sit down round the table with me. I join in but really I just want to finish my beer and go. I have that letter to write to my Daddy. Not before I have found out about Gregory's uncle though. This is my chance.

'Gregory,' I say in that, I want to know something, tone. 'Will you do me a favour please?' I suppose I have asked for the look he is giving me. 'I would like to meet your uncle, the one who used to work at the archaeological site of Malia Palace.' I can see that it is not the favour that Gregory is expecting of me, and I am very aware of my single status amongst a crowd of men. He brushes it off well though, and orders me a beer together with *raki* for the table.

'*Baba* Kostas,' he shouts across the room. 'The lady wants meeting.' I glance across to the card table where Uncle Kostas is pondering over his hand. He's an elderly guy with a big white moustache, and he is wearing a sports jacket that is well lived in, but at least he is a bit tidier than his nephew. He doesn't even look up but mutters something into his chin. 'After,' says Gregory, knocking a couple of stray olives from his beard. As he twists one end of his moustache and starts to pick his finger nails, I notice that the little finger nail of his right hand is about an inch long, whereas all the others are cut right down. It turns my stomach a bit but the moment passes.

Then all eyes turn to the television for the local news. The company listens in a very noisy sort of way to the four debaters who are debating, equally noisily, on the screen. Things start to get a bit rowdy. *Baba* Kostas throws his cards down in front of him and stands, fist in the air, shouting at what is being said. Someone else joins in. Everyone is shouting at everyone else and Gregory is the loudest. It's about Neapolis again, political trouble; time for me to go. I try to pay but no one will take my money. OK, next time.

It isn't going down well with Gregory that I am leaving, but he is in the thick of a heated debate with his mates, and the political situation takes priority, so it is easy for me to escape. It seems that I am fated not to speak with his uncle.

• •

The lonely exposed light bulb in my living room has dimmed because I have put the emersion heater on to warm up some water. Dam, it does it every time. Never mind, I can still see well enough to write to my Daddy. I know he is all right because I made a phone call yesterday from the village box. He has only just retired and is enjoying his freedom. "You have a good journey," he said to me as I was leaving, "Go and do your thing, and I shall go and do mine." Since mum died he has lived alone, and now he is planning a trip around the world in a camper van. I love my Daddy. I seal the envelope with a kiss. 'Love you Daddy,' I say. I am sending him all the details about my story. It's what we agreed before I left, that I would send him my book by installments. I'm not sure what he will make of it, I don't think Minoan history is quite his scene.

Hot water is always such a comfort. My new shower, the first repair that Aleko instigated, is so wonderful. I feel clean, relaxed, warm, and safe from the elements, in front of the fire in my little hovel, and I know it is time to light a candle and read the Tarot. I have studied the art of reading Tarot cards. It was one of my little comforters after Jack left me. Tonight I have a question. I need some help with my book - a little guidance to set me on the right track. Tonight the time is just right - there is a full moon. I will wash my crystals and let them have the benefit of soaking up moon-rays while I sleep. But first they can all help to give me an answer.

My table is ready; my crystals are set out on their familiar black cloth: amethyst - for intuition and for the go ahead to trust hunches, a piece of blue lapis lazuli - for wisdom, a green pebble from the beach - to help with affairs of the heart, (if only it were an emerald, maybe one day), my golden yellow tiger's eye that has beautiful lustrous stripes - it helps me with communication, and my clear crystal quartz that protects me and helps me to be creative. I am shuffling my Tarot cards and thinking about the life of Rhamu. Did he really exist? The more I have thought about him, the more real he has become. Maybe the spirit of Rhamu is trying to contact me in some way. My dreams have been very real lately and the story that is in my head seems very real. I hold my hand over the flickering candle and make a circle three times, whilst asking the powers of Earth, Air, Fire and Water, the powers of North, South, East and West, to be with me, to help me to know all that is to be known.

I begin to set out my cards in the form of the Celtic-cross, and quietly focus all my mental energy on my Minoan Prince, asking him to communicate with me. I know that my answer will come through the cards, and I turn them over slowly one by one. In the centre is The Sun, a masculine element, but it is cloaked by the Moon, feminine, yet dark and negative. There is Death in the past and hope of a reunion in the future. My Prince, he is here at my side in the form of the Chariot. The cards never fail me. It is so exciting - focus Kate. The Hermit, he influences the future like some timeless guardian angel. What's this, a magical seven? Supernatural powers, fate, wisdom, all my ideas coming into one. Seven colours of the rainbow; seven notes in a musical scale, the seven of cups, a water sign like me, Cancerian. What's next? The six of Cups, hope of the return of a lost lover. And finally, unity in the Ace of Pentacles - the balance between body, mind and spirit. A lost lover, is that Rhamu's lost lover? Did he lose his Sisi? Is Rhamu searching through time for his princess? How can I help? Let me look at it again, the magical seven. Am I being directed in some way? I don't get it, but I do feel that the guardian is going to guide me.

It is time to wash my crystals under the fresh-water tap in the yard and leave them in the moonlight for the night. I blow out my candle, give thanks for the powers that have helped me, and carefully wrap up my Tarot, putting them back into their wooden box. All my chores done, I am ready for bed.

5

Of course I dreamed last night. My mind was open and waiting for whatever came out of the blue. And come it did, the reason why my prince is grieving; the reason why he needs my help. Something tells me that it is not just fantasy, that there is more to this story than anyone has ever known. There is certainly more to it than I, at the moment, know, but it has given me a purpose, a mission. I shall help Rhamu to find his princess. I am probably the only person who knows how he lost Sisi. Did you know that an elemental, that is a half spirit, half man, will fade if he does not latch on to some sensitive being who anchors him to the earth so that he can fulfill his quest? I truly believe that that person is me, and in the state I was in when I arrived, my mind was open to his call for help. I know that Rhamu and Sisi were lovers and now I know who Rhamu was. Not just who he was, but who he was to become. Rhamu was to become the next Protector of the Hive. He had been chosen by the elders of the Palace of Malia as the person who would produce the next line of royal blood. As the son of a humble seal-maker and his wife, the daughter of a High Priestess of Demeter, he possessed all the right characteristics of natural goodness and intelligence that befitted a ruler. The elders had already marked Rhamu, but Rhamu knew nothing of his destiny.

• •

One week later, on the morning of the Festival of Demeter, in the workroom of the seal makers, the master craftsman speaks:

'Rhamu, I am to prepare the Royal Seals for the offering of the Princess to the great water-spirit, Tsuna. When the trees sing their loudest and the great fire in the sky burns the land, there is to be a feast to end all feasts, for it will be time to herald the coming of our next Priest-King. Sarpedon grows old and he must safeguard the hive.'

Rhamu is silent. His excitement for the day ahead is stilled. He feels a tightening of his stomach as his father's words echo in his head. Is his Sisi to be offered to Tsuna? It can not be true. Why, only last night they had met at their secret place. He re-lives the passion that had been between them. Even now he can feel the softness of her skin as they had lain together, naked, the heat of her belly as it had pressed on his, and the depth of her dark blue-blue eyes which had locked them in a single aura.

'Rhamu, stop dreaming and take these seals to the temple, now - the Priestess of the Miteres is waiting for you,' says his father.

As he crosses the central court to the Temple, Rhamu cannot stop thinking of Sisi. His mind is a cloud. As he skirts past the sacrificial altar, even the wild snorting and stomping of the bull does not penetrate his thoughts. He fails to hear the squealing pig. He does not see the land-child who is staked in the middle of an unlit bonfire. He simply slips into the Temple and delivers his basket of seals to the Priestess.

'You must stop and be blessed, child, for the work of your family, come,' says the young priestess, holding out her robed arm to direct Rhamu. She places him in front of the oak altar which is carved with ears of corn and is set on two great pillars of stone. 'You are now in the sacred grove of Demeter and must give thanks to our Mother Earth who is delivered of abundance to feed her children.' She hands Rhamu a seed. 'Rhamu, you have a great destiny to fulfill, has your father spoken to you of this?' Rhamu is a blank.

'I see that he has not.' The confident priestess blesses Rhamu and his family in the name of Gaia, the Divine Revealer, and making the sign of a cross in the air, she moves forward. The tiers of her long, bell-shaped dress rustle with every step. Bowing slightly from her tiny waist, she dismisses Rhamu. He flinches, sensing a certain reverence towards him, and suddenly, at the sight of the pink-brown nipples of a virgin priestess's breasts, he becomes conscious of his surroundings. He flushes pink, and leaves.

Outside in the courtyard the opening ceremony for the 'Festival of Demeter' has begun with the procession of the Elders. They descend the Palace steps, dressed in robes of blue Egyptian cotton; about thirty men and women, they move as a single body to form a circle around the altar. The bull, snorting and jerking, is already in its final death throes by the time Rhamu has climbed to a place on the arena steps to watch. Bloody and lifeless it spills over the edge of the altar pouring out a chunk of pale tongue through a foaming froth of saliva. A short dagger is pulled from its jugular and the blood is collected in a long silver cup. Words are spoken by the group, but Rhamu cannot hear, and signs are made in the air before they move on to witness the sacrifice of the pig. The pig goes squealing and screaming to its death, as its throat is cut from ear to ear.

Meanwhile, Sisi, from the roof of the Royal Chamber, sees her father put a torch to the pyre which flames orange and red as it sends the spirit of the land-boy as an offering to Demeter. His terrorized figure, naked and limp, soon chars to a blistering corpse, an unrecognizable black carcass that eventually turns to white ash in the purifying flames of the holy fire. Inside and outside the temple all turn to face the midday sun, and, covering their eyes with a clenched fist of the right hand in salute, they give praise to the Great God of the Sky:

'Come Spirit of the Earth, Mother of your children. Come Spirit of the Earth, make fruitful your body. Come Spirit of the Earth, to you we sacrifice our blood.' Thick warm blood is poured over the earth in front of the altar, where a stone slab has been removed to reveal damp, sandy soil which soaks up the rich offering. For the first time in her life, Sisi is not allowed to join the dancing and feasting of the afternoon. Together with her mother, Rheami, she can only attend from her tower, captive as she now is until her day of coming together with the mighty sea spirit, Tsuna.

• •

OK, glass of wine time, Kate. It is two weeks' to Christmas, and I am feeling very Vrahassi- bound. I seal up my letter to Daddy, together with part two of my story. 'Love you Daddy,' I say, kissing the envelope.

The weather, has improved at last, and I am planning a trip to the big city tomorrow, Heraklion. I will go on the bus, visit the museum, do a bit of Christmas shopping, and maybe even buy something new. This evening though, I will go down to the *kafeneo* where it is warm and friendly and, who knows, card playing *Baba* Kostas might just be in there, and I might just get to know a bit more about the Minoan seals.

6

I have joined the whiskery unwashed again, in their smoke filled habitat. I am feeling more at home in here every time I come in. The locals are pleasant, and I am beginning to feel part of the village. I have let it be known that I am writing a book, and that has given me a bit of kudos. It has taken away (I think) a bit of the "loose woman" image that I felt some of the guys were thinking about me. Anyway, by wearing trousers and an old sloppy jumper, I think my femininity factor is down to about zilch. Everyone is huddling around the tin boiler of a wood-burning stove, tucking in to blackened baked-potatoes. I squash in amongst them; to hell with the B.O. - it is another opportunity to glean information. Gregory is as loquacious as ever, albeit in some sort of strange abortion of the English language.

'Where have been to going? What to looking Malia? I am to having eating? I am to writing? I am to warming in?' I don't just get the gist of this last question but then I realize that Gregory's 'I am' really means 'are you', and that he seems to use a sort of half infinitive with a participle ending, and after that translation is, well, nearly impossible, but I'm getting there. Anyway, it is very cold outside this evening and I have no fire in the hovel, so the tin boiler and the black jacket-potatoes seem a very good option.

It is a normal evening in the *kafeneo*, until the door opens - and in walks a stranger - a woman. We are all silent. We all stare. She is blond, she is busty, about fortyish, and not afraid to glare back at everyone as she blurts out: 'Ooh, you lot never seen a woman before?' in a sort of "ooh-argh" Plymouth accent. Her escort is close behind her. He has dyed-black, curly hair that is hanging to his shoulders in great chunky ringlets. He is obviously Greek, and immediately gets into conversation. They sit at a table as near to the heat as they can get, and while the old men are leering at the woman, I attempt conversation.

'Do you live in Vrahassi?' I ask. I am almost sure that she doesn't but it is an opener.

'Ooh no,' she says, in a sort of disgusted-at-the-thought way. 'Back o' beyond up 'ere. No, I'm seaside. You live 'ere then? Watyecome 'ere for? That your man is he?' She points to Gregory.

'No, no,' I'm quick to put her right; perish the thought. 'He's just a mate.'

'Oh yeah?' she says, giving me a, you-expect-me-to-believe-that-one look. I don't want to tell her my life story but I am so hungry to talk with someone who can understand me.

'Really, he's just a friend,' I say.

'How longyebin 'ere then, Kate?'

'Only two months - You?'

'Ooh, 'bout ten years now. Why on earth d' yer pick Vrahassi then? Bit wild up 'ere init?'

'I found this place in an Estate Agent's window,' I explain. 'It sounded just right - a mountain village where I could get away from... (I hesitate not wanting to think about Jack right now, because of the tears that I know will always come) ...past things,' I say.

'Ooh, you got past things then?'

'Well, haven't we all?' I say, trying to shrug it off.

'I'm Suzy.'

'Kate,' I say holding out a hand of friendship. And from that minute on, we are like two travellers meeting on the road to Timbuktu, and babble away like lost sisters.

Around us, the old Greek men and some younger ones, swizzle their little strings of beads, as they, in their dreams, attempt to dive down Suzy's bosom. Well, OK, she is wearing a slinky, satin, low-cut number, but it *is* Saturday night, and she *is* out on the town with her boyfriend - though what he is thinking about, bringing her to a *kafeneo* in Vrahassi, I have no idea. While we talk, he joins the table of card players in the corner. There is no sign of *Baba* Kostas. Anyway that is good for me, because it means that I can continue in conversation with Suzy, and not have to get so close to Gregory, whose finger-picking habit sometimes gets a bit too much. Suzy tells me that she has recently split with her boyfriend of eight years and she's just a teeny-weeny bit bitter. Apparently he has been married off to an eighteen year-old girl whose family owns hundreds of olive trees and a hotel by the sea.

'Greek mothers want Greek daughters-in-law and Greek grandchildren; Greek men want an easy fortune to allow them an easy lifestyle, Kate,' she explains.

'They can bed whoever they want inside and outside of marriage, and love whoever they want, but their legal union should be totally *in the family*. I'm not going to allow the bastard to spoil my life though,' she says, 'From now on I'm going to, find'em, feel'em, fuck'em, and forget 'em.' I am not ready for that one, and I find myself looking around to make sure no one has heard her remarks. All right, I do say the occasional four-letter word, but it is usually *shit* or *hell*. The 'F' word has never slid easily off my tongue. It's not that I'm holier-than-thou about things; it is just the way I was brought up. I never went to university, so I missed out on the language of youth, and the company I kept was very staid, living in a backwater of Cumbrian society. When I did go into a bar it was the snug, where things were more genteel, and that was only on special occasions. Jack hated television, he said it was bad for you, and by watching it you were wasting your life, so we always read in the evening, or played music.

That is when I decided to become a writer. The thing is, writers need to have something to write about, and inside me there is another Kate - a Kate that wants to be a Suzy. Sometimes I wish I didn't live so much inside my own head. Suzy's conviction to party her way through life sounds like fun. We could go on talking, but the curly-locks boyfriend finally wants some attention, he is obviously not having any luck at cards. They leave in a flurry of *Kaliniktas.*

'You be sure to meet me tomorrow Kate, Heraklion, El Greco Square, 12 o'clock.' Suzy instructs, as she turns to make sure the geriatrics get a last look at her bosom and curvy backside.

'It's a date,' I shout back before facing the fire again to warm my fingers. Gregory, thankfully, has now joined the card table, leaving me alone with my plate of hot vegetables, chunk of bread and glass of beer. He calls across to me, 'You OK?'

'Sure.' I reply, thinking, I am really sure; you stay over there and leave me alone to sit and listen to the sounds of Vrahassi life.

7

Heraklion, capital city of Crete; there are neither bright lights nor merriment. No throng of shoppers, no Christmas songs, no Santa Claus. The great commercial Christmas has not caught on. On the way to El Greco square from the bus station I don't pass anything that looks remotely Christmassy. There are no office parties, no tinsel, no glitter, and no Christmas card shops – in fact nothing to indicate Christmas at all. What a let down this is. It is just twelve noon as I reach our rendezvous destination. Suzy is already there.

'Yer got 'ere alright then?' She asks in a sort of motherly way.

'No problem, only there were not many buses this morning.' I tell her.

'No, shouldav said - winter timings – 'ere I got you a pie.' Suzy hands me a warm cheese pie. I take a bite; it's good. Flaky pastry falls down the front of my t-shirt and I dribble soft, hot cheese onto my chin, but it warms me.

'We gotta shop first cos it's all shut at two,' she says.

A stray dog is rooting in the rubbish bin, so I throw the mangy thing a piece of pie. It comes closer and I can see that it is infested with fleas and has an abscess in its udder-like nipples.

'Don't you go feeling sorry for it; theres 'undreds same.'

Still, I do feel terribly sorry for it, even though I know that there is nothing I can do. There is a hint of mothballs on the warm December breeze. Dry leaves dance around the trees and park benches of El Greco Square, like lost paper cut-outs, and I wrap my scarf around my neck to keep out the winter chill.

Suzy knows all the best shops, but most of the clothes are very old-fashioned. My purchase of the day is a portable CD player-cum-radio. I have brought a few CD's with me from England, so now there will be music in the hovel.

'Here, take this, a present from me,' says the charming shop keeper. It is a CD of Traditional Cretan Music, *Zorbas, Zembetiko,* and *Hasapiko.* 'You can learn dance.' I accept the gift and am very happy with it.

'Let's go for a drink, shall we?' Suzy says, as she pulls me into this place up a side street. We abandon the idea of going to the museum; it really does need a day when I am alone anyway.

The bar is quite modern. In one corner a couple of old guys are sitting playing backgammon. A suited salesman chucks a couple of coins onto the counter for his drink, and leaves, as we perch on high stools at the bar. I try to look arty, or hippy, or something in between, and in my best Greek I ask for a beer.

'*Mia beera parakalo.*' The barman leans my way. 'So, you want a beer?' He speaks perfect English and his gorgeous smile and lifted eyebrows are very confident, and very Greek. He holds his hand out in welcome. 'What is your name? I am Adonis.' Well he had to be, didn't he? I am prepared for the usual chat-up lines: "Are you married?" "Do you live alone?" But no, 'What work do you do?' asks the sweet Adonis. We laugh.

'Maybe he thinks we're pros,' Suzy whispers in my ear. I immediately answer so as to leave no doubt.

'I am a writer,' I say quickly, and I am researching my current book (sounds better than, my first novel). That seems to do it. Adonis is interested in philosophy, and very soon we have spent the best part of an hour discussing Socrates, Saint George and everything from Christianity to Cosmic Phenomena. OK, Suzy hasn't much input, but she has her own philosophy, the four 'F's, and right now I am hoping that she keeps it to herself.

'My father is a *Papa*,' says Adonis. 'He is a teacher at the local Orthodox Theological College.'

'So, do you believe the same things as your father?' I ask.

'My father is a very learned man, but I am of a different generation. I have been taught to ask questions. I have been taught to reason answers. I envy my father's blind faith.' He pauses. 'What do you think about the Orthodox religion?' The question was turned on me in a very Socratic way. Before I can answer, however, Suzy comes in - she's been waiting her chance.

'The only thing I know about the Orthodox is that menstruating women can't go to church.' I cringe, wishing she hadn't said that.

'I don't know much about the Orthodox religion,' I tell him. 'All Christians believe in the same Jesus Christ, don't they? The difference, as I see it, is in the man-made rules of each particular church. The form of worship varies from denomination to denomination but the faith remains the same, doesn't it?' This only seems to get Suzy going more.

'Why should incense and bells, and all that crossing be any better than singing 'ymns?' she says. The argument, I know, is very naïve, and I feel that time is up. I look at my watch and am very relieved to be able to say:

'Oh, sorry, I have to go to catch the bus back to Vrahassi.'

'Come back another day,' says the sweet Adonis, taking our empty glasses off the bar, a faint outline of a smile lingering in the air after he says it. 'See you again.' I say, shaking his hand before heading for the street. As we walk back to the bus station we talk about Christmas and what we would have been doing back in England. How different things are in Crete; how very different.

• •

Suzy and I have become friends. The very hairy one has been found, felt, fucked and forgotten, and now we can get on with the business of planning our Christmas together. We have come to the butcher's shop in Sissi to buy a turkey.

Our choice is one of a chained gaggle that is sitting comatose, on the roadside. A freshly slaughtered bull's head is hooked to the guttering, and trays of intestines and other inner bits are piled up on the wooden counter-cum-chopping block. Suzy does all the talking; her Greek is better than mine.

'*Yasou* Manolis, *ti kanis?*' Hi Manolis how are you? That much I understand, as for the rest, well, she must have said the right thing because Manolis Butcher is unfastening a quiet turkey from its shackles and taking it to the roadside. I'm not really prepared for an execution, but before I can turn the other way the bird begins to flap its wings as its neck is sliced off with one big, sharp knife. Blood drains down through a grate into the sewer, and I am not sure that I want turkey for Christmas dinner after all. A few minutes later our bird is plunged into a bowl of hot water and very swiftly plucked of all its feathers, while Suzy and I sit and drink a tot of *raki* that has been poured for us by Manolis Butcher's wife. It doesn't seem to have affected Suzy, but I have to say, I am a little stunned.

It is Christmas Eve, we are at Suzy's house near the harbour at Sissi, and the turkey is in the oven, slowly roasting. That wonderful smell of sage and onion and roast vegetables feeds my inward breath, and all those magical delights of a proper home come flooding back to me: soft cushioned sofa, glass fronted dresser, a modern fitted kitchen and volumes of curtain fabric. They are just not to be my lot, at least for the time being.

'You've got a lovely home, Suzy,' I say.

'You'll 'ave one when you've been 'ere as long as me.' She hands me a flute and pours out the bubbly. It's Greek champagne, dry and extremely good. I lounge in decadent comfort in front of the television while Suzy produces a plate of pate on toast - little finger nibbles that remind me of kiddies parties. No! Do not go there, Kate. I can feel the memory causing a lump in my throat, and my eyes begin to water. I throw back the champagne. Thankfully, a knock on the door diverts my attention. It is the neighbours. All of a sudden the house is full of noise, like the interval at the theatre. It is unbelievable that two people can cause such a commotion with loud greetings, *'Kronia pola, kronia pola, kala kristoujena.'*

'Eleni and Manolis are my landlords,' Suzy says. They are a happy couple, dressed in best Christmas black, and all ready to go to Church at midnight.

'Come with us,' they say as they sit down. They are very friendly and Manolis (it's a popular name) hands a bottle of Greek brandy to Suzy. It is special Metaxa 7 star. She looks over at me as she takes it.

'Ooh, nice,' she says giving me a wink.

'No good offering you two a glass of wine or anything, is it? I suppose you've bin fasting for church?' They nod their heads.

I am feeling much better now, the company is good and the bubbly has mellowed me.

'Let's go to church, Suzy,' I say, 'I've never been to a Christmas service in Crete.'

'Ooh... don't know about that, let's see how we feel nearer to midnight, it's only early yet.' I agree, it is only nine and we have been drinking. Our visitors get up to leave, and once more there is a lot of throwing around of arms and kissing on both cheeks. I am quite relieved that they are gone; it is difficult to keep up with the conversation. Now I can relax again with another glass of 'happy juice'. Suzy fills my flute almost to the top and we giggle as I siphon champagne from the full glass so as not to spill any. All around me there are silver stars and tinsel and streamers and balloons. The white-tutued fairy is sitting on top of her be-jewelled Christmas tree, ready with her wand to grant me a wish. My eyes are closed tight and I make my wish. The room is an exciting vibrato of colour. It is the night before Christmas. Breathe Kate, and be happy.

Sometimes good old strong Greek coffee can come to the rescue. This is one of those times. Suzy is looking after me like a mother.

"Ere, sip this then weesalget ready for Church.'

'Thanks,' I say giving her a hug.

As we join the Christmas crowd in the small walled yard outside the tiny whitewashed church in the middle of Sissi, the noise crescendos then fades to whispers as the service begins. There isn't room for everyone inside the church, so we stand outside, huddling beneath our coats to keep warm. It is a bit much of me, I know, to expect Suzy to be religious and, while the chanting and crossing and swinging of incense is going on, Suzy begins to tell me about who, out of the congregation, she has, and who she has not, been to bed with. 'Call 'emseves family men…' she starts, 'th'r all more interested in getting th'r end away than anything else.' Her voice is very "ooharrh", very "Barkus is willing".

'Shush!' I say. I'm really embarrassed that someone might hear her. All I see are respectable family men proudly parading their wives and children at the candle-lit service.

'Yer don't know what th'r like, Kate, but yal find out.'

The priest comes out into the cold and swings incense onto us and onto the shivering crowd. Suzy, for once, is silent. I instinctively bow my head, and as he passes I notice the huge emerald ring that he is wearing on the middle finger of his right hand. It is a gemstone like no other I have ever seen, dark yet faceted, speaking of the power that the church holds. As soon as the priest is back inside the church Suzy starts up again. 'See 'im?' she says, linking arms, and speaking in a semi-whisper, 'We 'ad a picnic in the olive groves,' she winks. 'And see 'im?' She points to a seventy-going-on-eighty-year old. 'Dirty old bugger he is, wanted me to give 'im a blow job.

'Suzy, shush,' I say, but I can't stop her flow.

'Ooeh, look at 'im in his silk shirt - thing the size of a policeman's truncheon, he 'as!' Her commentary goes on. I wonder if the men feel any guilt at all about their extra marital carryings-on. Well Suzy certainly doesn't so I don't suppose they do either.

We get through the service without any undue embarrassment, and happily part until the morrow, when we shall feast on my roof in Vrahassi.

'Thanks for a wonderful Christmas Eve, Suzy, see you tomorrow.' We hug.

'I'd better get that bird out the oven. Me and 'im will be up at your place for twelve - Night-night.' And we hug again. My very good friend, Manolis is waiting with his taxi to take me back home - he too is looking his best in black leather jacket and new pullover. He smiles at me. 'You had good time Katy?' he asks.

I sigh, 'Oh, so good Manolis.'

. . . .

We're on my roof. It's Christmas Day. Two old plastic chairs, cheap wine and fresh roast turkey; vegetables a la Kate and "We Two Kings of Orient Are". The mid day sun is warm, there is hardly a hint of a breeze, and we nosh, we imbibe and we slag off men and their mothers. I like Suzy's company. She's good in a naughty sort of way. Then she hits me with her news. It comes as a shock when she announces that she is going back to England.

'When are you going?' I ask.

'Tomorrow,' she says, as though it's just a visit to the corner shop.

'No! Why? It's Christmas.'

'My old mum is poorly, gotta go, see... only me, see... so gotta go, see.'

Of course I see, but selfishly want her to stay.

'Can I do anything to help?' I know it's a futile question, but I have to ask.

'No, you just get that book written while I'm away and then weeselav a great time when I's back. And don't you get up to any mischief while I's away.'

We finish off the box of wine, inside by the fire, before Suzy leaves.

I watch her struggle into an old bashed up pickup truck, a pre-arranged lift down the mountain, not knowing when we would see each other again.

8

As the drums and timbrals of the Festival of Demeter faded to a mere echo in the spirals of a seashell, Christmas has faded to no more than a page in my diary, which simply reads: "Spent Christmas Day with Suzy". We had made the best Christmas we could, but without the hype of the western world there wasn't much back up.

Vrahassi seems deserted. Maria is eternally cooking, and I am, once again, working late into the night on my book. Tomorrow is New Year's Eve. Gregory has asked me to join him for a drink at the *kafeneo* but I know that it is the big gambling night of the year and a strictly male preserve, so I said that I would have a drink with him at lunch time instead. Before tomorrow I want to concentrate on the story of Rhamu so that I can put it in the post for Daddy. I wonder if Daddy has read the first two parts. By now he should have had time. I haven't heard from him but I know the postal service here is a bit - iffy. There is no post office in Vrahassi, which is a bit inconvenient for some people. The postman seems to leave most letters at the *kafeneo*, better for him because it saves him climbing the steep roads, and I suppose he can have a coffee at the same time. I must get on! Anyway, Rhamu waits.

• •

Unfortunately ego often demands greater status. The people of Megalonissos are no exception. Amongst them there is a faction who thirst for power, and these egocentric people vie to be personifications of their "Mighty One". In doing so a jealousy emerges; a jealousy that eventually brings about genocide.

The young Milu is such a person. He is full of ambition and leadership. He wants a cause to fight for, and more than anything else he wants to win. From early childhood he has not been like the other boys. He has always been in front, always the one who is obeyed, always the one who is feared. Though he respects both his mother and father, he manipulates them and holds them in awe of his brave deeds and sharp wit. He is a brash youth who has already planned his future. No-one is going to get in his way; Milu sees himself as the Priest-Prince, Guardian of the Royal Blood, Keeper of the Princess Sisi and father of her children.

On his visit to the Palace of Sarpedon, when he was five years old, Milu had climbed a tree and picked apple blossom for his cousin. They had sat amongst the yellow sorrel, making flower chains. Milu had flamboyantly adorned Sisi with a garland of flowers. The yellow-gold chain of eight-petalled flower heads which he now wears around his neck was a spring gift from Sisi. She gave it to him three years ago for his eleventh Spring Festival. As he sets of to hunt the wild boar, his eight-petalled medallion catches the rays of the rising sun as it powers over the mountain. There is a sudden rush: a disturbance through the bushes, an advancement of young hunters. Swiftly they spring between the cypress trees after a hog in the undergrowth. Most of the boys are dressed only in a short toga and leather sandals, but Milu, their leader, wears a gold printed cotton kilt. His silver amulet grips the muscle of his right arm, and his jet black hair falls about his broad shoulders in perfect ringlets. The kill is swift. Milu's spear pierces the chest of the exhausted hog making a low thud as it stakes the poor animal to the ground. Milu is pleased. 'I am Milu, son of Miletos and champion of my father's city,' he boasts. With triumph, their prize is proudly carried, trussed by its short legs to a long branch, down the steep slope to the settlement below. As they break through the line of trees, the metropolis spreads before them – a civilized principality of Minoan life. Sheltered in the basin of high cliffs, with an expanse of sea in front, and rolling mountains behind, each building seems to rest peacefully and in total contentment.

The peace does not last. On entering his house, Milu is greeted with news that makes him rage like a tormented bull. He bursts into his father's chamber, seething and ranting a venomous trajectory of sound.

'I Milu, son of Miletos, should be with the Priest of Knossos. I am favourite of Sarpedon; I, by my blood and my strength and my knowledge. I have lived each day knowing that I was the chosen one. Not this, this Seal maker. Who dares to raise him above me? It is I who will be the next Protector of the Hive, I, the great Milu.'

'Stop, my son, Sarpedon is my dearest brother, but I

know we are wronged. Even so, to act like the enraged bull will only bring defeat. We must retire and speak with the high Masters of our religion.'

The statesman Miletos has had to deal with his son's outbursts before. He understands him well enough. He can recognize the rebel ambition, for he knows that he too was not always so calm. He thinks back to when he was his son's age. He had, together with his brother, Sarpedon, been discovered trying to obtain the powerful Emerald Crystal from its underground chamber in the heart of the labyrinth of Knossos. It had been an act of bravado, a challenge foolishly accepted. He knows that the magical power of the Crystal is unequalled and whoever holds it holds all the secrets of the universe. For his part in the attempted robbery of the virid ice-like rock, he had been banished, together with Sarpedon, from Megalonissos for eight years. They had been taken one night and unceremoniously put out to sea in an unmarked caique, to live or to die, but never to return until eight summers had passed.

He thinks now about his brother Sarpedon and how they had returned with tales of adventure and a cargo of treasure. They had proved their worthiness and had inherited their rightful place as wise leaders. Known as the 'Sopho' who had brought back political links from far across the Great Green Sea, together with their brothers, Rhadamanthus and the mighty Minos of Knossos, they are now unrivalled princes of peaceful, civilized kingdoms

Miletos looks deep into his son's eyes and can see the anguish in him. He understands his disappointment; he too is hurt by the fact that his son has not been chosen, and he agrees to help him get rid of Rhamu. It is the only way to ensure that the succession to the throne of Sarpedon will go to Milu.

The next day Milu and his father set sail from a small natural harbour used mainly by hill farmers for their crude fishing boats. It is a little-used harbour and they are able to slip away unseen – their destination, Libya. There they will meet up with an old priest who Miletos knows will be sympathetic to their cause.

Together Milu and his father Miletos contact a triangle of powerful magicians as far away as Egypt and Asia Minor. Together they begin to plot the downfall of Rhamu. In secret they conspire to invoke the dark forces and to project their black will on the heart of their victim. It will take some time; to break through the powerful magic of the Emerald Crystal will not be easy. If only they can obtain the Crystal, absolute power will be theirs; they will even have supremacy of the High Masters of the Pyramid. Their appetite is whetted and a collective malevolence is created.

And so it is that the injured Milu and his father begin to fight the decision of the elders of Sarpedon who have decreed that Rhamu, son of the Master Seal-Maker, will be instructed and initiated in the ways of the high Keftiu Priests. Rhamu is to be prepared to host the mighty Tsuna. The elders have chosen him because of his innocent love, not only for Sisi, which they have observed, but also because of his love of all things. He is kind and gentle and his growing spirit is full of goodness. Rhamu has been chosen to become High Protector of the Royal Blood and Prince of the Kingdom of Sarpedon.

For two years Rhamu studies the customs of the High Court, and learns the most powerful earth magic. Meanwhile the Princess Sisi is held captive by Vestal Virgins who block her thoughts and keep her happy as she waits for her wedding day. And Milu, together with his father Miletos and some of the fallen tutelary genius of Egypt and Libya, plot black sorcery to support their cause. They return to Megalonissos with instructions to steal the Emerald and deliver it to the Brethren of Hades.

That will do for now. My shoulders are cramped with hunching over my laptop for so long, but I am pleased to have brought my story this far. I have had an idea to incorporate the story of Rhamu into a longer work about my life in Crete. Hopefully, I can pull it off. I know the village Crete that I am becoming part of, is quickly disappearing. How much longer will donkeys be used by the farmers to transport fodder, olives and wood? How much longer will toothless old folk in black be toothless, let alone in black? How much longer will people be allowed to smoke in the *kafeneo*? It may seem a long way off, but already the farmers are buying new 4 x 4 pickup trucks, and the old head-to-foot-black widows are not being replaced by the next generation. As for cigarette smoke, well, Crete is in Europe, and western ways and ideas are catching on fast.

I am not finding it hard work to write, as the information is all around me and seems to be inside me just ready to stream onto the page, as though it is being downloaded through my fingers. Nevertheless, the physical work of typing so many words is tiring and I am ready for a break. I'll just write a note to Daddy to put in with my story. Handwriting seems so awkward after using the computer; I am quite out of the habit. At least the world has moved on from the old quill pen, and writing with my new roller-tip is effortless and surprisingly neat, if I take care.

Dear Daddy,

Happy New Year, I hope you are OK and having lots of adventures. I just know that this year is going to be one of the best yet. Certainly, living in this mountain village is worlds apart from life in England, and I am learning so much. The people are very friendly, and there is no crime to speak of. I can safely go out and leave my door unlocked. Food is very fresh, and it is cheap to live here. My friend Suzy has gone to England for a while – I hope she will come back soon.

It is New Year's Day today Daddy. Last night came and went in Vrahassi without as much as a popped cork. I did go down to the kafeneo to meet Gregory, but he had gone off gambling somewhere and the village was deserted. He must have forgotten that I had agreed to have a drink with him. Anyway, the kafeneo was empty, and when I looked in they said they were closing, it was only 9 o'clock. I went home and spent the evening alone by my log fire, Mozart for company. I suppose you were in front of the TV, scotch in hand, listening to the Hogmanay programme. My New Year's resolution is to finish the book. Daddy, can you make it one of your New Year resolutions to read it?

Enclosed is the next part of my story about Rhamu and Sisi. Let me know what you think to it. I have started to think about publishing. The same publisher who produced my poetry book in Cumbria may be interested. What do you think?

The weather is really good here at the moment, sunshine and clear skies, of course it is not summer and as soon as the sun goes down it is quite cold, but the days are lovely. They make me feel good, and I must say that I am feeling so much better than when I first arrived. Don't worry about me Daddy, I am OK. Next week I am going to visit the museum in Heraklion, maybe even take a drink with the sweet Adonis. He is the owner of a cafe-bar in the town.

I'll end here Daddy. Hope you get this letter soon. I'll give you a ring next week.

Love you very much,
Kate X
P.S. And here is a little poem I wrote.

If the ocean were a puddle
And the street were golden sand,
Then the ripples I created
Would wash away the land,
If the ripples were a record
Of the love-song of the sea,
Then the puddles and the ocean
Would all be part of me.

There, that's that done: into the envelope, lick flap, stick down, add stamp and write address. 'Love you Daddy.' There is something very satisfying about getting a letter ready to put into the post.

9

The road down the mountain is busy-busy with Cretan farmers, out in the January sunshine thwack-thwacking their olive trees. Whole families are beavering about, scrambling up inclines on the many terraces and contours of the land. I pass one or two donkeys patiently waiting to be loaded up. '*Yasas*,' I shout to all as I pass, 'Hello, Hello my friends.' I am feeling like I have just found a lost treasure, they are looking at me like I'm crazy. 'Where are you going?' they call, 'Come and help us - *Ela*.' But I don't want to stop, I am adventuring in the countryside and I have a mission. I will walk down to the gorge where I can join the main road and catch a bus to Heraklion. 'Another time,' I call back.

Freedom! Utter freedom! Breathe Kate, breathe in freedom. I am free of the nest. Free of the herd. Free as the sixteen Griffon vultures which are circling above the monastery as I, light footed, head towards the gorge at Selinari. My spirit is in the sky and I am as a seedling scattered by the wind. I am a renegade with flowing mane and galloping fetlocks. I am a child of the universe - part of the earth but not on it. I sing to the sunshine. I sing to the sky. I sing to the clouds. It is so good to be out of the house, out of the village… Oh dear! Hang on! I thought it was too good to last. A teardrop touches my hand. It is raining!

- My friend is near. I feel him in the rain; the rain which has followed me from England, the rain which has brought such melancholy. I am not afraid. I am consumed in an embrace of living passion. The heavens pour down on me and I rejoice. The water leaves me clean, refreshed and wholesome. I inhale its opium; its elemental joy. My boots splash in play-puddles. My heart beats fast in my head.
Wet granite bathes in the torrent. Goat bells are a chinkling veil of seashells. I am a closed shoot opening into a verdant springtime. The newness of newborn green fizzles around me.
Paprika-red mud-clods make a soft soup-bed of the hard ground. Red, orange, yellow – each colour sings to me. A mix of musical tones sets me tingling from tiptoe to temple. All is vibration. My eyes are drawn to a high liquidy-ledge, and there, through the shivering and shifting blur of vapour; there through the rainbow of sunlight and sound, there in ethereal illusion, I glimpse the spectre of a mist-maiden. The Queen of the cloud-cliffs, resplendent in her iridescent gown of diamond teardrops, is looking down on me. She is as opaque as a moonbeam; translucent as a puff of gold dust. A laser-like brilliance shoots from the heaven – and she is gone. -

I begin to shake. Is the moment real or unreal? Whichever it is, it is mercurial. Globules of sweat drip from my iced skin. The rain stops. The vultures reappear.

A tiny shrew scampers beneath the barique. A white triangle, like an angel walking the sapphire water, passes across the horizon in the V of the gorge. I, stunned by the moment, sit beside an obelisk of carbuncled stone and take comfort from its solidity.

The *Stone* is unbelievably dry. It has somehow escaped the driving shower, even though it is as tall as a man. I need to discuss my vision with someone and who better than my new acquaintance. It is a bit one sided, but *Stone* is such a good listener. I shelter beside him. 'Am I going mad, *Stone*? Here I am in a foreign land, away from all that I was brought up with. My neighbours are friendly, but I will always be an outsider. I feel that I belong here, but like a weed in the middle of a crop of corn, I have to fight for my survival and be vigilant against *horta pickers*, who want me to become one of them. My mind keeps entering a world somewhere between awake and asleep; between day and night; between gravity and floatation. Where am I? Are my visions a trick of the mind? Maybe you also are a trick of the mind? Are you more tangible to my spirit because I can touch you? The eyes see. The ears hear. The nose smells. The skin touches. My eyes see a ghostly figure. My ears hear bodiless voices. My nose smells unknown gasses. My skin touches a warm aura. What is real? Are you real, *Stone*? Am I real? Does your spirit hear me?' - My head is very light.

- I am in the eye of an eagle. I am an infinite speck in the breath of the jet stream, I am expanding to become an infinitesimal particle that can merge with a rainbow and become a single raindrop. A tear slides down my cheek and I

hear a whisper inside by head. "Rainbows Herald Aquarius Magic Universe – RHAMU."

My spirit friend is inside the message. He has reached my inner self. The penny drops, of course, rainbows which appear when the sun shines. Rain tears - Tears from the sun, tears that are Aquarius magic. RHAMU, my water spirit, is in the rain. And the mist-maiden could she possibly be the spirit of Sisi? I pat my new friend, *Stone*, affectionately and say goodbye. I am in a slight state of shock. Rhamu has made contact again.

Five minutes ago I was feeling really good, but now it is raining and I am getting soaked, and it is not my idea of fun. Why don't they build bus shelters? I see one a little further ahead and rush towards it.

Enter into my life Pete. Crazy Greek drivers are whizzing by, down the gorge and on, in some obvious chase to meet an appointment with fate. I am feeling like someone just emptied a bucket of water over my head and this Jesus figure with long black hair and faded denims appears through a gap in the hedge. I'm not quite sure who is the most startled. He has obviously walked some distance in the pouring rain too. Water is dripping down his head onto hunched shoulders, and to say he looks like a bony whippet that has plunged through a stream is an understatement. Well, he dismisses any formalities and speaks to me as though I'm the local barmaid. 'When's this fuckin' rain gonna stop?' His accent is not quite Geordie, but definitely north of Carlisle. I'm surprised.

'You're English!' I say.

'That's fuckin' clever of you.'

I bypass the sarcasm and try to find out his life story. Pete has come to work in the olive groves. He's had a spell in Israel picking oranges, but fancied a change. He's living in Sissi (no wonder he's so depressed). I'm offended by his language at first. Every other word is preceded by the word fuckin'. 'Fuckin' weather stops the fuckin' work. There's no fuckin' money. I'm fuckin' fed up,' he moans. But he's friendly enough, and we chat till the bus arrives. It hurtles towards us, and miraculously stops so that we can get on through the side door at the back. No sooner are we on, than it's off again, before we have time to sit down. The crucifixes and hanging third eyes around the driver's mirrors don't have time to settle the whole journey. Fuckin' Pete (for that's what I will call him from now on) grumbles until we get to the bus station in Heraklion.

'Fuckin' Greek drivers... Fuckin' roads are not fuckin' good... Fuckin' dead dogs never get fuckin' moved... Fuckin' lucky we aren't over the fuckin' edge...'

In an obscure sort of way that last statement is close to being true – but the edge isn't that of the cliff, it is the edge of sanity.

I left Fuckin' Pete half an hour ago, but his words are still clanging around my skull like fuckin' bells. I shake myself like a dog just out of the bath, in the hope that expletives will spray out of me and get diluted on the wind. Ooooh! That's better! - First the post office and then for some serious research. I kiss the packet as I put it in the box. 'Love you Daddy.'

The museum is quiet: no tourists, no groups of any kind, just me, the guard and the remnants of a lost civilization. It is sort of weird - looking at bits of what are left from a great Palace, all out of context, in shabby glass cabinets, all broken bits of people's lives - a doll here, a fragment of jewellery there.

My mind starts to work like some automatic hologram machine, and I begin to put fingers around teacup handles, shiny bodies behind steaming cauldrons, brooch pins onto tunics, amulets around arms, and amphora onto shoulders. I hear babies crying, children playing, the rabble of the market place, the silence of the temple. There is a clanking and hammering of stone. There is a slop of wine. There is the stench of slaughter, and the sweet aroma of bees' wax and honey. I watch the seal-maker in his workshop. Now I can hear the music, watch the dance; see – Oh! What can I see? What is this here in front of me? It takes my breath. It is real. I can almost touch it - the *Sword of Right*, with its orb of clear crystal. But that's not all. There is something else. This is the reason I am here. This is the proof of my story. This is so unbelievable - so fantastic. Safely behind a glass case, calling me, speaking to me, sharing something very intimate with me, is the golden bee pendant, the very piece of jewellery that I have seen in my dreams. I read the card. "'This beautifully designed piece of jewellery was found inside one of the stone tombs at *Chrysolakkos*, the graveyard of Kings, at the archaeological site of the Minoan Palace at Malia.'" I can't take my eyes of it.

I am very cold. It is true, all of it. The evidence is here. Will anyone believe me if I tell them? Who is there to tell anyway? Suzy is in England. I can't get past, *what-are-you-cooking-Maria*, and Fuckin' Pete, well, we'll not go there. Oh! I'm so F...in' HAPPY. I want to fly out of the museum and tell the world.

I am in Lion Square in Heraklion, sitting in a comfortable wicker chair, with a very expensive cup of cappuccino warming the senses in my nostrils. I feel like I could be in *Paris,* or *Rome,* or *Vienna.* The city is revolving. So, my water spirit is in the rain, howling, crying, trying to feel his feet on the earth that he half belongs to, spirit without a body, his soul mate as elusive as a nymph in the shadows. I think back to the vision that I witnessed in the gorge, a vision that I can clearly recall. It was another rainbow-like water spirit – again confusion. Am I to understand that Sisi has not become incarnate? Is this illusory figure, yet another being of the heavens calling on me? The midday sun puts me into a somnambulant state.

- Sounds are muffled. People no longer walk on the pavement. I am surrounded by bodies that hover, neither attached to the earth, nor stable. They are jelly. Plasmic masses of vibrant jelly. They vibrate red and green, purple and blue. I am hanging upside down and I am in, or on, or part of a totally new world. Everything is crumbling around me. Dust to dust, to dust, to dust. But the atoms are singing.-

'Fuckin' deaf or what?'

'Sorry, you startled me. I was somewhere else. Would you like some coffee?'

'Fuckin' coffee, get real. How long have you lived here? Fuckin' coffee, no I fuckin' don't want coffee; you're in the wrong fuckin' shop. Come on with me

I'll take you for a fuckin' *raki*.' I have no choice in the matter. In a way it's quite exciting to be domineered, even if it is by Fuckin' Pete. I hold his hand like a schoolgirl, as he drags me through the town. We go between narrow streets, darkened by overhanging balconies of old Turkish houses, until we arrive at a very dingy *kafeneo* somewhere behind the bus station. Bedlam ensues. Sitting amongst the squalor and rabble of the old boys' conclave is Suzy, back from England, and bold as ever. We hug like sisters. Space is created for another two at the food-filled table and I squash in amongst toothless old men, fat butchers, out-of-town in-town shepherds and stinking fish traders. All have two things in common – they all stink and they all have the *raki* red-eye. It is a small *kafeneo* and the owner is a big guy who has to squeeze between the chairs. His breathing is bad, probably from spending his life in a box of smoke, and he appears to be deaf - well, everyone seems to be shouting at him.

'*Ferry moo mia beera* - Bring me a beer,' shouts one.

'Bring cheese' shouts another. And orders go out above the general din of the conversation.

Then we are noticed, Suzy and I - women. We had been noticed before, but politics have to come first. Women have to be ignored and made to feel invisible before the male pounces. But sure enough the male never fails to pounce.

'*Eh! Kookla - ti les?* - Eh! Doll, what you say?' I look bemused. What do I say to what? But I know that what he is really asking is - how do I feel about a quick shag in the olive groves. They never stop trying their luck, even when they are so fat that they probably haven't seen their manhood for years. I am disgusted with the company that I am keeping, but at the same time it excites me in a raw sort of way. Suzy seems to be quite at home. The music starts.

My head is definitely in trouble. The party is over. I haven't a clue where I am, or how I got here. Between me and the concrete floor is a very smelly goatskin. I can feel the warmth of a body at my side, and I am praying that it is not that of a toothless old shepherd. Close - it's Suzy, (joking). She's still fully clothed the same as me, boots and all.

'Owwerh! Is that you Kate?'

'I'm not sure.' I think I said that, but don't know whether the words just came in my head. 'Suzy, I want a wee.'

'Me too.'

'Can't move.'

'Me neither.'

Time passes. A strong smell of lanolin and sheep dung permeates my drunkenness.

'Suzy, where are we?'

'D' know.'

'Was it a good night?'

'D' know.'

Time passes.

'Suzy, I have to find the toilet.'

'Outside.'

I get to my knees, but I'm still dizzy. I stagger to the door, lift the latch and stumble into the blinding brightness of day. My mouth is like the bottom of

Maria's ash pan, and my throat is smoke-sore. I throw up into a bush, and wet my knickers. I'm not good, not good at all. A heap of shepherd is comatose on an old wooden bench beneath an olive tree, and we have slept the night on the floor of his bothy. He's a friend of Suzy's, thank God, and he takes us back to Sissi, but not before we've slurped copious amounts of thick black coffee. I never want to touch *Raki* again!

10

Suzy is celebrating with her Greek landlord and his family today. I was asked to join them, but prefer to stay in the village. It is the sixth of January - *Epiphany*. Barbecues are out in the streets, wine is flowing and *Papa* Zachariah, as is the custom, is visiting every house to perform a blessing. It is my place next. Maria, three children from the village, *Papa* Zachariah and I crowd into my little hovel; it is the first time that the *Papa* has been into my home. We have spoken many times at the *kafeneo*, but here in my house I feel the presence of a sage. He is always so gentle, so gracious, so kind. He is a black-robed guardian of the faith. The scene could have been an El Greco, with some name such as "The Blessing". Our illuminated *Papa*, with long silvery beard and hair knot at the nape of his neck, splashes holy water onto all present from a small brush of rosemary leaves. The three children clang their triangles and sing, and Maria and I watch trance-like, in a haze of incense. When it is over, I kiss the emerald ring on *Papa* Zachariah's middle finger, catching my breath at its brilliance. I place some money into his waiting palm, mesmerized for a second by the beauty of the jewel. The children rattle their collecting box for some coins, and they all leave. I am happy, the house is happy and all feels calm, in some sort of esoteric way. Let the feasting begin!

Maria's little courtyard is crammed full of friends and family. I join the table and am immediately made so welcome: food, wine, more food and more wine. Above us there is a canopy of trellis awaiting the growth of the vine, and around us there is a hotchpotch of potted geraniums and faded greenery. My dish is piled with spaghetti, my glass is never empty, and I tuck in to pieces of boiled turkey. I am here to share both the food and the company. Manolis, as ever, is very attentive.

'Katy, more wine?' he takes my glass and fills it.

'Manolis, I shall be drunk.' I say.

'Then you eat more,' he says, piling another knuckle of turkey onto my plate. Finally the revelry turns into song. It is the first time that I have heard Manolis sing, and what a voice he has got. The song is with all his heart. There is happiness in every note, every word; happiness and seriousness, as he makes sure that his performance is both understood and appreciated.

'Itan mia fora kai enan kero matia moo…' - It was once upon a time, my love…

It is a Cretan experience like no other, and now everyone is drinking again, and clapping another beat. The singing leads to dance, and the day ends in total exhaustion and sound sleep.

My peasant-farmer friends and neighbours are providing a secure environment for me. I am an outsider, and may just as well have come from another planet, compared with the way in which they have been brought up, but they accept me for what I am. Manolis hugs me as I leave. It is a generous hug; a warm and loving hug that sends me home feeling part of his world.

Evil spirits have been banished from every corner of my hovel, I have glass in the kitchen window, and most of the grime has been scrubbed away. My roof is still the most fantastic place to sit and contemplate, and I feel another episode of my story of Rhamu about to leap on to the page. I will not be going to Heraklion to post it.

. . . .

The Temple of Helios is set amongst a grove of oak trees, on a natural mound on the edge of the city of Sarpedon. From her tower at the top of the royal chambers, Sisi can see the tips of the two pillars of the sacred ground. They are obelisks of stone set close together, but far enough apart for a person to stand between them. Each one is carved with symbols of mysterious necromancy, which only the High Priestesses of the Temple can interpret and use in the sacred rites. In front of the two pillars is a pool of water, clear as the mountain spring which keeps it ever full. Around the pool are torches of eternal fire which burn night and day, their purifying flames taking messages and supplications to the spirits of the trees, who protect the grove and all therein. Constant communion and praise is given to the Great Shining One, Helios the sun. It is said that the priestesses can look into the mirror-like water of the pool and see the future.

Sisi wonders what they have seen of her future. She is now held captive in the very centre of her world, and, surrounded by her attendants, the vestal virgins of the Temple of Helios; she cannot expand her mind to reach the thoughts of her beloved Rhamu. Where is he? Why is there no word from him? She accepts her imprisonment, but is totally unaware that Rhamu has been taken to Knossos, or even that he is to be her prince. As she gazes out towards the mountains she longs for the touch of her lover.

After two cycles of the summer moon, in as many years, when balmy nights cradle the peoples of Megalonissos, the first signs of unrest are felt. It is a mere shiver of the reflected mountains in the Pool of Perfection that first catches the eye of the young Priestess Anthea. She knows of no reason why there should be bad portents now. On the contrary, the Master, Lendus is, at this moment, taking power from the Crystal at Knossos – she thinks. He is working with it for the good of all the peoples.

On a second look, deep into the eye of the pool, she can see the great magician raise his wand, and a stream of pure white meets it, like a silk antenna. Light emanates from the Emerald as if from a confident spider, which, sitting in the centre of its web, casts out razor-threads of energy. The grey bearded Lendus, his hair-knot tight to the back of his neck, fills with brightness, and all the joy of the worlds is in his consciousness, as he communes with the Great Shining One via the power of the Crystal. In his shadow stands Rhamu, the student, now standing taller and statelier than before. He steps forward to be by his mentor, the Master Wizard, and his face is alight with knowledge. With total confidence and tenderness, Rhamu reaches out his fingertips to gently touch the carved rock. It is cold to his senses, yet warm as a blood-brother. After reading the inscriptions with the sensitive pad of his middle finger, he draws a large cross in the air, bows to the Crystal, and withdraws backwards in respect. So is the initiation of Rhamu complete. His journey is about to begin.

The shiver, what does it mean? Anthea is worried as she gives praise to the messenger-of-the-water. She hurries away to seek the advice of her sister-priestesses. Before the day is out, further messages of ill, come on the winds to the priestesses of the Miteres in the Temple of Demeter. The High Priest to Sarpedon himself is aware of shifting vibrations on the ether. They all know to be extra vigilant in their protection of the Princess. With the heads of the priests and priestesses turned in the direction of the royal chambers, Milu takes his chance to slither into the dark passageways of Knossos on his mission to steal the Emerald Crystal.

Milu has no trouble weaving in and out of the little-used side roads and secret streets. His mind is locked with that of his father, who has made the journey before. He merges into the stone holes like a ghostly amphibian clinging to the slabbed walls, and in a sideways crawl he avoids the guard at the entrance to the throne-room. In his knee-length boot is a silver dagger, around his neck a soft pig-skin pouch, and slung across his bare shoulders, a black leather saddle bag.

Rhamu and Lendus, only seconds before, had left the throne-room after their final audience with King Minos. The once so beautiful boy-King is now, like his brothers, Sarpedon and Rhadamanthus, a mature and wise leader. As soon as Rhamu and Lendus have departed for their journey back to the Palace of Sarpedon, King Minos hurries to hold court with all his advisors.

The Throne-room is empty, apart from two guards who flank the high backed throne. Their tall double headed axes look menacingly dangerous, but they are mainly symbolic – no-one ever thinks of danger inside the Palace. On the walls are frescos of delightful scenes of nature: flowers and birds, trees, processions of noble youths, and bull-leaping acrobats. In front of the carved stone throne there is a rectangular area which is approached by a pillared flight of stairs. In the centre of this area there is a gaping orifice, which leads down and down, through the cold earth, to the epicentre of Knossos and to the Chamber of Power. The shaft that rises out of the darkness is interrupted only by the Throne-room before it continues through the roof, like an open chimney. When the sun is at its zenith, it blazes down through the perfectly round funnel, and sends a beam of life-force directly to the Crystal below.

Outside in the courtyard there is music and dancing and laughter, and the elaborately dressed court ladies sit about chattering. Inside, Milu crouches behind a bull's-head pillar. His heart races; he has got this far, now he only has to escape the gaze of the guard, and his plan to hide in the dark well will be complete. It is time for him to use the wind-bag which the magicians of Libya gave him. He carefully unties the knot, and can feel the force build. Pointing it in the direction of the guard he allows its contents to rush out. At once a freak wind gushes into the open, shrieking and howling, a blast of such intensity that the two unsuspecting men drop their staffs and can barely remain standing. Taking his chance, Milu springs up the staircase, and climbs down into the chimney. It is mid-afternoon; there is plenty of time for him to work his way down, down, down the long shaft to his prize.

The alarm has been raised. King Minos and his Council know there is an intruder. His magic may have shielded him, but it has also revealed his presence. Milu saves his most cunning manoeuver for his escape. He drops through the opening, his dagger drawn ready for a fight. The sky-light of the funnel is now only a round of blue in the heaven above him. Pouncing on the Emerald, he greedily wraps it in a square of brown silk, and pushes it into his saddlebag. As he moves, the round light becomes a crescent, and finally a void, as the Throne-room entrance is sealed. Protective troopers immediately begin to appear through the underground tunnels which lead to the vault. Milu is ready for the first wave. He fights with the strength of a giant, disposing of the unpracticed warriors. His silver dagger finds its way through soft gut with the practiced stab of a master butcher, and he litters the floor with writhing, dying bodies.

Locating an air vent in the ceiling, he swiftly climbs to find his escape. He rolls himself into a perfect ball of human substance and begins to tumble through the earth-pore; through the giant nigrescent worm hole, through the trackless tunnel of dragon's breath, until he shoots into the firmament like a blazing meteorite. The reddened atmosphere of a flaming orange sunset greets him, offering timely freedom. For now, he can call up the twilight forces and slip into the dimension of the imperishable. This he does, and is sucked into a zone of vile and grotesque forms, which claw to entrap him. In his mercurial transience he trembles at the sight. Yes, even "The Most Brave" Milu, shudders as he passes through the bilious plexus of the underworld.

This time Lendus, Minos, Sarpedon and Rhamu have been outwitted. Their protective leadership is in danger of crumbling. They are momentarily defenseless, however it will be some time before the boy Milu or his masters can decipher the Crystal. King Minos knows that he has no time to lose.

Within seconds, a network of consciousness is set up between the Hives and the Temples, and Sacred Groves. A warning vibration is soon emanating from Knossos. It creates both a signal against danger, and a barrier against any malevolent dissonance. Resounding as a low "omm" from a line of individuals, it eventually causes a total tonal blackout around the Kingdoms of Sarpedon and Knossos, and as far south as Phaestos, where the third brother, Rhadamanthus, lives in untroubled harmony.

Nothing else can be done until night has passed, and the sun is once more in the firmament to guide them. All night, in a triad of mysticism, the three brothers remain vigilant. For the first time in many dynasties, the line of the Royal Blood is in grave danger.

The next day it begins to rain. The golden orb of the sky is obliterated by an all-pervading nimbus; grey and barbarous in its relentless downpour. The growing echo of the Keftiu chorus continues to drone, like an amplified buzz of electric wires, and the usually active streets and public places are as unpopulated as a deserted garrison. Screaming cats scrap in the empty agora; dogs howl with sensitivity to the air-blast. The sea rises like a swollen flash-flood of an untimely storm, and a wash of burnt-umber mud swirls landwards in rivulets of the incoming tide.

It is Lendus, the Master Magician, who has caused the rain this mid-summer day. He has cloaked the island to shield it. For he now knows that the magic he is fighting does not come from his land, but from far across the sea. He knows that the island attack is coming from the Fallen Masters – the Brethren of Hades. The mating of Sisi must go ahead. When the moon has turned once more, the time will be right.

. . . .

I think it is time for a break, and a bite to eat. Computer off, coat on, hanky in pocket, handbag full of stuff to cover every emergency, and I am out into the cold, but bright afternoon.

'*Yasou* Katy. I am not you to seeing me. *Kronia pola.*'

It is Gregory. He startles me. I haven't seen him for ages. He is muffled up against the cold, scarf, gloves, and commando headgear. His hair stands up like a golliwog's, when he takes off his balaclava. It is caked in oil, as is the rest of his work-wear.

'*Yasou* Gregory. How are you?' I ask.

'Too much working Katy - Coming to inside?' He ushers me into the *kafeneo*. I am not protesting - I was just on my way there anyway. The February cold has really got to me, that and a bit of loneliness, so in a way I am happy to see him. It is like all the village is hibernating. I know they are not, because the olive factory is working late every night, I can hear the motors of the press. But people's doors are closed, the streets are empty, and there is a haze of wood-smoke hanging over the village.

For Gregory it is normal. He pulls up a chair for me near the wood-burner, and orders wine. 'Am to eating me together?' he asks.

'Yes why not?' I reply. It's too cold, and I'm too hungry to be bothered about his dirty fingernails. 'Where is *Baba* Kostas?' I ask. I never did get to talk to him about his work with the Minoan seals. 'Athens,' says Gregory, poking grime out of his ear with his lonely, overgrown fingernail. God! I am thinking. Did his mother never tell him not to do that? I smile at my own snobbery; the little voice in my head sounding just like Joyce Grenfell's when she did the sketch with the school children… "George, don't do that…" when all the time, I know that it is me who is the odd one out in the *kafeneo*, not him.

Our food arrives, a plate of hot meat and vegetables, it is kind of Gregory to look after me in this way, and he is not bad company. He talks incessantly, not just to me, but to the other guys. Most of what he is saying I can't follow, but it doesn't matter; his banter gets louder and louder. '*Then katalaves kala* - you no understand,' he keeps saying, backing up his side of the argument. And it does appear to be an argument now. 'Come on,' he says, all of a sudden.

'Come on where?' I say, as he begins to wrap up again, first his face mask, then his gloves. 'Milatos,' he says, 'you good to going on bike?' Now I have to make an instant decision. Do I want another adventure? Do I want to ride behind Gregory on his old Honda 50? Do I want to go to Milatos? Well, yes, I do, I really do.

I'm not sure what's up, but I don't want to miss out on the fun.

And it is fun, clinging on to Gregory's bomber jacket, whilst hiding behind his back out of the wind, as we putter, putter around the mountain and drop down the other side - down and around, down and around, down and around every hairpin bend, until we reach the coast at Milatos.

'Are you crazy or what?' I ask, as we come to a stop outside a closed beach taverna.

'Crazy,' he says. 'Crazy - *nai*, - very crazy.' He pulls the bike onto its stand, takes hold of my hand, and leads me into what looks like a closed café bar. It isn't closed. Inside is a tiny room with three tables. They are all occupied, all instantly re-occupied, to make room for us to sit down together with the other men. Gregory is well known. They eye me like I'm his floozy. Nobody speaks to me. Gregory is instantly in conversation, obviously fired up about something. It's four in the afternoon. The sea is bashing onto the pebble beach outside, and I'm wondering what the hell is going on.

'Gregory, tell me what's going on.' I say. 'Why are you so upset?'

'Katy - sorry,' he says, calming down and taking off his balaclava. Actually he looks better with it on, but who's counting? *Raki* appears on the table, together with a couple of fresh oranges. 'The Mayor is in prison...' he tells me, 'Tomorrow we to going Neapolis - many people.'

'Good grief! In prison,' I say. 'What's all that about then?'

'Political,' he says, in the sort of way that because I am a woman I won't understand, and he starts talking to the other men. Well, I did want another adventure, but all their shouting is getting to me, and I really want to take a look at Milatos, so I excuse myself and tell Gregory that I'll be back in fifteen minutes.

It is cold and windy on the sea-front, but the fresh air and smell of the sea effuse a menthol vapour around me, as I inhale its ghosts. Milatos - one of the hundred cities mentioned by Homer in the Iliad: where black-sailed boats left to fight in the Hellenic war; were Milu, in my story, stormed about, just like Gregory is doing; where the great statesman, Miletos, ruled his city; where right at this minute, in the history of the world, I am - and I love it. I love the time-wheel of history that has brought me here. Breathe Kate! Breathe and know!

The seaside tavernas are empty, and their awnings are blowing in the cold north wind. The best of the day is over. A purple-grey, turmoil of sky pours into the muddiness of the sea, dropping a curtain of night. A church candle flickers shadows over icons. Souvenir shops are closed, Rent-rooms deserted. Milatos seems no more than a cluster of buildings; a seaside hamlet battened down for the winter.

I focus on the hills, where so many people had found refuge in the caves. What would life have been like in those distant times?

'Come on Kate, we to going now.'

'No problem, Gregory, I'm ready.' I have had enough of this solitude, and I am glad to make the journey back to Vrahassi, and to the warmth of my own little pad.

11

I am not going to Neapolis with Gregory this morning; I will get a full report later. I just have to get stuck into part five of my story; the final part, the destruction of the Minoan Civilization. It is a fact that somehow, the great civilization that lived in wonderful style on Crete over 3,000 years ago, came to an abrupt end. There are various theories of how this happened. One of those theories states that a tidal wave swept the north side of Crete, and destroyed all the palaces. This tidal wave appears to have been caused by the eruption of a volcano on Santorini, an island only 88 miles (142 kilometres) away. If this was the case, then the skies would have been darkened with the fall-out of the volcano. This dusty ash would have covered the ground, making it impossible for crops to grow for years. There may have been fires. Well, Kate, your story is not a million miles away from this theory; it is just a little bit different.

Sisi remains ignorant of all else but her time in the tower, until one morning she receives a small parcel. It bears a grand seal, a Royal Seal, but she does not recognize it.

Then, as if it has spoken to her, she understands that it is the seal of Rhamu, and she tears into the package. Her breath is seized at the sight of its contents. An exquisite little wooden box, carved over its entirety with minute eight- petalled flower heads. She opens the lid. How can this be? How could Rhamu have obtained such a treasure? Who had given him the right to own a Royal Seal? Inside the box is a gift more beautiful than Sisi has ever received before: a jewel which she carefully picks up, feeling its warmth. She hands it to one of her attendants, bunches her thick blond tresses on top of her head and bares her young, downy neck to receive the gold pendant. It sits on her cygnet-skin reflecting beams of yellow onto her chin. As she looks down to admire its beauty, she sees the delicately-worked companionship of two golden bees. They are carrying a ball of golden pollen between them and they wear a single golden coronet. From the extended wing of each bee and from their joined abdomens, hangs a small golden disc, which represents the trinity of Rhamu, and the great sea spirit, Tsuna, and herself. With this gift all Sisi's fears are over. Now she knows that Rhamu has been chosen, and that they will be together again very soon. She is content. As she lies in the shade of a silver-tipped palm, she dreams of her love.

Meanwhile, the Master, Lendus, communes with the Temple of Isis in Egypt. He works day and night to keep the power of the Dark Brethren outside his circle. Sarpedon plays his part from the Sacred Grove of Helios, and meanwhile, Rheami joins her daughter in the tower of the Royal Chambers. Every member of the community is on alert, and the newly initiated Rhamu, as is the custom on the eve of his great day, is housed in the Royal Apartments below the sweet chamber of the tower where he is to make ready, both mind and body, for the coming ceremony.

The Festival of Tsuna is about to begin. The day is calm. A princess who has slept for a thousand years could not have awoken to a more pleasing morning. The cosmos is perfectly tuned, and each and every aura is vibrant with an essence of coloured clarity. A pellicular dome of azure light stretches from the horizon to the mountains, and the waters of the great green sea are milky-flat plastic, lazily rocking the morning caiques. A fanfare of happiness hails the rising sun, as its pale tones wash over the alabaster walls of the Palace, tender as a father cradling his newborn daughter, fragile in his wide arms. Every man, woman, girl and boy join the chorus of the dawn, in a single body of Keftiu people, to give praise for the day and to attune to the mighty power of the Great Shining One. The central courtyard of the Palace is a mass of faces as they make salute, with arms raised to their foreheads. In their all night cathexis, Lendus, Sarpedon, Rhadamanthus and the mighty King Minos have extended the shield of positive ions to protect the whole of the island, though in doing so it has left every one of them vulnerable. They are weak from the exertion, and welcome the energy of the rising sun. Whether or not the shield will hold, they do not know.

The ceremony begins. Led by their Priest-King, Sarpedon and his wife Rheami, the blue-robed elders make procession to the temple. As they pass the crowd there is a loud cheer; everyone believes that danger is over. All the citizens of the Palace are in party mood. There is music and dancing, clapping and jingling of tiny bells. Once inside the temple the mood changes slightly, though the congregation still chatter as they all bunch together to watch the proceedings. Offerings of fish and snakes are made to the goddess Demeter; this time for the fertility of the royal blood. On the altar are torches of fire, the flames of which are asked to send offerings to Poseidon, the almighty master of the sea. Poseidon is asked to release the sea-spirit Tsuna to complete the Trinity with Rhamu and Sisi.

A hollow note is given out by Sarpedon, and the Song of the Sea begins. It is taken up by the priests and priestesses. Soon the whole congregation is a trumpet of song, which echoes around the tall pillars and rises to fill the whole auditorium of the temple. The Song of the Sea carries in the still air over the olive groves and orchards, past the gardens, through the vineyards of drying sultanas and around the stadium of the horse. It resounds from the tall tower of the royal chamber, where Sisi is being prepared, and each and every wall of the Palace begins to vibrate in harmony with the sound. Not only that, but every individual stone begins to take on a golden hue which, seen from the hill of the sacred grove of Helios, makes the Palace appear to be a red-gold mass of molten ore. It is alive with a photonic radiance of harmonic beauty. The chant of the Song of the Sea enters the air and is sent over the flat calm waters. It calls the ancestors of the time that was, and the time that will be. On eternal ripples of an etheric disc, the music of that day is scored.

By mid-morning the bull is on the altar. There will be no human sacrifice this day. The gift to Poseidon is a golden caique draped with baskets of hooked prawns for his dolphin-like Nereids, and a bejewelled chariot in which he can ride the waves. As noon approaches, Sisi is almost ready. She is dressed as befits a royal bride, with a coronet of white and blue lilies and streaming peacock feathers. Her loose shift is woven with gold thread, and the bodice is cross-strapped with golden ribbon. It falls from below her open bosom in a heavy curtain of beaded rock-crystal. Each tiny prism reflects its own rainbow, as it turns and dances in the brilliance of the light. Between each diamante weight is tied a perfect sacral-knot, and at each side of the knots hang tiny, gleaming, mother of pearl shells which tinkle with every movement, like chinkling eastern bells. Around her smooth neck is the magic charm of the Golden Bee Pendant. She gently pats it into place before slipping her painted feet into the tiniest pair of golden sandals. With her flax-like hair flowing to her waist in a pour of virgin curls, she leaves the tower.

Escorting the Princess Sisi to her long awaited reunion with Rhamu are her mother, Rheami, and the High Priestess. Twelve vestal virgins attend her, carrying baskets of flower petals. The procession descends the steps of the tower, amid drumming and trumpeting and echoes of the sea-chant. They make their way inland towards the cedar lined track which leads to the grove of oaks – the Sacred Grove of Helios. Sisi stands in the centre of the two pillars and holds out her arms, while they are bound to the stones. She is an ethereal vision, waiting at the portal of destiny for her shining knight. In the water at her feet she can see her reflection; the glowing flames of the eternal fires flicker around her. Between two burning torches is the figure of a tightly-girdled priestess, she is ceremonially dressed in a tiered skirt with an open-breasted bodice. It is exactly midday. The High Priestess of the vestal virgins begins to read the symbols of the obelisks.

In perfect synchrony, Rhamu meets Sarpedon and Lendus, who are waiting on the cliff edge on the very spot which Rhamu and Sisi had thought their own. Both Sarpedon and Lendus look as though the life-essence has been sucked from them. In contrast, Rhamu is straight and strong and well prepared. Every inch a prince, the transformation of Rhamu, the seal maker's son, into Rhamu the Protector of the royal blood, is remarkable. Joining his mentor and the royal party, he bows low. He is wearing the holy robes of the ancestors – a green cloak of fish skin, scaled, fringed, and shiny. Beneath his cloak his white Keftiu kilt flashes with tiny ribs of silver and gold. Yellow gold amulets glint protective rays, and, sheathed beneath his cloak, he carries the mighty Sword of Right, its long silver blade is hidden, but its golden handle with a knob of perfectly cut clear crystal is positioned at his waist ready for use. As Rhamu holds his hand out to Sarpedon, the amethyst ring, which his father has made especially for this day, sits bravely on his finger. All is ready. The sun is directly overhead. The ritual begins.

Horns are sounded, sistra are rattled, and Sarpedon's troops close ranks to form an outer circle of protection around the elders. With tall, figure-of-eight shields they hide the royal personages from view. Lendus steps forward to face the sun. As if being charged with solar energy, his body begins to radiate. He raises his oak wand to touch the shoulder of Rhamu. The anointing begins with a splash of milk and honey from a small bowl; a posy of aromatic herbs is waved in the air, a triangle of candles are lit, and after purifying the group, Lendus raises his wand and cries out:

'Let the Shining Ones not have power over us. We are purified.'

Foreheads and wrists are anointed with oil and, swinging the aromatic posy between the three of them he says:

'We are anointed and strong and bring to you perfume and incense, O Glorious One.' He sprinkles the candle flames with incense and, starting with the east, places a flower to each of the four winds, saying:

'Let me place incense on this fire as homage to thee, Spirit of the Waters, Spirit of Earth, Spirit of our purifying Fire and Spirit of the Air. We supplicate thee O Great Shining One, to send our message to the al-powerful Poseidon, that he may release his spirit, Tsuna, to become our flesh and our blood, and to live with us to eternity. O Great Shining One, we adore thee, hail Lord of the Rays, thou art the God of life, Lord of love, and all people live when thou shineth.'

At this point the Master, Lendus, takes his dagger and swiftly slices a clean incision on Rhamu's arm allowing the fresh crimson blood to splash onto the rocks. Now Rhamu speaks:

'I make sacrifice to the Great Shining One, that by my blood, our people shall continue in harmony with all the forces of the universe.'

He dips the cut into the milk and honey, and then Lendus dips the posy into it. With the posy, he asperges east, north, south and west and, holding up the knife, he shouts:

'I show my mastery over all living things with this knife. I have made offerings to the Gods and sacrifice.'

With the gold ring of his right hand he traces the symbol of the sun above his heart calling.

'I become one with the Lord of Light.'

And, with a mighty crescendo, the all-mighty three, Lendus, Sarpedon and Rhamu, cry out:

'O Eye of Horus, grant unto us the secret longings of our heart.'

Filled with solar energy the cliff top group appears trance-like and possessed. Their breathing is loud and boisterous and they seem to expand in their circle of radiance. As if in some ever-inflating opaque balloon they grow tall, and as they become illuminated inside the halo of fire, they become as candle flames, undisturbed by the slightest breeze as they point towards heaven. The climax is a soak of fizzing white electricity, which brings them to their knees.

Descending into calm they kneel, bowed and silent, before reciting the words of consecration. After asking the Shining One to return to heaven, a gong is struck ten times, and the rite is completed with the words:

'We have walked beside the Great Ones, just as they pass close to God, who, mighty and resplendent, is the sum total of all things.'

The elders step forward to burn their flowers, and sprinkle the ashes over the edge of the circle. As the burnt offerings float down, surfing the smoke, they are caught in a whisper of breath that carries them over the cliff top and across the face of the deep, still, aquamarine ocean. And, in that same breath, a rumbling of the earth begins.

Soon the rumble turns into a low growl. It moves the rocks under foot overbalancing some of the less steady of the elders. A crack appears in the sandy shore below, and the low growl becomes a roaring bellow. With one cataclysmic split, a gaping chasm is ripped into the cliff face only feet from the magicians' circle, and a knowing horror flashes between the three Masters as the sun is obliterated by a grisly blanket of falling ash. Day turns into night.

There is instant panic. A scattering and fleeing of people! Pandemonium! Pelting hailstones! Steadfast and defiant, the three brave guardians hold their circle. Then, directed by Lendus, they begin to surround themselves with Ketheric brilliance. A cloud of splendid white light appears over their heads, which, with the middle finger of their raised right hands, they touch, and draw down to their foreheads. In total calm they allow the light to flow through their fingers, directing it to the solar plexus, and instantly it is joined by a surge of light from the ground. A band of unimaginable brightness is formed around each one of them from head to foot, and, streaming a trail of white fire from their right shoulder to their left, they complete the cross, thus becoming united within an expanding power. As a last hope of a final defense against evil and aggression, Rhamu unsheathes his long sword: it flashes and sparks with lightening. Stretching it out in front of him, he draws a circle around each of them, with the silver fire which emanates from its tip.

In their armour of light, they turn and flee through the spitting pumice which is raining out of the blackness. Along the great road from the sea they flee, inland towards the Sacred Grove of Helios, in an attempt to save their Queen and her daughter. Though they move without thought, faster than a thunderbolt, faster than an archer's arrow, faster than a falling star, they cannot beat the tearing blast which splits the ground behind them.

Lendus is brought down. He falls into the burning earth furnace, swallowed, devoured by its open jaws. Nothing can be done to save him.

Sarpedon is distraught at the sight. His own power is now dimmed to a flickering glow, like a waxless candle straining to keep alight. But keep alight he does and he battles on up the hill towards Rhamu who has already reached the outer circle of great oak trees which surround the sacred grove. Behind him he can hear the boom-blast of the Palace walls, as they give way to the angry sea, and the screams of his terrified people.

Rhamu, with sword outstretched, is pursued by the terrible roar. Finally he turns to meet it. What he sees is an indescribable volume of water; an intense density which appears as an expanding monster on the horizon. It grows and grows, until it reaches the land. Wider and wider it opens its cavernous jaws, to devour the chariot gift to Poseidon and the golden caique. The snorting curl of spumey ambergris becomes higher and higher as it coils over the vineyards and orchards, the olive groves and stadium of the horse, until finally the Palace itself is swamped in the ravenous blitzkrieg of the swollen ocean.

Turning to run, with the monster on his heels, Rhamu feels its baneful spit and he knows that he will have to turn and fight He shrinks back at the sight of the awful, raging gargoyle of the sea. With talons of a fabulous lion and the thrashing tail of a fearful serpent, it looms before him and gnashes at his minute body. But if Rhamu is repulsed by the demonic grotesqueness of Typhon, he is a pail of vomit when he recognizes the expanded ego of Milu. With a spear of green flaming tongues in his hand and Hades in his eye, Milu rides the aquamarine mane of surf. It surges shoreward, and he leaps towards Rhamu in a psychotic rage of evil.

And so they fight; steel clashing steel, white and green, blood and venom. They slash and slice and jab, and split each other open, until they are ragged with red-raw flesh, and gouged with burning blades. And Milu trembles at the sight of his own sanguine gut as it spills from his belly. Yet still he fights, calling on the power of the Brethren to sustain him. As they reach the plateau of the sacred grove, Rhamu has two adversaries, for Typhon is swirling a slimy wetness around the bound Sisi, whose high screams pierce the baritone roar of the titanic abortion. She strains at her bonds in hysterical frenzied desperation, but is bound by the magic of the stones.

Suddenly, like the sun falling to earth, a blinding shield of light drops before the Princess. It is Sarpedon, no longer flesh but a fireball of ketheric light. Rhamu knows that it is time. He withdraws his sword; bows respectfully to the mortally wounded Milu, like a matador before the kill, holds a stare of victory – then, vanishes completely.

With just as sudden a re-appearance, Rhamu springs out of the Pool Perfection. In a swirling spout of water, like a leaping dolphin, he flies through the air into the midst of the light. He is united with the summoned sea spirit, Tsuna, and becomes a fortified tower of a columned bodyguard. He swells, wide and bold, and continues to grow into an impenetrable waterfall-shield of iridescent silver. Together with Sarpedon he endeavours to protect Sisi, but their efforts are in vain, and only she remains in the wake of the planned noyade.

The demon, Typhon, is unable to battle with the purity of the holy light. Shrinking back, he is engulfed by the great tidal wave which brought him. Milu, however, is not finished. Though in anguish, he begins to battle with the now unrecognizable form of Rhamu-Tsuna, and the unearthly spectre of Sarpedon. He lets leash his spear with a mighty swing that sends it hurtling through the phosphorescent block. With one swishing slice of his sword, and the strength of Atlas behind its swing, Rhamu-Tsuna severs the tattered body of Milu in half. All that is left of the once beautiful Keftiu youth is a shredded shadow of grey-green particles that cling to the damp ground like stinking fungus in a stagnant pool.

But in his fight to the death, Rhamu-Tsuna is not able to stop the flight of the green spear. The venomous lance finds its prey and drives through Sisi's heart. Her limp, lifeless body is silent. Neither the spirit of Sarpedon, nor the strength of Rhamu-Tsuna, can save her. The music of the world stops.

In the aftermath of the maelstrom, Rhamu-Tsuna, half man, half spirit, master magician of a land that is no more, weeps over the broken body of his bride. He knows that his immortality will be a void of loneliness. His teacher and friend, Lendus, fallen into the abyss; his King, Sarpedon, metamorphosed into spirit; and his precious Sisi departed on her karmic journey. He floats her shell-clad body out into the wide expanse of the flooded land, and there beneath the waves, he encases her gently in the rock-tombs beside her ancestors. He places the golden bee pendant in her hands, and closes them together over her broken heart. The blackness of the sky is the emptiness of his soul, and his howls of grief resound throughout all that is. A thousand fissures scar the bloody hand of Gaea, whose open wounds are stanched by tears of heartbreak. The sorrow of a lost civilization blurs the moon, and the tears that fall that day are tears from the sun.

12

As unexpected as rain in July, a modern day *Zina* jumps into my life. Like an Amazon warrior she leaps from the back of a pickup truck and sends out a two fingered whistle that would stop a sheep dog a mile away. It sets up a ringing in my ear that is only deadened slightly by the booming depth of her well-exercised vocal chords. The animal I expect to heel to her command turns out to be a child, a young girl, but not like any other I have seen in the village. She is as filthy as a street urchin. Her long blond hair straggles out of its ponytail and drapes her face like bladder-wrack, and her wide blue eyes flash like the cursor on a VDU screen. She is wearing faded blue jeans, a black bomber jacket and modern, 'kicker' trainers, and she is the exact miniature of her mother.

'Baz, get ye' sorry little arse into this truck, I told you to wait for me at the bus stop. Can't ye' just once, do as ye' told?'

Like a gangly foal, Baz comes running. I and everyone in the vicinity have been stopped by the shrill air blast, but like the continuation of a melody after a sudden mezzo forte, the world takes off again. The formidable *Zina* look-alike instructs the young Baz.

'Get into this truck, and don't you dare move,' she commands, before she disappears into the supermarket. Suzy looks at me and shrugs her shoulders.

'She's a new one on me,' she says, and her eyebrows rise. 'Come on, let's find out more.'

We follow her into the shop. One packet of cigarettes later, the brusque *Zina* is pushing past us to leave. Her short blond hair is personalized by one thin plait, which starts from somewhere above her temple and hangs down the side of her face, like a feather from an Indian squaw's headband. Her shoulders are wide, and her arms bulge out of her short sleeved T-shirt like those of a fitness instructor after a workout. She is strong, confident and bellows out Greek words like a native. Suzy tells me that her flow of words is as full of profane expletives as the vocabulary of Fuckin' Pete. Gruff and aggressive, she comes out of the supermarket, draws breath up her nose, and spits in the street, before swinging her hips over the side of the truck and leaping into the open back beside her daughter, Baz, who is cowering down like a frightened dog. A single bang on the cab roof indicates to the driver that she is ready to roll. And *Zina* heads off, standing in the truck as if it was a chariot, and she was Boadicea. We can't get into the shop fast enough.

The gossip is juicy enough. Kelly, a hard woman from the north of England, who is shacked up with an itinerant from Albania, has appeared from the other end of the island. According to Esmina, the local newscaster, an old woman of the village where

Kelly had been living, had been head-butted by her after some derogatory remark. Consequently she was tarred and feathered by the locals, and thrown out of the house that she had not paid rent on for over a year. If that was not enough, the Albanian, who she is living with, is being hounded by the police because of his illegal presence on the island. The one good thing to be said for Kelly is that she can work in the olive groves like a man, if not better. We buy some chocolate, and leave the shop.

Our destination is Sissi harbour and an Ouzerie where we have arranged to meet Fuckin' Pete. It's just coming up to seven. I'm still thinking about the Amazon. Olive workers are rewarding themselves for the hard work of the day. Raki is on the tables. Fuckin' Pete is well ensconced with a thimble-glass of the clear spirit in front of him. With Fuckin' Pete are two fishermen. The fishermen are brothers. I have named them the Brothers Grim because they are so serious, but then, what have they to be happy about. They fish all night in an open caique, with only wheelhouse cover and a small tarpaulin for shelter. They live in stinking yellow oilskins, and they take consolation in *raki,* to make them feel good inside (And I know what it does to your insides). As we enter they get up to leave. They can't walk straight, partly the *raki*, partly a life at sea.

Anyway, we sit down with Fuckin' Pete.

'We just had an encounter with a woman called Kelly,' Suzy says.

Fuckin' Pete comes back sharply. 'We all have bad fuckin' days,' he says. 'Fuckin' frightenin' she is.'

Nothing more is said on the subject, because right at that moment all hell breaks loose in the street outside. Everyone rushes to the door. A crowd has already formed a human wall in front of us. There is shouting from every direction, and an obvious scuffle. Suddenly the air is charged with violence, the uncontrollable excitement of a crowd. Fuckin' Pete rushes forward to help the fishermen, but turns and grabs me by the wrist instead. He pulls me and pushes Suzy, at the same time, back into the ouzerie. 'Get back in,' he orders, 'this isn't our fuckin' fight.' There is panic in his voice. I protest wanting to see what is going on. 'No,' he commands, 'there's a fuckin' gun out there!

Everything happens so quickly - pandemonium. I hear the word gun and simultaneously the blast of a shotgun deafens us. A woman screams. Then silence. Oh Jesus! Fuckin' Pete goes out to investigate. Suzy and I, with grim curiosity, slip out into the twilight, and we too become stony statues in a battleground tableau.

One of the fishermen is flat out; face up, with his head lovingly cradled in the lap of the other. He is looking to the sky. His eyes do not see. Like a yellow crucifix on the black tarmac, he faces heaven. His body convulses. He chokes. His mouth fills with gurgling fluid. A flow of deep crimson blood begins to trickle over his whiskers. He's dead. Just like that, he dies, there, on the street. It is a violent, cruel death. There is no *Papa*; no anointing with oil; no last word; no, "well here I come, God, it's been a good one." Just bang, dead. His insides spill into his yellow oilskins like a gutted tuna, and his brother holds him together in a goose pimple embrace of heart-rending sorrow.

The police arrive, too late, and the blank-minded murderer is bundled into the back of their car. The ambulance men arrive, too late, and the uncovered fisherman is bundled into the ambulance. A north wind needles my face. The sea crashes into the silence, and a storm splits the air with a blast of thunder. We are soaked in a deluge of rain.

In a long pause of disbelief, time leaves us behind. Then, emotions begin to rise in an angry tide of discussion. Heads shake, fists bang on tables, opinions are loud and vituperative. "Women... It all boils down to women... Women are to blame...Women are the root... Women... Harlots... Fanny wagging whores." I feel uncomfortable. I keep quiet. Am I afraid? I suppose I am, a little. The mob is angry and hissing nasty things about women. Another *raki* or two, and the opinions are even harsher. This is not a time to air feminist views. The fisherman died because he dared to take another man's woman. It is worse. A fisherman dared to take the woman of a shepherd. And who is the villain? Well, the woman of course. Does it matter that the shepherd beat his wife? Does it matter that the fisherman lusted after a fresh bit of skirt? Does it matter that neither one of them actually loved the woman. She is to blame. She is the whore. She is the one who is never seen again.

There are endless conversations about the church, the law, morals, love, revenge, and a whole gamut of worldwide injustices. What is very plain to me is the fact that for the Cretan mountain man, although his woman is slightly higher thought of than his dog, she is on a par with his pickup truck, and a good woman knows her place. I look at Suzy, 'Thank God I am not involved with a man!' I say.

'You'll change your mind, Kate - Believe me,' Suzy says. But at this point in time, I thank God that I am totally independent of men; there is certainly no equality here.

The Brothers Grimm, are, no more, and the whole area takes on a very dismal appearance. It is as though all the people of Sissi, and Vrahassi, have one face. It is a sad face. It is a tragic face. It is the face of the fisherman, pale and cold, as he peers from beneath the blanket of purple-pink flowers that cover him in his open coffin. His beard is still encrusted with deep, dark blood. Can I mourn for him? I hardly knew him. I have no choice, my face is the face of the village, and the village is weeping. It is a communal emotion that is not hidden. The face of grief is open and wailing, as hundreds of people mourn as one.

13

It is time for some fresh air and open space. I am sitting on my roof terrace with a glass of wine, thinking about life. There is one thing that the murder of the fisherman in Sissi has done for me, and that is, it has raised several questions about my life. I am a woman, alone. What must the villagers really think of me? I am not a tourist. I am not working. I drink *raki* in the *kafeneo* with the men, and I go walking in the mountains. I have been so busy examining the lives of the Cretan people that I have forgotten to look at my own. In four months I have become another person. The walking and the drinking, the weather and the work in the olive groves have turned me into an unkempt tramp in old corduroy trousers and sloppy sweater. I have forgotten what it is like to get dressed up, to go to the hairdresser, to paint my nails, to feel feminine. Come on Kate, breathe this fresh air. I do just that, but it is so cold today, the sky is dark, and there are advance raindrops on the wind. It is time to get cosy inside. Will I ever change my thoughts about getting close to a man again? I will never love anyone in the same way that I loved Jack. How could I? Still, I suppose it would be good to feel wanted, to feel desired. Well, Kate, no one is ever going to desire you the way you look today. I take another sip of my wine, this time it can rain all it wants, I am safe inside my little hovel, and the door is locked.

I select my *Edge of Dreams* CD, plug in my music player, and sit back and relax. Oh, to be in love, Kate; that's the stuff of dreams for sure. Will some knight in shining armour come cantering up to my gate on a white charger, one day? And if he does, what will my reaction be? I pour another glass of wine. It is deep red and velvety smooth, a gift from Manolis Taxi. Well, Kate, what would you do? I must admit, right at this moment in time, I wouldn't mind if a knight in shining armour came cantering up to my gate. He could rattle it right boldly, summon me to his steed, hoist me up behind him and *commandeth* of me just whatever he *wanteth*. You are drunk, Kate? No! I mean it! Anything! It is death that has done this to me. It is death that has made me want to live; death, you bastard, you have taken everything from me, now give me something back. My head is reeling slightly as I listen to the synthesized music of the ocean. Sissi has brought me down again, but it will not hold me. The elements can howl as much as they want. Come, unseen powers of the earth. Come, unseen powers of the air. Come, unseen powers of fire and water, bring me life, bring me love - I dare you!

- I am sinking into the beach; face down, allowing some bronzed Greek, hunk-of-a-man, with lust in his eyes, and oil on his palms, to massage my shoulders and down my naked spine. I can feel warm bumpy sand between my legs,

the tingle of excitement in my breast, salt-spray surf in the sea-draught, and a rattle of shingle in the rushing ebb.

I can smell the after-shave of a waiter as it mixes with espresso, and the hardness of his apron, as he bends with my Lumumba.

An unsuspecting stranger accidentally nudges my knee, and, like a stalking cat, my toes reach for his bare ankles and climb, like a spider, up his soft hairy calves. I suck sweet coffee through a spangled straw, to the sound of his "Excuse me."

I am taken in the supermarket store room, amongst fresh cumquats, the smell of cardboard, and a spiked pile of paperwork. It is frenzied sex that lasts only as long as it takes to buy a box of matches.

I put out to sea, and make love in a rocking caique, with a man who smells of leather and wants only me. We are alone. Time does not exist. The sun is our incubator, and we hatch into a perfect world of purple eroticism. Clouds are pink-topped cotton blossom, and the wind is warm breath from his wide nostrils.

I even dare to step into a shower with a sensual woman, whose wine-dark nipples are large and firm in my sensitive hands, and whose experienced passion makes me cry out for her touch. Cool water drenches our hair; saliva meets on swollen lips. There is no danger in our lust, only the pain of wantonness in our penetration, as we roll, wet and naked, on starched sheets, our soft bellies feeling our soft thighs, feeling our female wetness, until we are dizzy with the flush of pleasure.-

Rat-a-tat-tat - Someone at the door! I shrink to a place somewhere down my spine. Oh no, not visitors now! I want to sleep! Maybe I can pretend to be out. Rat-a-tat-tat - Go away. No, Kate you have to open up, there is nowhere to hide.

'*Yasou Katy moo*, my Katy.' It sounds like Gregory. My pulse rises to that of a cornered chicken. Just at the critical moment of my meditation, I am yanked back into the reality of my flesh, by the unkempt, uncouth, Gregory, not quite the knight in shining armour that I was waiting for. He is obviously drunk to be calling me, his Katy. I open my front door. Sure enough, it is Gregory, but he is not alone; Suzy barges in and she's not alone either. Oh God! Tell me I'm dreaming. It's the *Amazon*: the woman who's as rough as a toad's backside, and has a reputation worse than Dame Hortense.

'Katy, meet Kelly.' Gregory is drunk, and the women are giggling, but I don't know who is looking more surprised, me, under the influence of wine and magic, or my visitors, at the sight of my candlelit pad, my crystals ,and the sound of whale song. Suzy switches on the light. The sudden brightness confuses my brain even more. I sit down.

'Come on Kate, we've come to take you out.' Kelly begins to inspect the house. 'Weird!' she exclaims. She picks up my stones. I resent her touching them.

'Who's he?' she asks drooling over a line drawing that I have done.

'Oh, someone in my imagination,' I brush off the remark. Gregory sits down, like he's in his own home, and lights a cigarette.

'Come on,' Suzy says again, 'we are going to the cheese-making.'

I protest. 'Suzy, I'm not ready to go out.'

'Kate, get your coat on, you are coming with us.'

There is no getting out of it. I put a comb through my hair, splash my face with water, apply a dash of lipstick and a spray of perfume - as though perfume will make up for sloppy dress. My protests go unheard, and I am forced out into the wind and rain.

Both Suzy and Kelly Amazon have experienced cheese-making evenings before. They are way ahead of me when it comes to having this sort of fun, and Gregory, well he is, sort of tagging on. With reluctance, I follow them into the wind and the cold, up the hillside, towards the shepherd's stony shack. The four of us enter the shelter like hungry cats charging towards a plate of liver. Our arrival is greeted by loud grunts of welcome, and we are seated at a table that is covered with husks of empty nut shells, spit out olive stones, orange peel, and stubbed out tab ends. We women, are instantly expected to become *one of the boys* (really not so difficult for Kelly), but I can't help feeling like some cowboy's moll, around a campfire, all grit and grime. Gregory fits in very well with his soiled work-wear and dirty digits. There is whisky on the table, and a bottle of Drambuie. I take a small glass of Drambuie. '*Yamas* - cheers,' I say, and begin to relax a little.

A cheese-making shack is a strange place to be when the wind is howling outside. It is a sort of makeshift

Bedouin tent, with cobwebbed hessian sacks draped under the old tin roof. What they are for, I'm not sure: maybe just drying out. One corner is stacked with animal feed. Along the back wall, there are shelves full of round cheeses. In the corner, behind the door, a big, blackened copper cauldron of milk sits on a one-ring gas burner. It's a really big one, nothing like you'd have in a house, more like a pot that you'd find three witches around. Anyway, one old shepherd, using one old paddle to stir the warming milk, seems to be all it takes. A single light bulb, which is hanging from a large meat hook in the rafters, blows and blinks every time the door is opened. And the small shed is soon filled with mustachioed bodies of the mountain, seeking a communal table.

It is definitely a gathering of tired bodies, and the blasting heat from the gas jets just adds to the aroma of sweaty-sock cheese - and sweaty socks. (Did I really need that splash of perfume?). But the company is male, very male. There are no namby-pamby types here. Oh no, on the contrary, the den is positively filling up with testosterone as we speak. Down another shot of Drambuie, Kate; even the Gregory is looking more a mountain poet now, his long hair falling in ringlets, and his eyes twinkling, as he recites a Cretan *mandinatha*.

'Do you see my little moustache? How it's beginning to grow. A pretty girl kissed it and soon it will overflow.'

Now it is my turn to paddle the curds. They are nearly ready. Of course, I cannot do it alone; it needs the confident arms of a shepherd to guide my strokes. We've reached the stage of giddy women, and we are enjoying all the attention. After a further half an hour of sipping Drambuie and nibbling nuts and raisins, we are all more than slightly mellow, and the sight of a dark, hairy, muscular mountain man as he puts all his weight onto a small basket of creamy curds, pressing out a trickle of warm whey, makes me give an involuntary groan. His strong arms weigh onto the soft cheese as he prostrates himself again, and the angle of his body shows off his firm thighs and his tight buttocks. It's almost too much to bear. Heavy gold falls loosely from his neck, past the open top stud of his black shirt, and I can see the outline of knee length boots beneath his black Levi's.

Bang..! Flash..! Sparklers… 5th November… 4th July… The second coming… I'm in LUST!

• •

It sounds unreal doesn't it? But I have fallen in lust. I know that it is not love. The thing is I'm not ready to be in love. I am waiting for my prince charming; my knight in shining armour - the white horse. In any case, I have got this feminist head on at the moment, free of all that *men* thing. How can I possibly fall in love with someone I have barely spoken to, anyway? No, it isn't love, it is lust. But I can't help thinking that I am free of my grief, free to get on with the rest of my life, free to be who I am, free to be me. I hold up my glass. 'Cheers everyone.' I make a toast: 'To life.' Suzy raises her glass. 'To bloody life, then,' she adds. And Kelly Amazon adds more, 'To fucking, arse-creeping life.' I cringe slightly. Then we three women clink glasses, knowing exactly what we mean.

'Hey,' shouts Gregory, 'What for the rest?' And he holds his glass in the air, saying God-knows -what, and smashes it into the flames of the stove, before slumping down onto a sack of animal feed, drunk out of his skull. And there he stays. We take it as a cue to leave while the going is good.

● ●

The cheese-making was last night, and now I am gazing across to the mountain-side from my rooftop viewpoint, to where I know my shepherd will be with his sheep. I cannot wait to catch sight of him again. Yes, I was drunk last night, and I have a thumping head this morning, but, I am still - in lust. I am not convinced that Cupid is to blame for the way I feel about the shepherd, but I am elated, and I long for our paths to cross again. He, of course, hasn't a clue as to the effect that he has had on me.

This morning there is a change in the weather. It is spring. The rain clouds have gone and there is a wonderful freshness in the air. Not only that, it is warm - warm and nurturing. I am feeling very optimistic as I walk around the village in bright clothes. I'm a widow, but I can do that. It is not the case for Cretan women though, they are confined to black. There are no merry widows here. No whooping it up, at the bingo, and certainly no falling in love a second time. I suppose lust is definitely out of the question. The hill people are not known for their finesse. They are rugged, hard-working farmers, and like farmers anywhere, they have been moulded by the land. There is no softness. Fancy education is not necessary for craftsmen. In the main, these short, tough hill folk are builders of stone walls, and masters of husbandry and agriculture. They have no need of letters, but they do need to know how to feed a family. Daughters are taught well: they can grow vegetables, milk goats, cook, clean, and be a comfort in their man's bed. Women at rest are never idle; their fingers work automatically to turn a ball of fine cotton into a strip of lace. Children play with dolls, and skipping ropes, and toy guns.

I am not of the world of Cretan woman, but I am learning its ways, and I hope to meet a half-way mark. The young women are becoming more liberal, they are working, they are educated and they see that there is an alternative to being owned by a man. The number of single men in the village seems to be on the increase as girls leave for a more sophisticated lifestyle. Divorce is definitely on the up. Is the Church losing its grip? No, there is no sign of that in Vrahassi, but things are changing, and I have always had respect for old ways. So, maybe a little temperance on my part wouldn't hurt. After all, I certainly don't want to end up like Kelly Amazon, and I don't want to go around, "finding, feeling, fucking, and forgetting." That's not to say that I don't want to enjoy myself, though. Oh, middle ground can sometimes be so very - boring. Maybe it won't hurt to be a little adventurous, Kate.

Well, for now my feelings are not hurting anyone. *My - lust*, is my lust – unseen - secret. I have shaken off the total misery of my grief, and my world has taken on a new colour. Now, I can move forward, happy in the knowledge that Cretan shepherds, at least, will always be Cretan shepherds.

14

Suzy's hairdresser, a young girl from Scotland whose holiday romance turned into marriage and motherhood, has invited Suzy and me to the baptism of her first child. The father is an electrician from the village. Oh joy! Things are just getting better and better. I have heard that baptisms are such good events. This one should be brilliant, with it being a village affair. It is to be held at the church of Saint George at Selinari, and the party after, in a big hall at Sissi. There will be food, music, dancing and - shepherds. He is sure to be there. Oh, please God, let him be there. I wonder if Kelly Amazon will be there too, hopefully not, I don't want any competition. Even though she obviously never read, *101 tips on How to be a Lady*, she is the sort of female that men go for. Oh bitch! Kate. For all that, there is something about her that I envy, and something that I recognize in myself. The total snob in me says not to get too close, or I shall be tarred with the same brush; on the other hand, why shouldn't we be friends? What makes me any better than her anyway? Well, I don't want to get bogged down with that one, after all, I've only met the woman once and she did introduce me to cheese-making. There really is something quite gratifying about being a little reckless. I mean, look at Suzy - she's not exactly Mother Teresa, but she is a good mate. In fact, she probably does more Christian acts than me, with all my church upbringing and moral hang-ups. It sounds like I'm making excuses for being happy, but being a bit, *devil-may-care,* has been like a tonic to me. The adrenalin rush of being, in lust, is very addictive.

• •

In this state of happiness, I watch the grey bearded *Papa* Nikodemus lift the naked baby high, to show him off to the congregation. Chanting and chattering echo around the church of St George, and there, for all to admire, is my night slaying the dragon with his spear. The holy icon, smeared with kisses, winks at me in the candlelight.

The baby is totally undisturbed, as he is plunged, naked, into the font - a giant challis, which has been positioned in front of the *iconostasis.* His proud godmother takes him in her arms, wraps him in a soft, white fleecy towel, and *Papa* Nicodemus anoints his head, hands and feet with oil. *Papa* Zachariah hands over the scissors, and a tiny lock of baby hair is cut and put into the holy water of the font. Three children, in flouncy white dresses, hold large candles, and follow the *Papa*, parents and godmother, in the ancient ceremony of circling the font three times. There is much kissing of the giant, gold filigree-worked bible cover that *Papa* Nikodemus holds before him. Baby Emanuel is dressed in oversized clothes, given by his godmother, and he is adorned with gold chains and crosses. He is baptized into the fold of the Greek Orthodox Church, amulets and all.

The whole scene is rich in colour; *Papa* Nikodemus, in a heavily brocaded, red and silver robe, and *Papa* Zachariah, in a white robe with blue crosses and flowers. Larger than life Saints tower down from the walls, in deep purples, reds and ochre. Lavish gold leaf - ornate and ostentatious, drips from chandeliers, double headed eagles, and icons. The baby is smiling, his parents are smiling, his godmother is smiling, the *papa*s are smiling, and the whole congregation is smiling - God is smiling.

Let the party commence! We all spill out of the church like a burst packet of hundreds and thousands, all dolled-up to the eyeballs in our Sunday best. A smell of mothballs permeates the church yard. It is a big party, probably five hundred people or more. There is a band, music, dancing. We are all stuffed with boiled lamb and spaghetti, more boiled lamb, boiled lamb bits, and then some. I am with Suzy, of course, on one side of me, and, yes, Kelly Amazon, on the other. Oh, what the hell, it is a party! The hall is filled with the sound of Cretan music. It is Eastern, it is three-time, and it is slow and gutsy. At first that is. Then it picks up, and the circle bobs about like a ring of swishing sword dancers. It is a ritual dance that is in the blood of every child from birth, and before. The cake is cut - baby Emanuel holds his first ceremonial knife. It flashes, mirror-like, and throws a ray of white light to the stars.

It hasn't escaped my notice that the trestle next to ours is filled with prime, young, dark shepherds, dressed in black. Some are too young to have a moustache, and they haven't quite mastered *raki*-control. They are falling about and giggling like teenage girls. These young bucks are looking to their elders in admiration as they rehearse their *mandinathas*. My shepherd is looking on. He appears to be happy, but a little topply, as he encourages his brother, who is a master of the verse, to recite and recite some more. Brother Nikos blurts out his improvised *mandinathas* one after the other. I cannot understand a word, they are said in broad Cretan dialect and totally over my head, but I do appreciate the skill - each verse carefully metred into fifteen syllables.

Baptisms, like weddings, are among the few occasions when men and women, play out together, and they make the most of it. The men are peacocks, showing off in front of the women with flamboyant acts of song and dance. Brother Nikos takes his place by the musicians. He holds one arm in the air, like a conceited impresario, and proudly recites his most philosophical rhymes, to the accompaniment of the very skillful lyre player. A group of bearded shepherds surround him, encouraging him to go on. They pass a bottle of whisky, one to the other, a communal bottleneck to get them in the mood.

Meanwhile, my sheep-man has caught my eye. With excellent control he makes his way to our table. We shake hands very formally. '*Yasou* Katy,' he says in that wonderful deep Cretan voice. '*Yasou* Manolis.' Yes, my shepherd is called Manolis, I call him Manolis

Shepherd. 'What a good evening this is,' I say and smile politely. Dam! That isn't what I wanted to say at all. I should have said more; I should have made it plain that I want to sit next to him, I should have... No! Stop it Kate - temperance, remember. I watch the handsome Manolis Shepherd return to his mates. He has made his move. Unfortunately it is his only move; as now he is fast asleep, head down on the table, his whisky bottle empty. Oh well, it is late and I am also getting very tired. The music never stops, and the circle of dancing is as big as ever. It is two in the morning, and there is no sign of the party coming to an end.

'Come on Kate,'

Suzy is calling me over to dance.

'I can't dance,' I mouth back, but she is already heading for me to pull me in to action.

'Yes you can,' she says 'it's easy.'

And before I can speak I am part of the ring, with Suzy's arm on one shoulder, and Kelly Amazon's on the other - my feet tripping along with the rhythm.

15

It will be Easter in two weeks time, and Maria is fasting in earnest: no meat, no milk, no cheese, no eggs, no oil, and no wine, but there is plenty of *holy bread* being handed around. Me, I will eat fish on Good Friday, a habit I was brought up with. Anyway, my mind is not on food. I have a princess to find for my Minoan prince. There are undiscovered secrets: undisclosed thoughts. It is dawn, I am on my roof, and I greet the sun. 'Come on, powers of the universe I need some help, just a clue. Where do I turn next? Rhamu-Tsuna, if you are out there, reveal yourself to me.'

'*Kalimera* - Good morning Katy,' comes a voice from the street.

'Good God! .You are about early.' It is Gregory the unshaven.

'I have to working,' he says.

'What work at six thirty in the morning?' I ask.

'Problem with water, I am to going fixing.'

'Oh,'

'I am to coming coffee after, OK?'

'Sorry, going out.' I say, thinking very quickly. The last thing I want is the travelling chimney to ensconce itself in my house leaving tab ends all over the place. And I don't want to put myself in the position of being alone with him.

'Where to going?' he persists.

'Hmm, walking,' I say, 'just walking.' It was an instant decision but a good one.

'You crazy English woman,' Gregory shouts up to me, and he carries on shuffling down the street. The minute he is out of sight I dash down to get washed and dressed, and get out of the house as quick as I can. Now, I am feeling guilty at my inhospitality to Gregory; he has always been so generous in the *kafeneo*. I decide to take him a present to make up for being so rude.

Adventurous, yes, that is how I am feeling today. Where shall I go? What shall I do? The sun is shining, the Griffon vultures are flying, and the promise of Easter is in the air. I can feel the energy bursting from the mountain and the trees, and I can understand those early people, worshipping the great divinity of Mother Earth. I feel like an apprentice, a born-again soul doing a quick course on life. Like Odin, hanging from a tree by his ankles, my world has turned upside down, and the view that I now have is something else altogether. The land is full of magical groves and sacred sites. I feel good, so good that I want to rush around to Maria's house and tell her what I am cooking. I am not so sure that Maria will understand, though, if I tell her that I am cooking up an adventure. A little bit of history and a little bit of dream; a little bit of magic, and something more than beans!

I have a fixation on one beautiful shepherd, and it is feeding my imagination with wonderful thoughts. The old cobbles are wheel-worn and hoof-trodden beneath my feet, as I trek along the old road, between the olive groves. I want to skip like I did when I was a six year old girl, plaits swinging. I want to twirl with happiness at the possibilities that are opening up before me. I know for sure that one day I shall be reunited with Jack, but for now, happiness is the quest. And part of that happiness is the help I can give to Rhamu; I have not forgotten that he needs help, and I know by the general lightness in the sky, that he feels my optimism.

Well, I didn't intend walking so far. It is noon, and I have reached the archaeological site of Malia Palace. Maybe I can re-live my dreams a little, and find a way to help Rhamu. The tide is blowing in like a swaying field of fresh green corn. It is a blustery spring day. There are one or two early tourists meandering in between the ancient foundations. If this place could only be built again as it once was: marble columns, private chambers, storage silos, a large central courtyard, and stone pathways.

I am on a stone pathway now; it is called *the great road to the sea*. I stop and look inland to the hill where the tiny church of Prophet Elias stands gleaming white in the sunlight. That is where my princess met her death. That is where it all happened. That is where I should go. Oops! I trip over my shoelace. I bend down to tie it and what do I find? Right at the tip of my toe is a small stone. In some silent way it says, 'pick me up,' so I do. It is only a rock, not a crystal or a semi-precious stone, simply a nut-brown piece of rock. It has no distinguishing streaks of marble or fossil imprint - no secret code, or hidden hieroglyphics, yet I recognize it instantly. It is an absolute replica of the obelisk in the Selinari Gorge, my confidant, *Stone*. *Small Stone* goes into the top pocket of my shirt, as I head inland to cross the main road, so that I can climb the hill to the church of Prophet Elias. As I walk along, I'm thinking - it can't be coincidence, that so many of these small hilltop churches are named after a prophet with a name so close to *Helios*, the Greek name for *sun*, when...

Thud...

No breath...

Blackness...

- I am sinking through the grass. I am sinking through the earth. I am sinking into oblivion. I am swaddled in the softness of a soft black fleece. I am falling, falling, falling into the black abyss of delightful nothingness until... I am scooped up by hands so gentle, so tender, and so full of love and care; hands that are warm and sure. Hands that hold me like a limp, new-born lamb, and carry me into the lightness of another world. Then, I am giddily thrust into brightness. -

· ·

'Ooer! Thatwereclose! You all right?' Suzy is sitting at my bedside. I feel sick. I am sick. Oh God! I'm sick all over Suzy. 'I'm sorry,' I say, not really knowing where I am. There are drips and tubes trailing from me, and my chest is bandaged tightly. Oh God! I'm hurt! I think I'm hurt.

'Am I hurt?' It's a silly question. Suzy is mopping herself up, but Kelly steps in.

'You're lucky to be alive,' she says, 'you've been out of it for two days.

'You see this?' She is holding up the small stone that I'd put in my pocket. 'This is what saved you. You were hit by a car, and a piece of metal skewered its way between your rib cavity and vital organs. This small stone deflected the metal just enough for it to have missed your heart.'

'I must have been daydreaming, but what about the hands, the hands that saved me?'

'Get some sleep Kate. We'll be back tomorrow.'

'No, Kelly, don't go.' I reach out to her. 'Give me the stone.' I'm in a haze, but I can feel the energy of my *Saviour* in the fragment of earth-power, that kept me alive.

White coats approach and retreat. My body is manhandled like some specimen aboard an alien spaceship. Unknown hands turn me. Muffled voices talk to me. Sweet fragrances mingle with methylated spirit. All the time, my mind is locked in the numbness of sedation.

Hospitals seem horrible places, unless you are the one that the doctors and nurses are making better. It doesn't bother me that I'm not washed every day. It doesn't bother me that I have no pyjamas, and have to wear a hospital gown. I couldn't care less. I am in pain, and all I want is that morning injection and that night time narcotic.

• •

Now, I do care. I've been lying in this bed for three weeks, and I'm sick of injections, sick of blood tests, sick of the whole smell of it all. I am obviously better and ready for home.

Manolis Taxi and Suzy come to take me home. It is ten in the morning. Behind me are all those sterile needles: chlorine floors and polished labyrinths of torture; the white-coated charioteers, the angels of death, the redeemers, the mercy givers, the second-chance makers. I have been given a second chance. I am redeemed; I am pushed through the concrete labyrinth on a urine-stinking, world-war-one-chariot, wheeled back into the world, and unceremoniously heaved into the taxi. Vrahassi is waiting, timeless, on the hillside.

Weak, but determined not to have a second-coming like the first, I get out of the silver Mercedes, like some celebrity attending a gala performance. We head for the shady veranda of the *kafeneo*. A vendor is opening up the back of his transit-van to display his wares: shoes, ex-army boots, combat trousers, jeans. The old boys are gathering. Women are passing by with their sticks of fresh bread. And shepherds are returning to base for their breakfast. One by one, battered 4 x 4 trucks, dock in their parking bays. Black figures dismount, like cowboys after their early morning round up. They amble towards the tables where, to my surprise, they all offer me a hand of welcome home. My suffering is acknowledged; their gesture of love is genuinely given, and genuinely accepted. I am overwhelmed and so very glad to be back with my family.

A diesel engine grumbles in low gear, as my favourite 4 x 4 manoeuvres into its spot. It is Manolis

Shepherd, back from feeding his sheep. He emerges, tall and straight, and proud, and he struts towards me like some unearthly creature that has no need of ground beneath his feet, (or so it seems to me). I hold my breath. My sultry cheese-maker takes my hand as though he were going to kiss it, but instead begins to stroke it tenderly, like calming a kitten. He continues to hold my hand in his while he speaks. His words are so kind, so passionate, and so unbearably *delicious*. I don't want him to let me go. I am a mess. This man is like a magnet to me. The very sight of him makes me tremble. His closeness is making me glow. Oh Kate, you've got it bad! 'See you,' he says, in that deep, sexy, dark-haired sheep-herder voice, before making for his house, where his mother has food on the table. His words go over and over in my head, "See you."

Suzy tells me that she thinks I am crazy to give him a second thought. She cannot understand my obsession.

'Don't let him take you in, Kate. He's a shepherd. They're different. They only think of sheep, and shagging. He probably visits the bordellos. He can't help it, he's eaten too many sheep's balls; too much testosterone. That's why they're so hairy,' I laugh. 'And besides, you are too weak to be even thinking about men.' I suppose she's right, but nothing she says seems to change my feelings for him.

My homecoming is perfect. It is warm, it is welcoming, and it is wrapped with a big red ribbon, as though every one of my new acquaintances is a beautiful bunch of red roses, and we are all gathered together in one bouquet of friendship.

There is only one thing I have missed, and that is Easter. The one big celebration of the year, and I have missed it. The lamb which Maria had hand-reared in the shed next to her house is gone. The ornate ark-like coffin of Christ has been carried in a procession around the village. Blackened crosses have been smudged over doors by the Easter candles - Christ is risen; Judas has burned, and firecrackers have frightened away the devil. Only the red eggs remain, to be passed from house to house until eaten, or thrown into the rubbish. Maria greets my return like that of the prodigal daughter, and hands me an apron full of red eggs, announcing, '*Christos Anesti.*'

Fuckin' Pete arrives at the house. He thrusts a bottle of wine my way saying:

'I thought you might be fuckin' desperate.'

It is his way of being kind. We drink the wine, but it's not enough of course - one bottle never is - so we head back down the hill to the *kafeneo*. As we arrive at the square, Kelly is leaping from the back of a 4 x 4. Crazy Maverick, so called because he has the habit of firing off a shotgun, whenever he is so happy that he can think of nothing better to do, is her driver. On this occasion, he is brandishing a pot of fish soup, which he has made especially for my homecoming. I am surprised to see them, and I soon realize that we are going to have a party. Stavros, the larger than life baker, rolls towards us, and before we know it, tables are being put together, bouzouki music begins to set our feet alight, and the wine barrel is opened. Of course, everyone that passes by, is called to the table, and of course, every time, we shuffle up to make room until we are all so close that another table, and another is added, and our trestle stretches the whole length of the front of the *kafeneo*.

A firm hand unexpectedly lands on my shoulder, and one of Jupiter's bolts courses through my veins. Of course, I know straight away, that it is my dark cheese-maker, and there is no argument when he brings up a chair and forces his way in to sit at my side. At my other side, totally forgiven for being so dishevelled, sits Gregory, and the feasting begins. We eat a banquet of lamb, goat, beans, *horta*, *fava*, fried cheese, misithra, octopus, squid, fish soup, *tzatziki,* salad, and bread. And it is all washed down, with wine, wine, wine, and more wine, until we can drink and eat no more.

Stavros is ready to dance – so Stavros dances. This great bulk of a baker dances like a giant not wanting to stand on the cracks. He rocks, and turns with precision, and he kicks out his leg and slaps his shin, as the music lightens his soul. He crouches to the floor, and pats the ground with patriotic passion. He feels the beat from the curl of his toes, to the third eye of his temple, as we swing our arms and clap a slow one-two.

Then the pace of the music changes, and the magic of a dance-circle expands, growing bigger and bigger in the haze of the wine, and the ecstasy of my mind. I can see, in the circle, spirits of time past and spirits of time present, all merging into one fiery circle of the *spirit-of-the-dance.* There is Stavros, and Michaelis, and Yannis, and Manolis, and Nikos, and Lefteris, and Yorgos, and Kostas, and Adonis, and Stefanos, and Dimitris, and Demosthenes, and Harris, and Babis, and Menelaus, and Miltiades, and Zach, and Christos.

The women join in: Maria, and Fotini, and Elaine, and Georgia, and Poppy, and Alexandra, and Ekaterina, and Dimitra, and Anna, and Yoanna, and Eleftheria, and Elizabet, and Sophia – they all dance with the shadows of generations of mountain people. I am dizzy with the pulse of Anavlohos, its children rhythmically treading down the ages, showing their joy in the middle of all their suffering - all their sorrow.

A blast, from the double barrel of Crazy Maverick's shotgun, highlights just how the mood can change to one of *Utopian Now*. Life is *now*, and *now* is as perfect as life can be.

I join the woven chain of dancers, my wonderful shepherd on one side, the incorrigible rebel, Gregory on the other. We pick up the pace, until we are on the edge of a spinning merry-go-round, held in a frenzied pirouette, a whoosh of a Dervish's skirt that becomes a blur of centrifugal time. My every sense is aware that the living flame of Sisi is being rekindled, as the wind of eternity blows from the mountains, to make a fading spirit into flesh. Rhamu-Tsuna is very near. The heavens open, water pours forth. This party is over, but another one is just beginning.

16

It is May. Birds are twittering. They are nesting in the top of the tree-trunk telegraph pole, at the corner of my house. Big black bees investigate every piece of old wood. 'Go out,' I tell them, 'You don't live here.' It is said, that they have the souls of the departed in them, trying to claim their house back. The geraniums are in full flood of colour: magenta, crimson, vermilion, powder pinks and ivory whites. There seems to be everlasting sunshine. From my roof terrace, I can see that the countryside is vibrant with new growth: yellow sorrel carpets the olive groves; pale pink asphodels stand tall along the lane sides, tiny woodland cyclamen and single orchids that are fairy habitats for sure. And the butterflies that flitter between the flowers of my balcony are little Tinkerbells in a transient rainbow of fluttering

My house is not looking its best. During my time in hospital, layers of dust have begun to form mini sand dunes over the furniture. A couple of dead cockroaches lie, legs up, in the sink, as though they've had a snort too many and just couldn't make it back into the dark crevices. The drains smell fusty. It is as though the house is dead and decaying around me. I have to save it. I have to let the spring in, let it breathe the newness of life; let it be filled with light, and warmth, and love, just as I am.

It is so reassuring to see my collection of crystals, but they are dull in the not-quite-light of early morning. My rock crystal, my amethyst cluster, my rose quartz dream-stone, my blue lapis lazuli, my green malachite, and my collection of coloured local stones, are all there waiting for me. Now, to keep them company, I introduce the stone which saved my life, the miniature of the obelisk in the Selinari Gorge. It looks like a drab-cowled monk, his identity hidden. As the light improves, the crystals begin to twinkle, and I know that each one of them wants to be cleansed. I can feel their whispers, their soft pleas to be taken outside. Carefully, carrying them into the yard, I hold them under the tap which brings cold spring water to the house. Next time I will bathe them under the full moon, and leave them beneath the stars, to soak in the power of the Universe. This morning, they simply want to be rid of a month's dust. Water gently falls over their geometric surfaces, bringing out all those deep colours of wet stone, and I know they are emitting happiness. The rising sun will dry them, but first I tap each one on its base, to wake it up fully. Now it is my turn to take a shower, shake myself off, and salute the dawn.

My crystal collection is awake, and absorbing the power of the sun. As I gaze, trance-like, at my stone collection, new *Small Stone* begins to vibrate. At first, I wonder if there is an earth tremor, but nothing else seems to have moved in my small yard, everything is perfectly still. The tiny rock continues to shiver with energy, and begins to glow with a red aura that shifts to green and back to red. Then, in a final tremor, it topples over on to its side, like a fallen domino.

Even I, who know the magic of crystals, am stunned to witness such a thing. I dare not touch a single piece. I am mesmerized by my little collection of rocks. Have the other stones in some way communicated with *Small Stone*? It is strange, but I am impelled to put *Small Stone* into my hand. I close my palm around its slightly warm surface, take a deep breath. The sun is on my face, my eyes are tight shut, and I concentrate on my breathing. Slowly, I enter the blue portal which opens in the middle of my forehead. I am in the blue, and of the blue, and I wait for a sign. It comes, silently, and swiftly, as if squeezed from a tube. The word **FIND** shows bold like the title of a film, only to be sucked into the blue again, where all exists. I hear my breathing, feel the substance of my body, and open my eyes. The sun is reflecting blinding rays from the white painted walls of my enclosure, and I feel decidedly shaken.

I am just out of hospital. The wine and the energy of my homecoming have done nothing to improve my well being. My mind is certainly in turmoil over the emotion that I am feeling for my sheep-man. Am I having hallucinations? Find what? What am I supposed to look for? Where do I begin? I know that I have to find the Princess Sisi, is that what the stone is telling me? Have I been so preoccupied with thoughts of lust, that I have neglected some other clue? Oh, I am really confused. One thing I do know is that *Small Stone* has given me a very clear message, one that I cannot ignore

- *FIND* - And find I must. Well, if one stone can give me a message, then so can another. I will go to see the stone of stones, my friend, the obelisk, in the Selinari Gorge.

I have gone through the mental pain that brought me to a new life, and I have gone through physical pain too. I now have to look deep into myself for the meaning of it all. I have reached one of those, *door opening and door closing*, periods of my life. The door behind me is well and truly shut, and there is no going back. I am like Alice in a new Wonderland, so curious to know what lies behind the door in front. Is it the spirit-world of Rhamu-Tsuna and the Princess Sisi, the land of magic and mystery? Or, will the door lead me on to a monotonous life of repetitive chores, boring social intercourse, and un-creative existence? If I could choose, it would be to go through a door beyond which there is a world of magic, of wonderment, of unexpected delights; a world of music, and colour, and passion. Well, you have free will, don't you Kate? Open the door that few dare to open. Open Alice's door.

. . . .

It has been a strange week. I have had lots of visitors. Food has been brought in. I have had plenty of sleep, and I must say that I am feeling on top of the world. So much so, that I know it is time for me to venture forth and *FIND*.

I am heading down the mountain in the direction of the Selinari Gorge. My mission is to visit *Stone*. We haven't had a chat for so long. Maybe I can share some of my new energy with him. I have this notion that if S*mall Stone* can communicate with me, then my old friend may have a few words of wisdom too. I am carrying my other crystals with me, in the hope that they can help. A silver-haired villager, booted and black, is just setting out for a day with his sheep. He twists the ends of his *Kitchener* moustache, and asks me to drink coffee. '*Evharisto* - Thanks,' I say, 'but I am going for a walk.' He doesn't understand me. Never mind - I don't stop, so he gets the drift. One hour later, I am down the mountain, confident that I have returned to the exact spot where I sheltered and chatted to *Stone*, but all I can see is a hole in the earth, as though a tree has been uprooted. *Stone* has gone. Has it fallen down the side of the chasm? No, my old friend has apparently disappeared altogether.

Well, it is a bit of an anticlimax. Here I am, all psyched up to hug a big rock. I have reached my destination, and my destination isn't here. It's like arriving at a party that has been cancelled. But suddenly the word *FIND* has a real purpose. Where has *Stone* gone? I have to find him. Something really deep inside tells me that I do *have* to find him. I take *Small Stone* out of the bag, and, holding it like a compass, I ask it where I should look next.

'Hey, what are you doing here?' It is a voice that startles me. I turn around to see a young man getting out of a little silver Fiat. What is more surprising, is that I recognize the handsome features of the, almost forgotten, Adonis from the bar in Heraklion.

'I thought it was you,' he shouts, smiling. 'What are you doing here so early in the morning?'

We shake hands.

'Oh, it's a long story. What about you? What are you doing here?' I ask.

'Me, I am on my way to Agios Nikolaos to see my father. I don't pass this way very often, and every time I do, I stop here to light a candle. Come for coffee and you can tell me your story.'

Of course I accept. For one thing, I am ready for a drink, and, for another, he is very persuasive.

'This is one of the most holy places on the island, Kate. Do you know, during the war with the Turks, prisoners were brought from Neapolis jail, to swear the oath on the bible here, because it was thought that they would not dare to tell lies at such a holy place?'

'No, I didn't know that. I have only visited the Monastery once before, when I came to a baptism here.' I tell him.

We are on the old road, which runs parallel to the new one at this point. Down here is a makeshift shelter of corrugated iron. We enter. Inside there are a few holy icons, candles in a sand-filled holder, and a string of little metal votives. Some of these votives are imprinted with legs, some with ears, some with children and others with adults; each one for a separate ailment. Little turquoise *third-eye* hangings are pinned to the frames of the icons together with a small bunch of rosemary. It is like a ramshackle bus shelter, but it works, and people on the old road can offer up their prayers as they pass. Adonis throws a few coins onto an old tin plate, and crosses himself, before lighting a candle and sticking it into the round, gilt holder. We are both silent for a moment.

'Come on, let's take that coffee.' Without thinking, we link arms, as we go up the steps which lead to the main road. The Monastery is before us. It is a formidable place, but very beautiful. One or two *papas* are going about their business. They are old, and Adonis tells me that they are retired priests who live in the monastery. First, we go to the tiny church where we light a candle and say a prayer. Duty done, we sit outside the coffee shop, in the cooling air that is being drawn through the funnel of the gorge.

The main road, which runs adjacent, is busy with tourists' hire-cars. Some pull in to the lay-by, for a closer look, others just stream past. A little further up from the coffee shop there is a fountain, out of which pours cool, fresh, spring water, from the mountains. A local guy is filling his plastic bottles and canisters. Just past him, a couple of bird watchers have set up their fancy camera. It is aimed at a ledge on the opposite side of the gorge. This morning they are lucky to see three or four Griffon vultures returning to their nest, casting shadows on the rock face as they swoop in to land. Once on the ledge they are so well camouflaged that it is difficult to see them.

I begin to tell Adonis the story of my life since Christmas, omitting all references to Rhamu-Tsuna, his princess, or the more recent events that concern stones. The one thing I do tell him is how I escaped death due to the stone in my pocket. I show him *Small Stone*. He is silent.

'I don't believe it,' he says as he stares at the stone. 'Do you know my father has a stone just like that one only bigger? It is in the garden at his new house near Agios Nikolaos.'

I am interested and excited. Adonis cannot understand my enthusiasm, and then… it all pours out of me, everything: my dreams, my visions, my unfolding story, everything. Adonis is silent again.

'Do you think I am mad?' Oh God! I fear he does. Finally he speaks.

'Look,' he says, 'if you believe in all of this, then who am I to say that you are mad. I am on my way to take these papers to my father. If you think that it will help you, come with me and see the stone for yourself.'

With relief, I thank him, and accept his wonderful invitation.

• •

A black-raven of a *papa* billows his way towards us, the happiness on his face forcing his eyes into little gleaming slits. Father and son embrace, and kiss each other on the lips. I am introduced to *Papa* Yorgos, who, I would say, is a little, but not a lot older than me, and I am immediately made welcome. He links his arm through mine, and walks me towards the shade. We all three sit beneath the leafy foliage of an old, knarled olive tree. The view is remarkable; a glistening expanse of morning aquamarine sea, out of which towers the crusty earth-core of living land. Across the bay is the metropolis of Agios Nikolaos. From our position along the coast, and half way up the cliff-side, we have an excellent panorama of the coastline.

'Welcome to my retirement home.' The *Papa* speaks tongue-in-cheek, for it is merely a plot of cleared land with the odd white stake to mark out the site.

'This is where I will live out my days when my teaching life is over,' he says.

And he goes on to explain that the land belonged to his grandfather, who had also been a priest. 'Poor man, he was killed when the Turks attacked the Monastery of St John in 1896. He was only a young man,' he adds.

I don't want to get into religious conversation right now, although it is tempting. Adonis winks at me. Father and son rabbit on far too quickly for me to understand.

'I have told my father a little about you, Kate, especially how the stone brought us all together.' I am intrigued by *Papa* Yorgos' calm reaction. Then, he says something that really surprises me.

'I too understand the power of the stone.'

What can I say? I think it best not to interrupt, and I let him continue. He points towards the sea. 'Look.' I follow the line of his finger and, astonishingly, there on the cliff edge, some ten meters in front of us, firmly planted in a bed of soft earth, is the eternal watcher - *Stone*.

Quietly, and in very good English, *Papa* Yorgos begins to give me a history of *Stone* as he knows it, and as his father had known it:

'My first recollection of the *Stone* was as a child. I used to tell it all my secrets. According to my father, it was found on land just to the south of the archaeological site at Malia, at the base of the small hill which has the tiny church of the Prophet Elias on its top. It was removed when the land was being cleared to plant new olive trees. My father took a liking to it, and had it placed in our garden. At that time we lived near Malia, where my father cultivated the land.

'For me, a small, imaginative child, with no brothers or sisters, the *Stone* provided friendship and fantasy. I always felt safe when I was near it. I could hide behind it when I did not want to do chores. I could pretend it was my horse, as I sat on its shoulders and battled the Turks. I could see much more of the world - way out to sea. In short, it was my childhood playmate.

'Much later, when my father died, and I was a young student, the old family home was left to decay. My mother carried on living with us in Hania, where I continued my studies, and the *Stone* was left to guard the land. Eventually some rich man, from the mainland, sought me out with a proposition to buy my land; it was a prime site on which to build a hotel for the tourist trade. Well, it was of no use to me, and his offer was more than generous, so I accepted with the proviso that the *Stone* be removed, and remain my property. He agreed, and I had the S*tone* put into one of my olive groves.

'Finally my mother died. She spent her last days at Selinari, where she was looked after, being the daughter-in-law of Yorgos, of the Monastery of St John. Well, one day, she wandered down the gorge, and was found at the side of the road. She was sitting in a little hollow, her eyes wide open as if searching the horizon for a lost sailor, however, the life had gone from her and I had to go through the total misery of incarcerating the body of my beloved mother.'

Papa Yorgos reaches for the hand of Adonis and sighs, 'Just as you did my son, not so very long ago.' Both father and son are held, for a moment, in their thoughts. 'To continue,' he says, 'we had the *Stone* erected in the gorge at the very spot where my mother died.' He catches his breath again, 'And there it remained, as guardian of the gorge, until progress came along and wanted the very place for a telegraph pole. I had the *Stone* brought here where I can take care of it - and it can take care of me.' He smiles -a calm knowing smile.

Adonis breaks the solemnity of the moment with a quip. 'Well, I hope you do not expect me to adopt it when you die, father.'

I am impressed by the compassion that this teacher of Christ has for *Stone,* and the thought strikes me that he is truly a guardian of the old religion. I thank *Papa* Yorgos for sharing his story. By now, the teacher has found a pupil with interest in his subject, and his eyes twinkle with enthusiasm as he goes on.

'The mysteries of the universe are vast indeed. We can only expect to learn a fraction in our lifetime. That is why we must always seek out those erudite people who have made specific studies of a particular subject, and have been blessed with extreme talent and wisdom, in order to expound their theories. We must acknowledge their genius, and have faith in their conclusions. We must take their work and not waste time repeating it, but rather move on; use our life to climb the next rung of the ladder. Only in this way will mankind attain his destiny.'

'So, what is mankind's destiny, *Papa* Yorgos?' I ask.

'In my opinion, it is to know the mysteries. Maybe *Stone* knows more than we do.' I think *Papa* Yorgos is going to explode with excitement when I ask my next questions:

'What is your special study *Papa* Yorgos? How are you going to climb the next rung?'

There is no hesitation. 'Music, My child – music,' he blurts out, animated like a mad professor. 'Music is the key.' I have asked the right question, and the exuberant *Papa* doesn't let me get a word in for the next ten minutes. He tells me about harmony; the harmony of the cosmos, the harmony that we are all part of - the harmony of the Creator - God.

'He is the father from whom we all came, and the father to whom we shall return.' As he speaks, his eyes flash towards the heavens, as if he is visiting some other world. He draws breath. 'Oh, I am sorry to go on so young lady; I cannot expect you to understand any of this.'

But he is wrong. I am quite aware of the things that he is talking about.

'You are speaking of the *Harmony of the Spheres*, *Papa* Yorgos,' I say quietly. There is a silence. *Papa* Yorgos, calm again, gently takes my hand in his, smiles at me and says, 'Tell me what you know.'

I take a deep breath, and begin to tell him the story of Rhamu-Tsuna as it had been given to me, through dream and vision. I leave nothing out; the worship of Demeter, the slaughter of the bull, the burning of the child, the magic, the mysteries, the music. He is particularly interested in how the Keftiu people protected their city by setting up a deep resonance, a vibration which had created a force-field of energy that even halted evil thought. He shares my story without interruption and without emotion, until finally, a single tear appears in the corner of his eye, and trickles down his cheek.

'I have prayed for a key that would unlock the door to the next level, and here you are child, with that very key.'

My story is so fantastic that most people would think me crazy, yet, out of all the people on the island I have found the one person that believes every word of what I say. Yes, the message was, *FIND* and I have certainly found. I have found *Stone,* and I have found *Papa* Yorgos. But it obviously doesn't stop here, there is much more to *FIND* before my quest is ended. I explain my feelings of belonging on Crete, and my thoughts on the subject of *spirit* and *soul*. We discuss the writings of Johannes Kepler, in particular his physical explanation of the workings of *sympathetic vibration*; how, when a violin string is plucked near to another violin, then the same string on the other violin will resonate in sympathy. It is the same with a glass that is shattered by the high notes of an opera singer, or a tuning fork that is sounded close to another fork of the same frequency. It is a known fact that everything in the universe vibrates. At this point you could say that *Papa* Yorgos and I are on the same wavelength. We have certainly found a common ground.

'I am convinced, Kate, that *Kepler* was right in his conviction that the source of the human response to music is to be sought in the soul and the intellect. Through my study of sound, I will eventually be able to communicate with the spirit which, I believe, resides in *Stone*. If I can find the exact vibration of the spirit of *Stone*, then I will be *in tune* with it, so to speak, and in this way, I hope that maybe, just maybe, I will be able to climb the next step and discover a great mystery.'

All this is very strange coming from an Orthodox priest, a learned theologian. We both promise not to speak to anyone about his work, and, slightly phased by the revelations of the day, I make to leave, but I cannot resist going up to *Stone* and giving him a big hug first. Adonis, who all this time has been talking to the architect about the building plans, drives me back to Vrahassi where I go home to sit on my roof.

-I am the rock of ages. I am a thought within a thought. I am all, and I am nothing. I am the eternal nous that is, that was and that always will be. I am Faith. I am Hope. I am Love. I am all that is known, and all that is not known. I am in the earth, and in the air. I am in every living flame, and every drop of water. I am in the sounds. I am in the silence. I am in the darkness and I am in the light. I am the Creator and I am the created.-

Now I know that everything is possible: and knowing that makes life so simple.

17

I have come to Agios Nikolaos to get that present that I never bought for Gregory. I haven't seen him about lately, but I am sure he will be lurking in some *kafeneo* or other, arguing and imbibing. Anyway, I am in a most wondrous shop. It is filled with massive geodes and minerals of every shape and colour. Some have been polished, some rough rock; there are clusters, and chunks, single and double pointed crystals. There are crystals for healing, and crystals for meditation. If you lack vitality, feel insecure, are of a nervous disposition, or are simply stressed to hell, then look no further, for there is a stone for you. The shop is filled with power so heady that I make for the door - and, oops! That is when it happens. I literally trip over this big woman's gypsy skirt, as she bends down to take a piece of rock from a low shelf. My foot gets inexplicably ravelled up in a volume of Indian cotton, and I am brought to my knees. Now, both on the same level, we come face to face, and simply laugh at the situation.

'Well, hello,' she says, easing to a standing position, and offering her hand to help raise me off my knees. 'I'm Maggie.'

'Kate,' I return, we are already shaking hands. Maggie has risen, with me in one hand and a piece of golden-yellow tiger's eye in the other. It has a beautiful lustre and rich striped markings.

'Well, I'm obviously meant to ha' this one,' she says, looking at the stone, 'but I'm not sure what I'm supposed to do wi' ye'.' She let's go of me and we laugh again.

Maggie is voluminous, like her skirt. Her bosom, though well strapped to her, could have suckled a litter (and probably has for all I know). She has flaming red hair, thick and curly, about shoulder length, and she speaks in a broad, loud, Glaswegian accent. (Och I de noo Jimmy) which I have trouble deciphering.

'De ye ken what this stone is fer?' she asks, not waiting for an answer. 'It helps wi' communication. If ye'r looking for a stone, stop now. It's stones as find ye, ye know. Take this fine piece o' tiger's eye,' she holds her trophy on the palm of her hand. 'A was ne' intending to tek a piece today, but a think, mebe a should.' Maggie is convinced that the Tiger's Eye in her hand was inexplicably linked to me, and she is so grateful that she asks me to visit her. She's very direct. 'A'd like ye to cum an' visit me. Ye can catch a bus fri Neapolis on Friday, and cum stop the weekend. A live alone, but 'ave got a wee bed fer visitors.' I accept without hesitation. A little trip to Maggie's house on the Lassithi plateau sounds like another adventure.

Coincidence is not an option. I have come too far along the path of life to realize that the people I meet are not simply wandering in the woods. When our paths cross it is a coming together that has to happen, like molecules that are attracted to certain molecules. I have come to know that when two people do meet, then it is for a reason. Maybe I have a message for them, or maybe they have a message for me. This has been highlighted so much during my brief time in Crete. Think about it? Maria just happened to be the mother of Manolis, my taxi driver, and just happened to be my next door neighbour. Suzy turned up when I really needed someone to show me how to live a little. Pete, well he is part of it all, and he does seem to appear just at the right time. And then there is Adonis and *Papa* Yorgos, who, you have to agree, I was meant to meet. Not to mention my sheep-man, who, brought romance back into my life. Even Kelly Amazon, with all her brusqueness, has taught me a thing or two. And now Maggie – I wonder what part she has to play in my life.

• •

It is Friday; I have just arrived in Tzermiado, a small village on the Lassithi plateau. The bus ride, up and over the mountain, was a treat. The great Dikti mountain range cradles the flat land; vast tracts of cultivated fields spread out around small villages; they are planted with potatoes, mainly, and there are orchards of apples and pears. It is a vast fertile plain, which seems to me as though it is on top of the world. I have ascended about three thousand feet and the air is fresh and the temperature slightly cooler. Tzermiado is festooned with local produce. Intricately woven Cretan designs drape the fronts of shops in the form of runners, and rugs, tapestries, and samplers, hand-crocheted tablecloths, embroidered napkins, linen shirts, and knitted jackets.

Other shops display hand-carved olive wood; spoons, bowls, ashtrays, egg cups, ornaments. Yet others have hand-thrown pottery, painted plates and plaques. It is a tourist fly-trap, and I have been deposited right in the middle of it. Still, it is colourful, and so too are the people. 'Nice tablecloth madam...' 'Plenty more inside...' I try not to look at the vendors as I make my way towards the outskirts of the village, following Maggie's directions. Away from the market place, at the centre of the village, are the hovels and stables with their old grannies, and old goats. Let me see - up this ginnel, here, I should find...

'Ach, a was just comin' te look for ye, come in.'

Maggie's living room is scattered with candles, Celtic symbols, runes, and ritual insignia. Her bookshelf reads like a *Who's Who of the Occult*, and the music, which is playing as I enter, is of dolphins calling. The atmosphere is otherworldly; it is almost like walking into one of my dreams, (ooh, scary!).

'Wow!' I exclaim. I am in Old Mother Shipton's cave, Madam Arkartie's Séance Chamber and Alester Crowley's study, all thrown into one updated emporium of the *New Age*. Charts of the heavens hang unevenly over the bulges of a natural stone wall; soft chimes of angel bells catch the stillness of a celestial breath; candles flicker in every corner and crevice. A large rock-crystal stands, proud and gleaming, like an opaque glass Cleopatra's Needle, an energizing core of pure knowledge. Low wooden beams and an ancient stone archway lead to a sanctum of an esoteric nest, which snuggles between immovable boulders of the hillside, to create a microcosm of calm.

We sit on big velvet flour cushions, in front of an old, round, wooden table - Japanese style, and Maggie lights a joss stick. Her green kaftan deflates, like a grounded parachute, around the great bulk of her formidable clanswoman's body, and her red frizzy hair falls around her big, rounded jowl. She tosses her head back in a very confident way, and the audience begins.

It turns out that Maggie is a Celtic seer, who was drawn to live near the cave of Zeus. There is nothing timid about her. In another time and another place she could easily have been a fearsome Scottish freedom-fighter.

'A'm afeered of nothin' Kate, especially the wee Greek bodies who live roond 'n aboot. A canna be doing wi interfering biddies, 'n men wi' th' brains in th' balls.'

Had I been the Kate of a few months ago, I would have crumpled at her feet, but hey, this is The One - The Only, - The invincible, - Would-be ruler of the world, Kate, who has been energized, and has opened the door which leads to a thousand and one exciting magical moments.

'You're right, Maggie. Do what you want; go where you want to go, that's what I say.' I take a sip of the most welcome glass of village wine, and enjoy the fire which it sends to my stomach.

'So, Kate, what de ye want, and where de ye want to go?'

'I have quite a story to tell you, Maggie,' I say, 'I'm sure that our meeting was no accident, and I am equally sure that you are going to help me in my quest.'

'Look around ye Kate; maybe I know more about ye, than you know about me. We've all neet; we've plenty o' vino and av med tatty ash fre later.'

I give her it straight, all of it. She doesn't speak, or move, as though in a trance. There, crossed legged on the cushion, all that is missing is a great chief's pipe to suck on, as she takes in the wisdom. Then, with a sigh, she shifts her weight from an obviously numb thigh, rocks onto all fours, rises onto solid tree trunk legs, and pours us both a 'wee tot' of something very strong, with a, 'If ye de ni need it, a dee.' The only person I do not reveal is *Papa* Yorgos, whose confidence I will not betray.

'It's obvious that we've work to dee, Kate. And if ye agree to let me tak' ye back, we can start toneet.'

'Take me back where?' I ask, thinking she must mean to Neapolis, or even Vrahassi.

'Tak' ye to find ye self.'

'Are we talking, regression, Maggie?' I am curious, and curiously nervous.

'It's the neet for it Kate, but ye 'av to want it.'

I think about it for a minute. Do I really want to go back in time? Do I really want to know who I was? Shouldn't I just be content to know who I am? 'Can you really do that?' I ask. Maggie obviously senses the fear in my voice.

'De nay be afeared, Kate, we shall tak' the path together and no harm shall come to ye.'

Well, Kate, you have come this far, and you know that meeting Maggie was not a coincidence, so there is nothing for it but to go along with her plan.

'OK, Maggie, let's do it.' I say, throwing back the whisky, and agreeing to do everything she says. And from here, in this cave-room, at the foot of Zeus' mountain, I set out on yet another fantastic voyage. Yes we smoke. Yes we trance. Yes we touch the stars. We call on the spirits of our grandfathers, we enter the female consciousness of the moon, we turn to the harmony of the universe, and, in the body of a wolf I cleverly cover the grounds of the ancients in my search for Sisi.

A time has passed. I am weak, and mentally exhausted. I return to my flesh to the sound of a loud, click, and I am now staring at the ceiling as if paralyzed, trying to make some sense of my surroundings. What I don't know is that I have reported everything to Maggie, who has carefully recorded every single detail of my flight. As she hands me the dictaphone, she says: 'This aught te gi ye somethin' te think aboot.'

• •

I am playing the recording for the third time. Even for me with my dreams, my beliefs, my theories of consciousness, my stones, my music, my Pythagorean faith, never did I for one minute expect to encounter such a journey when I entered the door that led to magic.
This is a transcript of that recording. I tell of times in which I meet familiar faces, including that of my own. I see from outside, whilst feeling from inside, who I was in a previous life. I watch a mind video of me being me, but being someone else at the same

time. I am I, the viewer; I am I, the viewed; two totally separate beings but at the same time one totally whole being. In a confusing abstraction of time and space I overlap with myself, and meet the group of people who have, like some molecular cluster, always joined me on my earth journey, those kindred spirits who I will always recognize. On the wings of the wind I fly through time.

MAGGIE: Relax Kate. A'm by ye side but ye must speak to me, a canna see what ye see, but a can hear ye. Tell me where ye are and what ye're doing.

ME: I am on an open hillside. Wait... I can see someone coming... Oh! It's m - can it be me? I am carrying an earthenware pitcher on my shoulder; it is sitting comfortably on a piece of woven cloth. My dress is a simple tunic of white cotton, sashed to my waist by a tasselled cord of purple-dyed threads. My hair is long, blond and tied back with a piece of the same chord. I am barefooted. I am so happy. I am singing. Up the path I go to the top of the rise. It is grassy and fertile. Around me are oak trees and myrtle. When I reach the top I can see the boggy flat lands that merge into the sea below. I feel the safety of the high point...Oh..!

MAGGIE: What, what can ye see?

ME: It is a temple. My heart is light. I can hear voices, sweet angel-voices. They are here, my friends, they are here, it is Suzy and Kelly. I'm sure it's them but it isn't them. We are all very young, and very happy, and we are making our way together towards... towards - an altar. It is an altar but it is something else... Oh..!

MAGGIE: Tell me Kate, what is it?

ME: It is perfect. It is a perfectly carved dolphin in gleaming white marble, sleek and powerful. The sun is rising directly behind it. We are all on our knees and we are singing the Song of the Sea. There is such a pure sound rising from my head. It is curling around the whiteness of blinding marble. We are shielding our eyes against the glare. We are greeting the sun.

MAGGIE: And noo, Kate, what is it ye are doing noo?

ME: Now, I am pouring water over my cupped hands. It is cool and soft as a kitten's ear. I am pouring the living water over the hands of my companions. We are carefully rinsing the dolphin, massaging and cleansing its warming body.

MAGGIE: Who are ye Kate?

ME: I'm Kate... No, wait! I'm someone else. I am a virgin maiden. We are three virgin maidens gently bathing our master.

MAGGIE: And who is your master?

ME: He is the god, Apollo Delphinious. Every morning we bathe the likeness of our god, for the tales of our ancestors tell of a great battle that was fought between a mighty sea dragon and our people. They tell of how the priest-king had fought bravely but even with the help of the great Sun-God, he had been defeated. Now the great Sun-God, in the form of a dolphin, remains in the waters to protect our sailors and to keep the island safe.

MAGGIE: Move on Kate, look for the others; journey along the path till ye meet 'em all. Ye are on the wind - go where ye want to go.

ME: I am at the foot of a mountain. Around me are sheep. I am in the middle of a flock of sheep. I am wandering to the sound of chinkling, grazing mouton-musty creatures that look more like goats than sheep. They have floppy ears, spindly legs and fatless lamb-chop chests. I am a shepherdess, with a long crook. A boy is tethering his horse - do I know him? Yes…it is my Jack… Oh Jack, Jack… I am coming… wait… I am running towards him. I am kissing his sweet lips. He is holding me so tight. He is calling me his own Ieisha. But it is me Jack, your Kate. No, what am I thinking, look at me, I am Ieisha, the 14 year-old daughter of *Ieira*, of Praisos. And Jack, who is he? Jack is *Diyamah* the son of *Diyana*. Our mothers were guardians of the flame at the temple of our Goddess, Artemis. We are children of the priestesses, conceived at the spring rite, where our fathers had performed their duty at the festival of fertility. After our birth, our mother's left the temple, and younger virgins took their places. Mothers rear their children communally in the village until they are old enough to give back to the temple, if they are daughters, and to their fathers, if they are sons. My father is the sheep-keeper and butcher, *Kriyadah* and *Diyamah's* father is known as *Stratagah*, the leader of the guard. I will return to the temple this year.

MAGGIE: What guard? What are they guarding?

ME: It is the holy sanctuary of Diktaian Zeus.

MAGGIE: Why are they guarding the sanctuary?

ME: Wait - I am crying, *Ieisha* of Praisos is crying - Diyamah is saying that he has to leave to fight a battle. An army has come from across the sea to retake the power. I am loosing him again. No! Don't let me lose him! Oh, no! Please, wait. He has gone. I'm leaving too. This is too much.

MAGGIE: Kate, take hold. Fly de nee flee. We're together. Move wi' the wind Kate. Move.

I've switched the dam recording off a minute. I hate that bit where I meet Jack and lose him in the same instant. OK, I'm composed. Switch on:

ME: Oh, this is better. I am on a mountain overlooking the sea.
MAGGIE: What mountain, what sea?
ME: I am at a place called Anavlohos, where the watchers guard, and the black sails wait. I am thinking about my words, words for a verse that I am writing, *"...In the eminence of emerald drifts the idea of Menelaus, leaving Crete with the power of Mycenae crusted on his feet, and venomous blood surging those bronzed pectorals of a thwarted youth."* The meter must be just right. *"... And woe betide the bold Paris and his bride, stolen or otherwise – conjecture; but so devised as to create a war, so terrible, so prolonged, that ten years passed and heroes lost, before they saw their brave prince home, wearily to Sparta come, with the fair Helen so unhappy won."* I compose my words carefully for a celebration. That which was taken has been found, and returned to the guardians. I am at a place called Anavlohos, whose sirens herald the wakening that is to come.
MAGGIE: Who are ye?

ME: I'm not sure, I could be lost but I'm not. I am on the earth but only just. I can hear music. Oh, such sweet music. It is carrying me up to the light.

MAGGIE: KATE MOVE NOW! IT'S TIME TO RETURN!

ME: I can hear you Maggie.

MAGGIE: Then fe God's sake get ye feet on the ground and return, NOW.

That's where the recording ends. I remember hearing a loud, *click* in my head, and feeling like a lead weight in the bed. The rest, well, like a dream really, and if it wasn't for this recording I would scarcely remember any of it. I stay with Maggie the whole weekend, and we visit the cave where Zeus is purported to have been born. I even buy a small woven rug with a picture of two dolphins on it, a souvenir for my little hovel, and finally find something for Gregory, a new string of *cumboloy* beads for him to twiddle in the *kafeneo*.

• •

Now I am on the bus again. A little piece of me is thinking that I have had enough magic for the time being, but I know that there is more to come. I am trying to relax and enjoy the ride - it is not easy. The road snakes down the mountain, and is so unmade that it is almost scree in parts. Travelling on the edge of the unfenced track does not feel safe at all. At least we hugged the mountain on the way up. Down is another matter; it is very precipitous. I keep having this premonition of the old charabanc not quite making a corner, suffering brake failure or else simply being driven, like some microlight, into the space between up and down. Maybe the driver has had a raki session? Maybe he will have a heart attack? I prepare my soul for a fall into oblivion. Finally the bus swings around a corner into the high street at Neapolis, and stops just past the kiosk. Beaded crucifixes and lucky third eyes, which dangle in the front window screen, sway to and fro for a second while the driver lights a cigarette. I feel as though I could do with one as well, even though I don't smoke, - apart from whatever I smoked at Maggie's that is. There are sweaty bodies pushing and shoving past me as I step down on to terra firma. It's time for a beer Kate!

I love Neapolis. It is a local town which was once the capital of Lassithi, and there aren't many tourists. All services and shops are within a short walk of the main street, which is a beautifully wide, tree lined boulevard with pavements full of tables and chairs. That is where I am heading. I have spotted just the right place for me at the top of the street under a spreading leafy canopy of mulberry trees. Yes, this will do fine. *'Mia beera parakalo.'* I take a bottle of *Amstel;* it is long and bitter and very cold, and it slides down my throat, feeling like water would to a parched kangaroo, leaving me with a moustache of white froth on my upper lip. Ah! Wonderful! Neapolis - continental - and crowded with real people doing real jobs: chemists, doctors, dentists, solicitors, architects, contract makers, pastry makers and *papa*s. They are all zigzagging across the road as though it were for pedestrians only, a much practiced weave between, trucks, cars, motor bikes, scooters, the occasional bus and the odd appearance of a motorized lawn-mower-cart, complete with farmers from the hills. For a moment I think about the Mayor of Vrahassi, and the time he was in the jail up on the hill. It was a short stay apparently, because his mates managed to buy or bribe him out. The passion: the politics of Crete, I love it all!

Spotting the tourist is very easy. They are the ones who are totally undressed in shorts and t-shirt. They dismount from their hired scooters and wonder if they dare cross the road. Then, not being able to find sliced bread or cellophaned cheese, and, seeing bloody carcasses hanging freely outside open-fronted butchers' shops, they beat a retreat to the safety of the seaside, MacDonald's and English Breakfast. I, on the other hand, am almost a local (well I have been here for nearly eight months), and I am feeling very at-home in Neapolis.

So, what do I make of my experience with Maggie? I can't wait to tell *Papa* Yorgos, but first I have to scrutinize the tape for clues. I really want to find the Princess but I also know that I must find the Emerald: the source of power, that magic crystal which was taken from Knossos and used by evil forces to bring about the downfall of the Keftiu. That was the purpose of my astral flight, but I never once came across even a hint of a precious stone. Or did I? Yes I did, but it was not in my astral journey, it was on the hand of *Papa* Zachariah in Vrahassi. He was wearing a beautiful emerald ring when he blessed my house, and I noticed it again at the Baptism - coincidence? Hm, I am not sure. The afternoon sun is making me drowsy - that and the beer. The smell of fresh ground coffee and the pungent market-day cologne of mountain men, mixed together with that formaldehyde musk of fat village women, scent the breeze. My thoughts turn to history, and I can see a parade of enemy forces marching down the high street; the stamp of feet through the ages: the Dorian, who swept down from the Balkans, the Romans, whose power ruled most of the Mediterranean, the Byzantines, whose split with the Roman Empire gave them control of the Eastern Empire, the Venetians, the Turks, the Germans. They were all here. Their blood is soaked into the land together with all those Cretan people that they killed. Land they wanted to make their own. But that has nothing do to with my search - or has it?

Let us go back to the beginning - or the end, as it were, of the Keftiu. I imagine that some of the people, if not from the Palace at Malia then from the surrounding area, survived the tidal wave. They would be the ones that settled in the hills. They were the original Cretan people. All would know of the loss of the Emerald and would have wanted it back. Maybe it had taken centuries, but, let us say in all the fighting that went on, (and Libya was involved with much of it), that eventually they did get it back. Is there any evidence of that? And, where is the Emerald Crystal now?

Was I, in a past life, one of those very early survivors, a maiden singing at the temple of Apollo Delphinious? Are Rhamu-Tsuna and Apollo, God of light, of music and of prophecy, one and the same? And if he is Apollo, then Artemis is his twin sister, and wasn't my mother in another time, a priestess at the temple of Artemis?

What was it *Diyamah* said of the Guard? They were going to fight to save the power. What power? Could it be the power of the Emerald Crystal that was being protected at the ancient Cretan site of Praisos? And, let us say that 'all that' Trojan War thing, was not really over a woman, but over the very powerful Emerald Crystal; and that all the Helen story was just a cover up for the real reason for a war that went on for ten years. Let's imagine that Menelaus finally won, not Helen, but the Crystal, and returned to Sparta with it. Wasn't it Achilles that sneaked into the Temple and stole the 'Luck of Troy'? Could 'The Luck of Troy' have been the Emerald? And Artemis fought on the side of the Trojans. Who are the good guys then? Hang on, don't get carried away Kate, but why not, myth and history, it all makes sense when you enter fairyland.

I feel like a bloodhound that has just picked up a scent, and I have to know more.

18

For three weeks, I have immersed myself in as many history books as I could find. I am preparing a dossier of information to uphold my theory about the missing emerald; a dossier which I will present to *Papa* Yorgos on my next visit. It is a good job that I don't have to work this summer, this project is giving me quite enough to do. I have not seen Suzy or Kelly in all this time, and I have only been to the *kafeneo* once, to give Gregory his present. Maria, at the sight of my house, full of books and maps, has stopped asking me what I am cooking, and instead has taken to bringing me a plate of food every day. 'Fuckin' Pete is working in a bar in Sissi and, can you believe, I haven't given one thought to my sheep-man, who obviously doesn't care whether I exist or not.

Recently, my only contact with the village has been my occasional visit to the little open-all-hours emporium. The elderly couple who run the shop cannot understand me so we don't say much. It really is a wonderful shop where I can buy everything including post-war Tide (hand washing powder) or dried salted haddock, if that's what I want. Fresh meat is a problem because there is no butcher's shop in the village, but I'm not bothered about that, you can give me wild spinach anytime. Anyway, Maria's shepherd-friend butchers his own lamb in his back yard, so she has a regular supply, and that means that I certainly don't get the chance to become a vegetarian.

I have read so much about the history of Crete and the various conflicts which have involved Libya and Egypt that I feel it is time to see for myself some of the places which I think may have come into contact with the Emerald Crystal. The one place which keeps cropping up over and over again is Ierapetra, an ancient Minoan port from which the Keftiu sailed for the coast of Africa; Libya is 180 miles over the sea. Ierapetra in Greek means *holy stone*.

The air is still, and the temperature is pushing 30 degrees. I am on my roof terrace. The opposite hillside is a blend of pink-beige as it, and I, breathe in the subtle reflections of the rising sun. Every ancient tree bark eases from the cobalt shades of night into the soft sun-soaked chestnut of a new day. Baked protrusions of sandstone shale glow and radiate like warming cooker-hobs, slowly turning from ochre into umber. Sleeping citrine flower-beds unfurl into golden grounds worthy of Elysium. *Dia* Island wallows like a snoozing, granite-dragon in the ultramarine water of the Aegean. White domed churches are pearls of the hilltops. Ten Griffon vultures circle on a thermal and another day begins. My bag is packed and I am all ready to travel to Ierapetra for a few days to see if I can find out anything about the anything.

The Sun-God is smiling as the bus to Ierapetra pulls out of Neapolis. It picks up a handful of people at Agios Nikolaos then hugs the coast road. What a wonderful journey I am having. The unspoiled coastline, which the cliff top road follows in a round and round up and down way, dangerously near the edge in places, is stupendous. The bus ride from the Lassithi Plateau scared the pants off me, but this one is not scary, it is exhilarating. Golden sandy bays hook into the rugged cliffs like jig-saw connections, making perfect crescents of blue and yellow. Here and there, outcrops of rock almost sway to and fro as they are lapped smooth. Like the backs of hippopotami wallowing in the shallow waters, these wrinkle-worn beings are infants of their time, even though aeons have passed in ours. There are wild bits and cave-y bits, and tiny private-beach-y bits. White sea-surf edges the land, as though a barber is fuzzing up foam on a gentleman's cheek. Tropical foliage thrives in the well-tended gardens of *posh* villas which dot the hillside. I am in undiscovered territory, for me at least, and I am absorbing the scenery as though it were some memory game that I will be tested on later.

The imposing khaki-coloured block of the Sitia mountain range gets closer as we travel east. They are called the Thripti Mountains. They remind me of some fairytale badlands where the wicked witch lives. Maybe there are trolls. Certainly there is a feeling of foreboding about the dark, creviced fissures that lead to the cold, black bowels of the earth. Ooh! It makes me shiver. Round the next corner, down, over a narrow bridge that spans a ravine, up the other side, and we pass by the narrowest point of the island. Just off the coast is the tiny islet of *Pseira*. Oh! This is great! I have got a fantastic view of the ruins of the Minoan town of

Gournia as we drop a gear to take the hill between the site and the sea. I can almost see those people going about their daily duties: fishermen returning home after a long day; town officials organizing festivals; young children playing in the streets.

Now we have turned away from the coast, and are heading south to the most southerly town in Europe, Ierapetra. I am so looking forward to being in a town again - a metropolis. Oh the joy of it! Shops, goodies, and all those things you cannot buy in Vrahassi: high heel shoes, expensive clothes, jewellery, birthday cards... what would I do with any of them anyway. No, this is not a shopping trip, Kate, don't forget your mission. First I have to see if there is any evidence that the precious Emerald Crystal was ever in Ierapetra. Surely with a name like *Holy stone* there has to be some connection.

Wow, I am amongst it all again. Life in the fast lane, well, not exactly, but it is a lot faster than village-time. Talking of time - I am hungry. So, this is Ierapetra. I have found the seaside and I am ensconced in a soft-cushioned wicker chair under a big flapping umbrella. Relax Kate. Fresh orange juice, a sandwich, and then find a room for the night. This is such a change. The sea is a deep green colour and there is a busy port. Even the locals are different - yes they are definitely more African looking, dare I say it, more Libyan. After my lunch I will take a walk along the quayside.

This seems a good place to start; it is an old fortress. Let me see what the guide book says. It was built by the Venetians in 1204 on the site of a former Byzantine fortress; it was remodeled in 1626, but was conquered by the Turks in 1647. Before all of that, Ierapetra had been one of the principal eastern ports of the Roman Empire for the rich province of Cyrenaica (Libya). Here we go again, that eternal connection between the Crystal and Libya.

What is this? It is a ticket office for boats. I wonder where they go. It is a trip to a small island about forty minutes away, Chrissi Island. The boat leaves at ten thirty every day. Well that lets me out today but I could go tomorrow. It sounds interesting, remnants of an ancient cedar forest, remains of a Minoan port, and the boat is named "Iphigenia" who was the daughter of Agamemnon, King of Mycenae, who was offered as a sacrifice to Artemis. That settles it.

I have bought my ticket for tomorrow, and I am now sitting on a wooden bench by the port. I have been joined by a very tiny, very old lady in black. Her face has been imprinted with the creases of life, whiskers sprout not only from her upper lip and chin, but from the bulbous mole on the inner fold of her nose. She is very long in the tooth, *the tooth* being *the truth,* for she appears to have only one and it catches on her bottom lip as she speaks. What she is saying I have no idea, the only thing I make out is her name, Kalliope. Her tone is a sort of half moan, half wail. I can tell she needs sympathy so I make those sort of noises, 'tut'… shake my head, 'oh dear' - that sort of thing. What else can I do?

'Oh *kakomira, kakomira,*' she keeps repeating, and with a wide, half-crazed grin she offers me her hand. I ask her if she has a home to go to, but of course she does not understand me, and besides, she is busy rooting in her bag for something. Finally she unearths a couple of

Greek biscuits that are covered in a piece of grubby linen. She hands me one. What can I do but accept? Then she is in the bag again. This time (to my relief), she pulls out an old tattered photograph and shows it to me, again going off with the *kakomira, kakomira* thing. It gives me a chance to put the god-knows-what-germs-it-has-on-it biscuit down, to look at the photograph. What have we here? It is a young boy standing by a large black cauldron with a cheese-making paddle proudly held for the camera. Behind him is a perfectly built stone wall, probably part of a sheep fold, and in the distance the mountain. It is a well-handled, well cracked, black and white photograph and I presume that it is some relative of Kalliope, maybe even her son. Finally, she puts it back into her bag, shakes her head and shuffles away. Well, what was that all about? Without a doubt there was some message in the meeting, but what? I am so cross with myself for not being able to speak her language a little better.

The day is rolling on and I have nowhere to stay yet, so I make that my next mission. It isn't difficult to find a room... This one is OK, The Smaragdi Hotel, it looks clean enough.

I have had a little nap, have taken a shower and now I am getting ready to hit the town. Yeah! Give me music, bring it on, come on Rhamu baby, help me out, show me a good time, Yeah, Kate you are looking good tonight. I am enjoying a wee aperitif; it's a drop of wine I bought to start the evening off right. Well, I am on holiday - sort of. Yep, I'm relaxed and just know there's plenty of magic out there. One last preen in the mirror, black trousers, little strappy top to match, best silver flip-flops, lipstick, flick of the hair, bag over the shoulder and I'm out. It just feels so good to be somewhere I haven't been before. It is another little adventure. I am going to go out for dinner and let the evening take me along. Who knows, I may meet my prince charming! Well, you can see what sort of mood I am in - devil may care. What a pity Suzy isn't with me tonight she really brings out the worst in me. What am I saying? Keep a level head Kate and an open mind.

Water - it always draws me back. Oh yes, tented tavernas and jingly Cretan music. It is very touristy but just what I want. A green-tinged Libyan sea is lapping the sandy shore only a few feet away. The *Iphigenia* has returned to port for the night, and the sea front is vibrant. That seaside saltiness is in the air - that and the succulent aroma of barbecued pork. Happiness and hunger and the promise of a hunk of a waiter to faun over me, add up to me finding myself sitting at a lamp-lit table in a busy, but not yet crowded, taverna. The menu is huge, and it is in three languages, Greek, English and German. There is so much choice - delicious Cretan food: all that oil, all those herbs and spices, soft *misithra,* salty feta, sun-ripe tomatoes, stuffed peppers, wild greens, giant beans, octopus, squid, sardines, snails, *stifado, kleftiko, souvlakia, paidakia…* it just goes on and on. And then there are all those sweet things: *baklava, kataifi, galatoboureko,* cheese pies, yoghurt with honey… how hungry can one person be? I order a Greek salad, grilled octopus and a half kilo of white wine.

'Half a litre, madam,' says the hunk.

'Oh excuse me,' I say, 'In the village they ask for half a kilo.'

'That is the village,' he says in a very snooty sort of way.

That's the trouble with waiters; they do think they know it all. Well the cat's out of the bag that I live in a village so I suppose I've blown it. I've seen better butts anyway.

Half a litre is quite a quantity of wine for one person to consume on the top of a couple of glasses in the hotel bedroom so I suppose I deserve to feel a bit wobbly, and, I admit, a tiny bit randy. Oh, where is the sheep-man now? He is far away Kate, and probably in some brothel as we speak - so get him out of your head. No sooner said than done, boss! Ah, I don't know, maybe the waiter has got a good butt after all. Kate, did you say that? I'll just sit here a while longer - 'Coffee madam?'

I deserve a little headache, don't I? But last night was all clean fun, and after a couple of thick black Greek coffees I found my bed - no problem. I'm up early this morning because I want to make the best of the day. I have a lovely balcony overlooking the sea. Breathe Kate, fresh air, fresh sea air - how freeing it is, how free my spirit seems this wonderful new hour of my life. The sun is causing opaque peacock-feather patterns on the water to bob and shift, like tiny mirrors that catch and reflect darts of pure light. If I had more time I would just sit on my balcony and watch the sea. But, *Miss Marples* has a job to do. Oh come on, Kate, ten minutes isn't going to make any difference to your life. You only have this room for a few nights, so relax and enjoy it.

The room is not so great, but it is cheap, it is a standard box-type with a built-in bathroom. There is a dressing table and a mirror, small bedside tables at each side of the bed, with little green lamps to match the green silky bedcover. The paintwork is pale green with dark green woodwork. Come to think of it, it is all a bit too green for me, better on the balcony. I pick up the hotel welcome letter, take a seat in the fresh air and begin to read:

Dear guest,

Welcome to the Smaragdi Hotel. On behalf of myself and my family I wish you a pleasant stay and good holidays.

Many years ago a young shepherd boy was herding his sheep in the hills behind the town when it began to rain. He took shelter in one of the caves and there he found a magnificent, green crystal. He showed that crystal to a teacher of the town, who said he would take it to the museum. No one ever heard of the crystal again. However, the teacher became very rich from that day on. The young shepherd boy was a member of our family. We think that the crystal must have been of pure emerald and therefore we have called our hotel "The Smaragdi" which in Greek means, The Emerald.

We hope that you will agree that our hotel is like a jewel in the middle of Ierapetra.

Should you require assistance with anything, please contact reception.

Mr Yannis Spanakis
Proprietor

Well, it is unbelievable - totally unbelievable. The boy in Kalliope's picture, could he have been the shepherd boy mentioned in the letter? Was that what she was trying to tell me? How poor they were, and how rich the other chappie had become. She was bewailing something that is for sure. I wonder what else she knows. I bet somebody in the family got some money from the find, to be able to build this hotel. Oh God! I'm all excited again! I've got to find Kalliope.

19

It is typical isn't it? When you want something so much, you just can't find it, or in this case, her. I thought Kalliope may be a creature of habit and spend her day wandering around the port area, but as yet nothing and it is ten o'clock. I am going on the boat at ten thirty, and really don't think I should be doing that now. It is crazy - just crazy. Where is she? Where is the one toothed crone? How can I enjoy my boat ride with this in my head?

'Excuse me, did you loose something?' He has a very deep voice.

'Err, no, um…' Who is this… pirate? Short, square, very broad hairy chest, bare feet, loose green pantaloons, longish hair, gold tooth, (watch out Kate, you've seen one of those before), lovely twinkling brown eyes, and a parrot on his shoulder, no - that's a lie - there is no parrot.

'Are you going on the boat?' He sounds concerned. 'Come on, have you got a ticket?' To be honest, I am not adverse to holding his hand as we go across the gangplank and onto the boat. There is something very secure about the way he is looking after me. He is getting me a drink at the bar; I think I have been picked up by a bare-footed pirate who, seems to know everybody on the boat.

I have christened my pirate Smee. He is about the same age as me, and speaks passable English. Is he a Gigolo? Does he hang around the boat picking up stray women? I ask him. 'No,' he says, 'I live on the island.'

'But I thought no one was allowed to live on the island,' I say.

'I'll show you my house.' I bet you will I'm thinking.

'Oh thanks but I …' He's off… Where's he going? Oh, he's helping with the gangplank. Maybe he works on the boat. The boat is full to overflowing with tourists who have been coached-in to Ierapetra, and backpackers, who have made their own way cross country. The tourists are seated, very orderly, on comfy seating around tables, or else exposed to the sunshine on the deck above, their swimming costumes and towels neatly packed into coordinating PVC bags. Bikini-clad hippies with big hoop earrings decorate the deck, together with their be-drummed and be-guitared partners; their badge-covered sacks, tents and boxes of water tell me that they are obviously not on a day trip. I have excellent company for the journey, not only Smee, but a veritable pandemonium of parrotless pirates, are squashed into the half-moon shaped seat with me. There is beer on the table, and suddenly I am part of yet another party. I am not the only woman either. The company is very good. I ask Smee what they are celebrating. 'Life,' he says, 'We are celebrating Life.'

• •

We have been celebrating 'Life' for three hours, and there is no sign of it coming to an end (the celebration that is). The boat leaves at three-thirty, and the way I feel, I don't care if I'm on it or not. In fact, I think I will just doss down with Smee. The way he is acting towards me, I don't think he'll mind at all. 'Yamas matey.' I am reeling a little; there goes another *karafachi* of raki.

'Pass the *smoke*, matey… Ooh – God! I'm high as a...' 'Did I miss the boat?'

'There's one tomorrow.'

'Where am I?' I am, in fact, in some sort of bed. Well it is a mattress anyway. My cheek is pressed against the soft snug broad chest of my pirate matey and his muscular arms are around me. 'Did I miss more than the boat?'

'No Kate, we just crashed.'

'Oh.' Where the hell am I? It is not a house, it is not a cave - it is a… nest. Well it is not quite a nest. I am inside a tree. At least, I am underneath the branches of a tree.

'Welcome to my house,' says Smee, 'It took me two years to build.' Sure enough, he has waffled twigs in between all the main boughs of an ancient cedar to create a dome of interconnecting branches. The cedar has been so bent with the high south winds, and the sand dunes so formed, as to create a cave-like effect beneath the tree. A sandy floor makes two levels, with a step out of the 'bedroom' into a semi-covered living space complete with table, chairs and cooking area. A second bedroom has been added on as an annex, under some low, sweeping branches. It is fantastic - remarkable. I have found a real live Robinson Crusoe.

Happily, I see that I am still dressed even if it is only in cossie and sarong. And I smile inwardly when I see another couple, still fast asleep in the second bedroom. Smee passes me a drink of water and slowly, slowly I come round.

The morning drowsiness passes, but I am still not sure whether or not I have died and gone to heaven. I can hear Mozart melodies coming from a battery-operated CD player, but apart from that all is still, there is hardly a breath of wind, and it is hot - very hot. Four scarab beetles have found a temporary haven in a box of rotting tomatoes especially put there for them. Smee gently lifts the box down off a shelf to show me. They are unbelievably beautiful, like living brooches of iridescent titanium. Then he reaches up into the tree and brings down a small snake. It wraps around his wrist like a coil bracelet. 'You see - I'm never alone,' he says, stroking the underside of the snake's head softly, to make it sense the air with its tiny forked tongue.

'There is only one thing to do in this heat,' I say, 'I am going for a dip.' It is past six o'clock but still blistering. 'Me too,' says Smee. We go for a swim together. The water is like crystal, it is green and opaque and sparkling, I have never swum in such clear water. I feel as though I am part of some jewel, a cameo of shifting shell-sand, an appliqué of sun-warm earth and vegetation. Chrissi Island is a paragon, set in the midst of shimmering liquid quartz that meets the blue horizon in an almost perfect line. The emerald water holds me, possesses me.

When Smee leaves the water I can see that he has the muscular form of an acrobat. His naked ape-like body tromps through the sand to where he has left his cargo-pants and he senses me looking at him. Turning, the epitome of a bronzed south-sea islander complete with shell necklace, he bites his teeth together. They glint gold amid his grey whiskers, in a flesh-eating smile that looks like it could chomp through a coconut. Oh my God, I'm in lust, again. I feel my face flush crimson and I want to dive to the bottom of the ocean like a mermaid.

I know it is a temporary feeling, but I am going with it. The stars are coming out, I am on a desert island, I have wonderful male attention, and the musicians are tuning up. When I was a child I used to draw desert islands; a circle of yellow land, one tall palm tree with a brown trunk and green leaves surrounded by blue sea and blue sky. My Daddy would add two small matchstick people on a yacht with three portholes and a triangular white sail. In my imagination it bobbed up and down on curly waves. In the sky I put a bright orange sun with star-like rays, and an m-shaped seagull. I can feel the crayons in my hand now. The times I must have drawn that picture; a primitive scene of the imagination that has become real. Chrissi Island is the treasure island of my childhood.

Refreshed after our swim, we have come to the one taverna on the island where the-ones who-were-left-behind, are gathering, to pass the evening together. I have been adorned with the obligatory shell necklace, and I am well-sprayed with mosquito repellent - sarongs are wonderful evening attire. Smee, bare-chested and always the pirate, is so at ease. There are people of all ages here, but everyone is a desert islander, tanned, skinny, semi-naked and extremely relaxed.

Out comes the raki again, but I have learned my lesson. I sip it very slowly so as not to have an empty glass, and I have a tumbler of water at the same time. I want to remember this night, not just blow it away in a drunken stupor. We have small plates of salty cucumber and tomato to help the raki down before the main food appears. We are all seated at a long, wooden, makeshift trestle, crudely nailed together. There are no frills, no, you-mean-litre madam waiters. It is very communal. The food has been provided by the host of the evening, an emaciated looking seventy year old who I am told lives in an old shack nearby. He was the first to stay on the Island way back in the sixties. He lived like a hermit, but was always there to greet the occupants of passing boats, (that was before the tourist boats). He offered hospitality, they brought booze. Thirty years on, his liver must be completely pickled, and his body is wasted, yet he still throws back raki like his life depends on it.

Smee is very attentive; we seem to have hit it off. The barbecue smells delicious. Somebody must have had a good catch; there are little fish and big fish, and even bigger fish all charring nicely over a drift wood fire. There is not one sign of boiled goat or spaghetti, not one descent moustache at the table, not a hint of black-boot anywhere. No, this is another world altogether.

No matter how much I try to avoid drinking the raki that is put in front of me, a quantity of it passes by my tonsils, and consequently enters my bloodstream.

Add to that a balmy evening and a shared spliff, bongo rhythms, a Greek version of Bob Dylan, scantily clad nymphets with hair down to their waists, and young Tarzan look-a-likes, soft sea-washed skin on soft sea-washed skin, and the result is absolute bliss.

Now, in the middle of all this absolute bliss-ness another person joins the group and sits, guess where, right in between me and my pirate. Like some guest of honour to be made room for, a chair is brought for her, and she pushes her way to the table. I can't speak. You just don't know how stopped-in-my-tracks I am. Dressed in traditional black granny-gear, (what was it I said about no hint of black?) and standing not more than four feet high in her cotton socks - there in the middle of us, her one tooth catching on her bottom lip as she smiles, is Kalliope.

No sooner does she sit down, than a glass of raki is set before her together with a plate of soft fruits. I look at her, and with a glint in her eye she holds her glass up to mine and croaks '*Stini yamas*'. And there's no sipping, on her part anyway, she takes a shot better than any Brit on the beach road in Malia. While Smee refills her glass, she rabbits on to me as though we were long lost friends. 'Smee, what is she saying to me? What is she doing here? Help me out. I don't understand any of it?'

'Katy, this is my *Yaya* – my grandmother.'

I don't know what to say. It is all so surreal. Kalliope is so out of place and yet she fits in like a lobster at a shrimp's tea party; the very Queen of all. We eat and drink and clink glasses.

Her Royal Highness Granny Kalliope is tucked up in bed safe and sound as Smee and I walk barefoot along the water's edge. It is a very romantic moment: a desert island, waves gently lapping, stars twinkling, and the light of the full moon illuminating our sandy path.

'Tell me about your *Yaya*?' I plead. 'She must have had a very difficult life.'

'Yes, my *Yaya* has had a hard life.' We sit down between the bleached, white carcass of an ancient cedar tree, its skeletal branches lying twisted and knotted across the sand. Smee puts his arm around me.

'Katy, I will tell you my story, and then we shall swim in the moonlight, yes?'

'Yes,' I say, enjoying the softness in his voice and in his eyes.

'Kalliope was brought up in a hill village above Ierapetra. Her father was a poor illiterate farmer who knew nothing else but his crops and his livestock. Her illiterate mother was the hired hand, and the producer of his ten children, out of which only my grandmother survived. The others either died in infancy or joined the rebellion against the Turks and were killed. At the age of 15 she married a man thirty years older than her, Manolis Spanakis from over Malia way. They carried on living at the farm together, with Kalliope's parents. In the space of five years, Kalliope had three children, Nikos, Fotini my mother, and Yannis. Her forth pregnancy was still-born. My uncle Yorgos, Kalliope's fifth child, appeared much later, a good twenty years after the others. My mother, Fotini, gave birth to me six months later, so my uncle Yorgos and I are like brothers.

'So where are they all now?' I ask. 'How come Kalliope is living here on Chrissi Island?'

'Be patient, Kate, you will have the whole story. My mother was not educated; she was expected to help Kalliope in the house and in the fields. It was a woman's place. But she could weave, make lace and sew beautiful clothes. She was only in her twenties when she died. That was when I was born. My *Yaya* brought me up alongside her youngest son, then only a few months old, and my father? It's not a pleasant story, Kate. My father had violated my mother during his wife's pregnancy, and I was the result. Yes, my father was also my grandfather. Are you shocked Kate?'

I am shocked, but I am also intrigued with Smee's story.

'My father couldn't bear the shame. He wasn't a bad man. He was hard, he had had to be. By all accounts, he was as strong as an ox. He built walls, he wrestled rams, he herded his sheep and goats, he harvested his olives, and he made his own raki. When Nikos and Yannis found out what he had done, they beat him up. They were not farmers, they were educated but they were young bucks with morals, and fists.

'My father hung himself on the day of my mother's funeral. Kalliope had two babies in her arms, and no-one to work the farm. The Germans had invaded, and nobody was safe. Nikos was already a teacher in Ierapetra, and Yannis was studying to be a lawyer in Athens. It was a catastrophe, as they say. To outsiders, I was a bastard; rumour said I was half Italian. Nikos and Yannis would not look at me. They said I had killed their mother; the wound never healed. But my *Yaya* loved me and brought me up, she needed me, and for as long as I can remember, I have looked after her.

'In the 1930s when Nikos, Fotini and Yannis were growing up things were a little better here in Crete. All those rebellions to force the Turks out had paid off and Crete was finally united with Greece. Education was on the up, and Nikos, who hated the farm, took his chance at school. He walked miles every day to get to school. It was difficult for him during the war, but he carried on teaching, undeterred by the occupation. He didn't get involved with any of it, though many young men of that time had more adventurous spirits, and whenever a boat landed munitions off Ierapetra they would be there to help unload it. The Italians who had control of this area didn't bother him. He was far too clever to go out there and invite death. Kalliope on the other hand, was fearless. She slept with a gun under her pillow during the war, and still does. But Kalliope's war is another story.

'Yannis was also a scholar, but he was more energetic. He always boasted that he could get to school and back much quicker than Nikos, even though he was five years younger than him. He did help on the farm, but Kalliope could see the advantage of educated sons. Yannis was sent to Athens when he was fifteen, where he lived with family and continued his education. He finally became a lawyer, and stayed in Athens until the sixties, when he returned to Crete, and built a hotel on land left to him by his godfather.

'Only the women were left on my father's side of the family; his mother, Fotini, and her daughter, Katerina. They were not so poor, because old Manolis' family originally came from over Malia way, and he was big in the production of carob. They had a warehouse in Sissi, from where the carob harvest was loaded onto small boats and transported away. Anyway, I never knew my grandfather. Apparently, he, together with his father, had been killed in a brush with the Turks when they were visiting his other son Yorgos, who was a monk at the Monastery of St John in Anopoli. They got caught up in the slaughter.'

'So who found the Crystal? I blurt out.

'Oh, you know about the Crystal? Be patient Kate, I want you to know my family, and know why Kalliope and I live here, away from the world of deals and double crossing before you make judgments. The monk, Yorgos, who was murdered at the Monastery of St John, did have a wife and son, and his grandson, my cousin Yorgos, also became a priest. He is the only member of my family that I truly love, apart from Kalliope that is.' Smee flashes his teeth and opens his eyes wide in a totally crazed look, and makes me laugh. He is slightly crazy - that makes two of us I suppose.

'But I thought that monks were not supposed to get married.' I queried.

'Oh, Kate, he was a man first and a monk second. He did not live with his woman but the child was his.'

Is it possible that my *Papa* Yorgos is Smee's cousin? Surely he must be. The story of the monastery of St John is far too much of a coincidence.

'Smee, I think I know your cousin, *Papa* Yorgos.' I explain the connection and I am right. Once again fate, or call it what you will, has brought a circle of people together. Now, I am totally convinced that we are all connected, all meant to play some part in the search for Rhamu-Tsuna's soul-mate. I am not going to tell Smee too much of what I know about *Papa* Yorgos; maybe he knows about his obsession, maybe he doesn't.

'Please go on,' I urge him.

'Well, I have no school, only life, but I work with tourists, and for many years I am with an English woman. We lived together here on Chrissi for a long time. When she left, *Yaya* wanted to come here to watch over me. So, here we are my Yaya and me, poor survivors. My brother George joined the priesthood. He never married, and now he is some fancy bishop with glittery robes. We do keep in touch, but he never comes here.'

'Why did your English woman leave you,' I am inquisitive. I get that pensive look, and I can see the memory is hurting him. 'Oh never mind,' I add quickly.

'No, never mind,' he says, and goes on with his story. 'We carried on living in the farmhouse, and the rent from the land, together with Kalliope's weaving, gave us a living. Then, one day something happened to change our lives. I was up in the hills where I felt free. It began to rain. I headed for shelter in a cave. The rain was pelting down, worse than I'd ever known it. It was unusual because it was July, and we never get such heavy rain in July. I went deeper into the cave than I'd ever been, even though it was very dark. The rain began to make mud of the earth in the entrance, and I climbed onto a ledge to avoid getting wet. There I sat, enjoying the solitude, for almost half an hour. Then the stormy skies cleared and the sun came out, like an angel directing a beam of light right into the cave. And then I saw it: sparkling, dazzling, flashing light like a black-green diamond, a diamond the size of a dinosaur egg. The rain had washed away enough earth to uncover the most remarkable rock I had ever seen, the precious Crystal that you are looking for.'

I am speechless. It's like until now I wasn't sure that the Crystal really existed. 'Smee, it's a fantastic story.'

'It is not a story Kate, it is true. How the thing got into the cave I have no idea, pirates' treasure? Who knows? I took it home to Kalliope, and it sat on our kitchen table for a week. I knew that I was looking at a fortune but if the government should get hold of it I would get very little. I told my *Yaya* that I hadn't stolen the rock, but she said that it wasn't mine, and I should not keep it. We agreed to ask brother Yorgos when he came home. Well, to cut a long story short, my brother Yorgos, at this time training to be a priest, could utter no wrong in the eyes of Kalliope, and he persuaded us to allow him to contact our other brothers. He could obviously see that the thing was valuable and thought it only right that all the family share in the proceeds.

'Nikos and Yannis descended on us like eagles swooping on a hare. The hate we had for each other soon became tenfold. They argued as to who should do what with the Crystal. The teacher wanted to take it to the university, the lawyer, who had contacts in Athens, said that he knew someone who sold antiquities to America, and the priest said the Church should have it. I had no say, and I said nothing. I just picked up the rock and slung it out of the window, and then, in a rage that seemed to come from nowhere, I reached for the old shotgun, and blasted a hole, right through the roof. That silenced them all for sure, but it was only temporary.

'In the end, it was agreed that Yorgos would ask a question of the Church superiors, if such a thing as the Crystal was ever found, would the Church be willing to purchase it? Nikos was to ask the same question at the university, and Yannis was to see how much such a thing would fetch on the open market. They left.

'Well, the Crystal went to the Church. They had the most money to spend on such treasure. Nikos and Yannis took the money and became very rich. Yorgos stuck to his calling and wanted nothing, though his promotion was rapid. Kalliope was an old woman, and what did she need at her time of life? She had shelter, her old donkey, chickens - what more did she need? And me, well I was a bastard brother, a murderer in their eyes. They lied to me about how much they had taken for the Crystal, and they gave me a sum of money which, at that time, I thought was a fortune. Later I discovered it was nothing to the amount they had. Anyway, I have no need of money or brothers - *As to diavlo...* they can go to hell. The Crystal brought us nothing but trouble. They aren't happy. Nikos went to America and we never heard from him again. Yannis, always the lawyer, made sure that no one could touch his money. He built the hotel and has lived a life of debauchery; now he suffers from gout and has a bad heart. His children are just waiting for him to die so that they can get their hands on his money, but they are rich wasters who have never wanted for anything - Agh Family!'

I am dying to ask where the Crystal is now, but somehow I know that it is better to keep quiet and wait for the whole story to come out. Smee is seething underneath about his family and he needs to calm down.

'Ah Katy, you are so beautiful,' he says. I am not ready for the compliment, but just squeeze his hand. His eyes are big and brown and wide and I feel as though I am entering a portal through them into his past.

'What is your real name?' I ask, 'You never said.'

'Lefteris, it means 'freedom', it is a good name, no?'

'Yes, it is a good name. Let's swim,' I urge, and, in the moonlight, we enter the cool calmness of the Libyan Sea. Floating, we entwine in a warm embrace of friendship and we look deep into each other's eyes. Then our lips meet and we kiss, tenderly. Our friendship is suddenly something more, it has turned into affection. We separate, tread water, and turn to face each other again. We both want the same thing. Passion sparks, and this time we are kissing long and hard. We find each other in the water, burning with desire, wanting more, taking more. And under the water we cling to each other, holding on to the beauty of the moment, surfacing to see, to feel the reality of our naked bodies. And when we are totally exhausted, we float together in the pale moonlight, bound by a fire that even the ocean cannot extinguish.

–I drift into an octave of resonance and reach out for the hands of my prince. Within me, the rhythm of my

*heartbeat becomes a double echo, my pulse is a growing surge of life-force, as invisible as the blackness of a deep cave, yet as visible as the vision of a blind man's dream. It is as unsubstantial as a rainbow; as solid as a charged fence. Above the ancient earth I hear the whisper of a boy. I feel the soft brush of his cheek. I embrace the warm body of a lover. I am lost in the blackness of the cave. I am alive in a chromatic fantasy of colour. I am a shape within a shape. I am splintered in a blast of whiteness. Every particle of **me** explodes and implodes. –*

There are no more questions, only the cool air on our bodies, as we lie on the sand contemplating the starlit heavens above. A streak of light shoots across the firmament, and I don't know what to wish for first.

20

Is it love? Was it lust? I didn't see the white charger stomping sand, but have returned, as on the back of a dragon, with a slight tint of emerald in my aura. Now, I am on my roof pondering over the unimaginable information that Smee imparted to me. One thing is sure, he had touched the Emerald Crystal, it had touched him, and now it has touched me. It seems that it was still under the influence of the dark power to have affected his family the way it did. The cult of Artemis was directly connected with a holy stone, and she was the Goddess of war, of the hunt, of the moon. Does she still control the stone? Does she control me? I don't know exactly where the Crystal is, but I have a very good idea. It is in the hands of the Orthodox Church, and it is in a very safe place. Surely, if it is in the hands of good Christians, then its power of good will have been restored.

Content with that thought, I gather all my evidence and ring Maggie to tell her about my trip. Tomorrow I will try to contact *Papa* Yorgos with my news.

The garden, that I have been nurturing on my rooftop, in a variety of old tubs and pots, is desperate for water. I have neglected all things to do with the house, so I fix a hosepipe onto the outside tap and set about trying to save my wilting geraniums. Water gushes everywhere as I quench the thirst of every plant, and swill clean the soil-stained concrete of my terrace. Now I know why Greek ladies have such a fascination with running water, it not only washes away all the sand that is deposited on the south winds, but used correctly, it can be powered to clean every inch of outside space. I am enjoying creating a waterfall down the stone steps, watching every splish and splash that forces its way out of my hosepipe when a gravely voice behind me says:

'*Kalimera Katerina*, how are you?'

It is Aleko, my lecherous landlord, flashing his gold tooth at me. 'As you see I am getting very, *Greek woman*, Aleko. *Ela*, come in.' I un-stack a couple of plastic chairs, wipe them dry, and we sit down amongst the drips and drops of draining water.

'Can I get you a drink,' I offer.

It is only ten in the morning so I don't expect him to want anything but coffee. However, he says he'll have a beer, and that suits me fine. I hate having to make Greek coffee, watching it every second as it boils, to catch the rising froth, and, more often than not, missing the exact moment to pour it into the cup. Anyway, I feel like a beer too; July mornings are oven warm.

It is not usual to have a visitation before the rent is due, so I doubt that this is just a social call.

'You are here early Aleko,' I say intimating the question, 'why?

'I am here to make you an offer *Katerina*.'

Now what? I'm thinking, better not get too close. But he's all serious over something, so I wait for him to speak.

'I want this for you, *Katerina*,' he begins, in the best English he can muster, 'because I like you.' Ooh! Flattery - warning signals, Kate. 'I know you like this house, and life here is good for you, no?' I nod. 'The camping is very busy. I think (he hesitates), you know a little typing?' Oh God, he's offering me a job, and I'm quite happy not working, anyway I nod again.

'Listen, come work with me in office - talking little - watching shop - until October.' He sees the look on my face and holds his hand up. 'Wait - because I like you *Katerina* (oh here we go again); you work for me and - because I have no money, (what?), I will give you this house.' (WHAT!)

Have I heard him right? Is it a joke? No. He goes on to explain that if I will work for nothing until the end of the season, then he will have a legal contract drawn up, and sign the house over to me. He does not need the house, and he does not want to spend money on repairs. Well, Aleko is a wily old fox, but this is an offer, I MUST NOT turn down. At the worst, I will have worked the summer for nothing, and if all goes to plan, I will have my own little Cretan hovel before the year is out. 'Have another beer, Aleko.'

• •

So, here I am, working on the campsite, a paradise of lush vegetation, with grassy bays for tents and caravans. I have hired a scooter to get me to work every day, and put my quest on hold for the summer. It is on hold, but it is not out of mind. Position-wise the campsite could not be better. It is on the coast between Sissi and the archaeological site of Malia Palace. Every day I can survey the sweeping bay of Malia to the peninsula of Hersonissos and beyond. The work is easy and the company good. A myriad black pipes snake between the oleander bushes and almira trees to quench the garden, but the scorching heat has turned the grass into straw. Flowers blossom, blackbirds sing, bees buzz, butterflies wisp here and there, and I think that I am in the Garden of Eden. Aleko may be a rogue, but he has created a beautiful environment for happy campers. Mrs. Aleko is a bouffant lady from Heraklion, with gold-tipped shoes. Thank goodness she only puts in an appearance at the weekend, because she tends to be on the bossy side. When she isn't ordering me to do this and that she is lording it over Aleko, who seems to take it like a little pussy-cat. Anyway, the camp site is not her natural habitat, so she never stays around longer than necessary.

The toilets are of the hole-in-the-ground variety, and the showers are a bit grotty, but they work, most of the time. The electricity supply is dodgy, but the shop-cum-office is pleasant enough, and the old Remington typewriter is fantastic. There is a cannon ball the size of a melon to keep the door open, it was found on the site, and various other worn-away stony relics are dotted about here and there. The smell of grass is everywhere. I am here happy as a wart-hog in a bog, inhaling all sorts of *happy-smoke* on the wind, while my friend, Suzy, is working at a taverna on the harbour in Sissi, and Kelly is serving tables at a hotel, with arms strong enough for a tray of twenty plates. Fuckin' Pete, is working in a bar where he can 'f' and 'blind' with last-minute cheapies from the north of England and the 'al royt gal' brigade from the south. It is summer, hot, happy summer!

Sissi is an arena of tattooed flesh, pierced flesh and naked flesh. Drooling waiters hang around menu stands like she-devils in Soho. Disco music vibrates around pool bars. There are women with painted claws and Marilyn Monroe lips, all keep-fit firm and sun-bed brown. They drape over sun loungers with slipped down cossies, like undressed mannequins, and melt in the mid-day shadows of giant umbrellas, sipping tall-glass cocktails full of citrus fruit and cherries. At night they vamp around the discos in masks of Max Factor; bra-less, back-less and bejeweled. Clouds of eau-de-toilette scent a trail for the hounds. Men sniff out women; women are on heat. Men love men; women kiss women. Licit, illicit, the village is an orgy of licentiousness; ouzo, fish, fresh bread, and condoms. And I love every minute of it.

• •

July - it's my birthday, yippee! Hoorah! I telephoned *Papa* Yorgos last night to tell him about my trip to Ierapetra, but he is still away. I tried Adonis, but he was busy in the bar and we couldn't talk for long and Maggie says that birthdays are not her thing. Daddy is somewhere in the middle of Europe, so I can't share my day with him. Anyway, I've asked if I can leave early tonight, so that I can get ready to go out. I'm going to meet Suzy and Kelly at the Kera bar in the middle of Sissi, for a girly night, yeah!

Suzy and Kelly are always in Sissi at night, but I have been going home after work and have not tasted the mid-summer night scene. If I had seen Manolis Shepherd I suppose I would have invited him along, but I haven't set eyes on him in weeks. Gregory, on the other hand, is always about, especially since I gave him his present, so I dare say that he will be in Sissi tonight. In hindsight, I am not sure that the present was such a good idea. Still, he has never done me any harm.

The music is loud and full of bass. 'What's love got to do, got to do with it… what's love but a second hand emotion?' Kelly throws another whisky down her gullet and, like Tina, she gyrates, mini skirted and bare legged, to the throbbing sound which bounces round the walls of Kera Bar. It is small inside and squashy. People have found their own place at the long bar, and thirty men and women look like a hundred in such a small area. The walls are decorated with strings of big iron keys, old musical instruments, and black and white photos. Large mirrors double the space, and low lighting creates a cave or cellar-like feel. Best of all is the music, which is drumming through my veins and making it impossible not to dance. The low bass and disco lights make everything pulsate, and we order another round of drinks.

It is ten, and we are all a bit tipsy. I know it is ten because something so unusual happens that I look at my watch. My focus is not all it should be, and the light not good, so I ask Suzy to confirm the time. There is one cannon-fire blast of terrifying thunder that shakes the building from the outside and, would you believe it, the heavens are open in a diluvial downpour that is bringing even more people into the bar. All the people who know me start shouting, 'Rain-woman, Rain-woman.' It is a sobriquet, from the days of my arrival and the wetter than usual time which followed. We all start dancing again. Drinks appear in front of us from a Greek guy at the corner of the bar; we turn around, and it is Gregory, lurking in the shadows. We shout, '*Yamas!*' I must be under the influence, because I go over to the bar and link arms with my little ragamuffin friend. 'Hi, Gregory, come and dance with us.' I pull him towards our table. He doesn't resist. He dances with us, his little legs not really knowing how to move to western music.

    I am resigned to a girly night, when - guess who makes an appearance? My dark prince - THE shepherd. I have not seen him for so long, and all those feelings come rushing back into my brain and into my skin. I am high and bold and just ready to be his, when I notice, coming through the door behind him and draped all over him, is the most ugly, gothic sorceress that you have ever seen. Her black lips and black eyes match her black finger nails and the tips of mine begin to curl over. My eyes narrow and he - he has the audacity to take my hand in his. 'Yasou,' I say coldly, catching a glimpse of green light surrounding my fingers, and I turn back to my friends. So, Suzy was right. Obviously, by the way he is walking, he is stuped up on drink (not that I have any room to talk). His eyes are blurred; he is unshaven, and he is reeking of sex. Rain welts down outside, and I want to run into it to wash away every thought that

I ever had about the *good shepherd*. Memories of Jack flood back, I wish he were here with me right at this moment to share my birthday. Oh, Jack, Stuart, Annie... The alcohol is making me morose; I have to shake it off. I look at Gregory, fighting back the tears, and think, not in a million years, mate. There is nothing else for it but to have another drink and start dancing. I throw my hair back, and the bitch inside me says, "Just show that shepherd what he's missed." Jack would have liked me to be positive.

The rain has stopped and the evening continues in a hazy way. It is so good to be with Suzy and Kelly again. I have had my limit of drink, and it is time to get away from Gregory before he thinks there might be something in it for him. Suzy looks at me, and I know what she means.

'Come on.' She nods her head in the direction of the door, and, still dancing, we form a conga into the street to make our escape. Just across the road, waiting at the taxi rank, is Manolis in his silver Mercedes. Ah - safety, I think, and say my goodbyes to Suzy and Kelly.

'You always seem to be there when I need you,' I say, as I fall into the back seat of his limo. I don't remember the ride to Vrahassi, but my faithful friend once more escorts me up the hill to my little village house.

21

I have received a letter from *Papa* Yorgos. It is written in Greek, and I am at this moment pouring over the dictionary in an attempt to translate it. What makes it even more difficult, is that it is handwritten, and some of the letters are nothing like the ones in my text book. Anyway, I am getting through it. It has taken me two hours to translate *Papa* Yorgos' letter, and I am very pleased with myself. The contents, however, are somewhat puzzling.

> *Dear Kate,*
> *Are you well? I am very well.*
> *I know that you have been trying to reach me by phone, and from this I think you must have some news. I too have some news. I hope yours can wait, because I shall not be home until August, when I must attend to my church duties during the weeks before 15th. As you probably know, we have our big festival of the Virgin Mary on that day. Well, nothing can be done before then so I ask you to be patient and make notes. Our dreams are very important, Kate, remember Daniel?*

I look forward to hearing more about your dreams, and hope to see you again very soon.

Love, Y
P.S. Be vigilant Kate clouds can bring more than rain!

The post-mark is not easy to read, but the stamp is Greek. Where is he? What does he mean clouds can bring more than rain? And what is all that about Daniel? I have bought myself a mobile phone, and I am ringing Adonis to give him my number.

'Hello, Adonis; it's Kate.'
'Kate, are you good?'
'Yes, thank you, how are you?'
'I'm good.'
'Adonis, write my number down - I have bought a mobile phone.'
'You are already in mine.'
'Oh, OK, that's good.'
'Kate, are you all right?'
'Yes, sure, only I had this letter from your father.'
'What does he say?'
'Have you time to listen? I'll read it.'
'Go on.'

I read him the letter, and he tells me that when his father writes a letter he always wants you to learn something.

'First you must learn about the festival of the Virgin Mary, Kate. Then you must take your bible and read the book of Daniel, and finally, you have to be careful in all things. You know my father, Kate, he is very wise, and you are of special interest to him. Do as he says and Kate, ring me if you need me. I put the phone down thinking, Adonis really is a beautiful person.

Maggie is going to visit me for the August full moon. That is a few weeks away, so in the meantime I am going to do what *Papa* Yorgos says. It really is not easy in this heat. I don't feel like doing anything after work. The evenings are fresher, but that is mainly due to the Meltemi that is blowing from the north. It is two o'clock in the morning, a dog is barking, probably a late worker coming home, and I have just finished reading the book of Daniel. Thank goodness I brought my bible with me. I have been engrossed in the story of a master magician, a high priest, a man whose visions changed the world. I am reading how Nebuchadnezzar, a king, had a strange dream and he asks his magicians, astrologers, sorcerers and Chaldeans to interpret the dream but they cannot. Daniel, however, with his special gift from God, can. After telling the King what it means, Daniel goes on to speak of God saying: "… *he giveth wisdom unto the wise, and knowledge to them that knoweth understanding: he revealeth the deep and secret things: he knoweth what is in the darkness, and the light dwelleth with him.*" Giveth, Revealeth, Knoweth, Dwelleth - there is something magical in the sound of biblical words. Is God revealing deep and secret things to me?

Balshazzar, Nebuchadnezzar's son, is reveling at one of his feasts when he sees the fingers and part of a hand appear. He watches in terror as it writes a message on the wall. Daniel interprets the writing as foretelling the downfall of Balshazzar, because he worships nothing but silver and gold: *"...the God in whose hand thy breath is, and whose are all thy ways, hast thou not glorified: and this writing was written."*

I begin to wonder if the *hands* of my dream are somehow connected to the hand of Balshazzar's feast. Are the hands of Rhamu-Tsuna and the hands that plucked me from the blackness of destruction at the roadside the self same power that the Church acknowledges as 'God'?

It is late, and I have work tomorrow. I fall asleep thinking about Daniel.

• •

Today is the eve of the celebration for Saint Panteleimon, 25th July, and the villagers are holding their annual festival. Of course I am going along, with Suzy and Kelly Amazon. Kelly is going to bring her daughter, Baz. That is quite unusual because she prefers to go out without her daughter, but Kelly's Albanian boyfriend has been hauled in by the police and transported back to Albania, so she doesn't want to leave Baz in the house by herself. Already the young Greek guys have their eyes on the nine-years old. Young Baz has cleaned up well; her long blond hair is crinkling down her back, let loose from the plait that usually keeps it together. Her worn jeans and t-shirt match her worn trainers, but her confidence over-rides anything she may be wearing. She is already teasing the young boys with the promise of her beauty. I hope she doesn't grow up to be as masculine and uncouth as her mother, but I somehow know she will. Kelly has told her to "bugger off and play," and we three unattached find a seat at one of the paper table-clothed trestles. The school yard has been laid out with long tables, and chairs, and a band has set up at the front, leaving a big circle of empty space for the dancing. The atmosphere is quite party-y, as all the locals get together for an evening of food, drink, music and dance.

'Here, Kelly, will you go and buy some wine.' I give her some money, and she heads towards the booze. Suzy and I settle down at a long table, reserving a seat for Kelly. More people funnel up the drive and take their places at tables. There is a sound of Cretan cackling going on, as the band begins to tune up. I always think that the sounds produced by a Lyre's three strings are very limited, but on occasions like these, no other music would do, Der-de, de, Der-de, de, Der-de, de. It drones on and on, but it is hypnotic. Kelly brings two bottles of wine - pork chops arrive - and everyone is happy. It is a big outside party that by midnight is just getting going.

CRUNCH… Two heavy hands drop onto my shoulders and squeeze. A deep voice smolders *'Yasou Katy.'* I freeze. A crowd of shepherds has surrounded us, and they are busy bringing in extra chairs. Manolis Shepherd looks at me strangely, deeply, questioningly. I don't think he understands me. Well there are four of them and three of us, so it is a group rather than couples. Suzy throws me a wink; I move my chair back a little. They are all cleaned up for the night, best black uniforms out for parade, gold chains, waxed whiskers and a slight aroma of lanolin following their every move. A bottle of whisky arrives on the table. Oh God! Where do I go from here?

'Well, it looks like we are the chosen ones.' I shout over the music.

Suzy comes back with, 'Oh just go with it, Kate, you know what he's like now, don't be so serious, have a bit of fun.'

I pick up my glass, 'I suppose you're right,' *Yamas.* We all clink our glasses, and the party begins. It is surprising, but the hate that I had for my shepherd on the night of my birthday has disappeared and I am, once again, thrilled to be in his company. We are all three flirting like teenagers; our heads are back, our manes flowing. It is obvious that we are enjoying the tactile company of Vrahassi man, and they are enjoying ours.

'They think foreign women are begging for sex,' Kelly bellows knowing that they don't understand what she has said, although they do catch onto the word "sex," and perk up.

'Well, are we?' returns Suzy, and we all throw our glasses in the air and shout in unison 'Yes,' as though England has scored the first goal.

It is a good job we are sitting on one of the tables at the back, because most people are turned towards the musicians and are totally oblivious to the party that is going on behind them. Baz has joined the big circle of dance, with her schoolmates. Bottoms are flapping and bosoms are bouncing, as the music picks up speed. Our shepherds do not want to dance tonight, they think they are in with a chance, but we three have made a pact to get a taxi back to Kelly's, and stay the night there. We are the power of three. We raise our glasses again, and toast, 'the power of three,' we proclaim, and, like some sign from the Almighty, the whole arena is thrown into blackness.

The electricity has tripped (probably one light bulb too many), and the music has stopped. We sit there in the dark. There is silence, but only for a split second. I feel a hand on my knee, and another around my waist, and my head turns straight into the bristly lips of Manolis Shepherd. One minute later, the lights are on, and our taxi has arrived. My shepherd grips my hand for me to stay, but our minds are made up and I pull away. It is all part of the game, I suppose. 'He's not going anywhere,' Suzy advises me, and of course, she is right.

I sometimes think that I am such a pathetic creature. The truth is I wanted him to kiss me so much. I want him to lust after me. I don't care about the other women. Well, that's a silly thing to say, Kate, of course you care. He has to want you, and only you. But will he? No, just go with it as long as it lasts. Remember Suzy - eight years and then he dumps her for a Greek girl. I suppose a fraction of that time would do me with the Casanova of Vrahassi.

• •

Well, the pork chop of last night has worn off and I am hungry. I have a bit of a headache, but it is not too bad. Suzy, Kelly and I have decided to walk to the harbour in Sissi for English breakfast at the bar where Fuckin' Pete works. It is not far from Kelly's house. We all sat up late last night, talking and putting the world to rights so we did not get much sleep. But it was a good night.

'So, how do you feel this morning?' Suzy asks, 'Do we have Kate back, or is she still in cloud-shepherd land?'

'I'm OK - really I am - but I'm still a bit smitten.'

Well learn to live with it,' says Kelly in a curt, Greek-hating, man-hating, tone of voice, 'because he'll never settle down, his mother won't let him.'

I am thinking, what does she know, but I don't answer. In fact I do have other things on my mind - *Papa* Yorgos' letter for one. He will be back in a couple of days and I still have not done all the things that he asked of me. Next on my list is the Virgin Mary, not a very apt subject to slot in alongside my carnal thoughts.

'Hi Pete,' we say in unison, as we approach the cafe-bar.

'Well, look who's fuckin' here. You three look like you 'ad a good night.'

'Pete, what do you know about the Virgin Mary?' It is not a serious question just one that pops out and I know it will force a reaction.

'Which fuckin' virgin Mary? There ain't any in this fuckin' place.'

He takes our order and disappears into the back. Good old fuckin' Pete - always the same.

'Where on earth did that question come from?' Suzy asks, 'It's a bit of a leap from sexy shepherds to Virgin Mary.'

'Oh, it's just that I know the big festival of Mary is coming up and I want to find out more about it.'

'Well, all you need to know is that it is another bun feast like last night, only bigger. We can either go to Neapolis where the whole town comes out to eat in the main street or we can go to Milatos where the party takes place on the harbour. Take your pick.'

'Is it a churchy do then?'

'If you are churchy, yes, and if not, it's another good excuse to go dancing.'

Our breakfast arrives and we tuck in to bacon, eggs, beans and sausage.

'Anyway, if you want to know the church side of it, there is *Papa* Vassillis over there, he speaks a bit of English, go and ask him.'

Papa Vassillis is ensconced at a *kafeneo* table playing backgammon with an old boy. His grey suit trousers show below his simple black tunic, and his head is bare. His hair is fairly short, dark and straight, and his black beard covers his cheeks in a bush of hair that has probably never seen a razor. He is nothing like *Papa* Zachariah, with his knotted white hair and long silver beard, or *Papa* Yorgos, who also has long hair and a long beard. No, *Papa* Vassillis is obviously a more modern type, or is it just that he is younger? Anyway, I am reluctant to approach him while he is playing backgammon.

'Better ask him now before he starts on the raki,' Kelly buts in, 'and make sure he doesn't fall down your cleavage while he's talking to you.'

'I get the picture.' I turn to take another look at *Papa* Vassillis just as he is lighting up a cigarette and he catches my eye. 'I'm sure he knows we are talking about him Suzy.'

'Of course he knows; everyone talks about him.'

'Hey! It's Gregory. Over here - come and join us.' Kelly Amazon has spotted Gregory in the street. He looks like he never went to bed last night. 'Where were you last night, Gregory? We didn't see you at the festival.'

'Well me to seeing you. Playing good time,' he stares straight at me. I can feel the red begin to grow on my face, and I feel guilty.

'Sit down and have a coffee Gregory,' I say, meaning, don't be so petty just because you didn't get the attention.

'No, not,' he says 'another time,' and gets back onto his old put-put, and goes.

'Oops, I think I have upset him,' I say. 'Maybe we should have asked him to join us last night.'

'Come on Kate, you don't really mean that, do you?' says Suzy.

She is right, of course, but Gregory has become part of my life in Vrahassi, and the last thing I want to do is upset him. Maybe the present was not such a good idea, I think he has got the wrong signal from it.

I finally find the courage to ask *Papa* Vassillis if he can explain the reason for the celebration of the Virgin Mary. He welcomes the question and is at my side in a flash telling me all about it. His English is very good. He begins, 'Did you know that in the Orthodox religion, Mary does not die but rather falls in to a deep sleep? This is known as the "Dormitian," and is celebrated on the 1st August, and thereafter a period of fasting begins: no meat, dairy, oil or wine. The day that Mary is taken up into heaven is the "Assumption," and it is celebrated on the 15th August.'

'But what about the Virgin Mary: why do people worship her?' I ask. 'Of course I know that she is important because she is the mother of Christ, but I have searched my bible, and she is only mentioned about a dozen times; a devoted mother, no more.' *Papa* Vassillis totally ignores my question, maybe he has not understood what I asked. Anyway, he seems eager to get back to his backgammon mates, so I thank him for his answer and he leaves. I am left pondering over what happened to make people worship the mysterious Virgin Mary like a goddess? When I see *Papa* Yorgos I will ask him. Meanwhile, I think he will be pleased that I have at least answered a few questions that his letter asked. What I still cannot fathom is his post script about clouds. What was it? Clouds can bring more than rain? And why should I be vigilant? Is there something I should be afraid of? Thunder or lightning maybe; does he know something I don't, about the future? Oh, I don't know, the sooner we get together the better. We all decide to go to Neapolis on the 15th August, and I head for the campsite for the rest of the day, just in case there is anything urgent to do - a letter to write, a stamp to sell.

Back in Vrahassi after a slow day trying to get rid of my hang over, I take a couple of *Depon* paracetamol tablets, and head for my roof terrace where I have a fantastic view of the starry night sky. I relax in my old plastic chair and go over the events of the last couple of days, with the constellation of Orion high in the dome of the heavens above me - the three stars of his belt twinkling in the clear night sky, echoing the scheme of the great pyramids. Sirius, the brightest star of them all, seems to have a sort of wobbly oscillation like a suspended ball of white fire. I know that the Ancient Egyptian Goddess of fertility, Isis, is watching over me. 'Thank you Ancient Goddess for my wonderful life,' I say, and throw my arms wide open to invite her embrace.

• •

Adonis has been in touch to invite us all to eat together in Neapolis. It is the night of the celebration of the Assumption of the Virgin Mary, 15th August. I cannot wait to see *Papa* Yorgos to tell him about my trip to Ierapetra. Suzy, Kelly and Baz, are going to meet me here after work, which could be late as the restaurants of Sissi are very busy now. It is nine o'clock, and the great bell of the big church sounds the hour. I have just arrived from Vrahassi with Manolis Taxi, and I am amazed at the scene. Market stalls have been erected on the road, in front and up the side of the church. There are lots of goodies for sale: toys, handbags, miniature icons, religious bric-a-brac, biscuits and sweets. A gypsy girl, looking like *Mary Poppins* about to take off, is swamped beneath enough helium balloons to take her to the moon. Musicians are wiring for sound on a huge stage which dominates the centre of the town, and every café-bar, souvlaki shop and *kafeneo* has arranged trestle tables outside their shops to make the high street resemble one great big wedding venue.

The church is brightly lit, its doors wide open, and I have promised myself a peek inside. There are well dressed families milling about the paved forecourt. Some are going in, some are coming out. I can't make out whether a service is about to start or has just finished but I push on intrepidly, boldly going where I have never been before. I have time to kill before I meet the others, so a bit of research seems a good idea. Churches are quite sobering places aren't they? This church is known as the Cathedral of Petra, Peter "the rock," how very apt! Wow! It is fantastic, it is ornate, it is rich with silver and gold, and the great wheel of a golden chandelier dominates the centre isle. It is held in place by guide-rope chains that suspend it from the domed ceiling like some frame of a *big top*. The silver-edged icon of the Virgin Mary, which is festooned with votives, jewellery, silver and gold crosses, hearts, bracelets and other trinkets, is before me like some oversized Mona Lisa hiding behind a strange suite of armour. A painted Virgin and child peer out from beneath their clothes of silver, looking on as devotees bend to kiss the glass which separates them from humanity. I take it all in, thinking about Isis, Artemis and Mary; all worshipped as Virgin Queens of the Heavens. I ponder the thought that they are all one and the same, and that people throughout the ages have given the *Mother-power-of-the-Universe* a slightly different identity, but have kept the philosophy of supreme purity the same. To be quite honest at this moment in time I can understand how, if I were in deep trouble, I would be able to ask the sweet

Virgin mother for help. It is to do with unconditional love: the love of a mother for her child, love that has no boundaries, love that provides all answers, solves all problems, the safety of being held in loving arms that will not let anyone or anything hurt you, knowing that your all-loving mother can ease any pain. I light a candle, and thank the Virgin Mary for being there to ease my pain.

Right at this moment I could so easily break down again, thinking about arms that held me as a child, my own warm mother who was always there to encourage me, to stand up for me, to provide for me, to love me. But I have to stop myself thinking about such things. They are over, gone - those past times, all those wonderful people that I relied on for love, now in heaven. So, Mary, Queen of Heaven, if you are there, wrap your arms around my mother, my children and my Jack for me; I am sending love with this flame. Let my thoughts cross the boundary between earth and heaven and let my love warm their souls. Sitting quietly at the back of the church, I block out all else and for one split second Kate is an infinitesimal spark in the great scheme of all that is.

In a self-induced calm that has relaxed me, I gaze at the tall wooden cross that the Bishop is holding in front of him as he processes down the isle towards the altar, and I am aware that a service is about to begin. The polished gold medallion of this obviously hierarchical priest catches my eye as he climbs the circular steps which wind him up to the pulpit; from there he peruses his audience like some wizard looking out from his tower. Revered father of his flock, senior father of holy fathers, dressed like one of the saintly icons, loved by some and feared by many, he opens his speech with 'Love is all...' and as he does, a firm hand takes hold of mine and the familiar face of Smee settles down beside me. We don't speak. We just look at each other so happy to be together. I realize now that the high priest is Smee's half brother, the one who rose in the ranks of the church, the one who determined the whereabouts of the Crystal.

My pirate translates for me: "'In 540 AD, a mosaic in which the Virgin Mary sits enthroned as Queen of the Heavens was created in the centre of the apex of the cathedral of Parenzo in Austria. In France, at the same time, mighty churches rose in tribute to her, and all over the world there have been reports of visions of the holy mother, swathed in light, often bearing her child as she spoke. That Mary, mother of Jesus, mother of us all, Queen of the Heavens, exists is not to be doubted. We are here today to honour her.'"

Smee gets fed up of translating but I have heard enough. The address does not last too long, and I have got the gist of it. A short anthem follows, and various priests of the area swing incense about before processing down the central isle and out into the warm, festive air of an August evening. We sit and wait for the church to empty, stunned by each other's company.

Once on the forecourt of the church, we are spotted by *Papa* Yorgos, who is heading our way at the rate of knots; his black gown is billowing around him like those black sails of Cretan ships which set out to fight for Helen. I am enfolded in clerical cotton and embraced warmly. Following on the heels of *Papa*

Yorgos is Adonis, who is accompanied by his uncle, Yorgos, the Bishop of Hania. This is a reunion indeed; a family affair that I was not expecting. I am among esteemed company that is for sure, and together we make our way to a table that has been reserved directly opposite the platform-cum-stage, that is surrounded by amplifiers, and festooned with flowers.

As we take our seats, Suzy, Kelly and Baz arrive. They are obviously surprised by the company. 'I didn't know you had connections in the church, Kate,' Suzy whispered. I had told them that we were meeting an Adonis and his father from Heraklion, and that was all they knew. Suzy is wearing her best glam - a blue fitted dress and high heels, she has had her hair highlighted and cut short. Single sapphire droplets hang from her ears and match the blue of her outfit. Kelly is wearing a short, tight denim skirt and V-neck body-hugging T-shirt with little cap sleeves; it has a flash of a sequined stripe running diagonally across it which matches the glitter on her eyes. She seems to tower above us in her heels; I don't think I've ever seen her so done-up. Baz, as always is a miniature image of her mum. I feel positively short in my flat sandals, but I love my black trousers and strappy black top. We are glamorous company for the illustrious Fathers. They seem to revel in it and put us at ease straight away by ordering wine. There is so much I want to ask, but this is not the time. No, it is party time. Adonis is getting on famously with Kelly, Suzy is doing her best to find out what she can about Smee, and *Papa* Yorgos reaches out for my hands across the table, squeezes them tightly and just says, 'Ah, Kate, it's so good to see you again.'

The music begins: a live band and singer. Various people keep coming up to the table to speak to the Bishop. There is a lot of kissing of his ring, another chunk of emerald. From time to time he disappears to engage in conversation with suited ones, but in between he talks to us, asks us questions and genuinely seems to want to know all about our lives. I desperately want to ask him about his, but I dare not. Suzy on the other hand comes straight out with it.

'You seem to be a very important person Your Eminence.' I want to shrivel up but George the Mighty, as I call him in my head, enjoys the bluntness of her question and answers simply.

'Yes, I am.' Then he goes on. 'You see, Suzy, the higher up in the offices of the Church one goes, the more chance one has of being able to do things, alter things, make things happen.'

George the Mighty speaks very good English; I butt in to alter the course of the conversation. 'Do you speak any other languages Your Eminence?' I ask. What a difference there is between Smee and his half brother; there is a family resemblance, but that is all. I can't help thinking about his old mother, Kalliope, and how she has had to live. And how different *Papa* Yorgos is, how much kinder he looks, how gentle his manner and how, to me, so very Christ-like he behaves. Soon, a big black limousine arrives to collect the Bishop, who is ushered away surrounded by men in black. He has been the perfect host at his table, and I, for one, feel honoured to have been one of his guests - but I am glad he has gone, and now I can breathe a little easier.

There is so much I want to talk to *Papa* Yorgos about but I know that as long as we have company I must remain silent. Smee is fantastic company, and he looks a million dollars in his cream linen suit and soft pig skin shoes - very *Zorba*. I remember our night together on Chrissi Island, something else that must remain our secret. We are all a little more relaxed now that the Bishop has gone.

'So, Kate, it appears that you have met my cousin before,' says *Papa* Yorgos looking across the table to Smee, 'I had no idea that you two knew each other.'

'Oh, we met quite by accident in Ierapetra,' I hastily explain.

'Ah - by accident,' repeats *Papa* Yorgos with a slight raise of his eyebrows. 'Tell me dear cousin, how is Kalliope?'

It is the first mention of Smee's grandmother, and the enquiry is very polite, with no hint of how *Papa* Yorgos feels about the unfortunate old woman whose history he must certainly be aware of.

'She is well, cousin,' is all that is said. How different Smee is tonight from the semi-clad pirate of Chrissi Island, but the twinkle of his gold-toothed smile tells me he is not going to be drawn into conversation about his family.

Our taxi is booked for 2 a.m., though the party will continue in the wonderful cool of the night. When we leave, Adonis hugs us all. Smee does the same but plants a very affectionate kiss right on my lips, and tells me we shall meet again very soon. *Papa* Yorgos shakes hands, and kisses both cheeks, whilst at the same time handing me a note which I quickly smuggle into my handbag. The company has been wonderful and we all agree to get together again before too long.

Agapiti moo Kate, My dear Kate,

I have been away for a few weeks and have missed talking with you about your dreams. I know that tonight we shall not have the opportunity to discuss our mutual interest, so I hope you will be able to meet me on Saturday, early, so that we can have a good chat before the moon rises. Be ready at 5p.m. and I shall pick you up in Vrahassi, unless I hear otherwise.

Y.

Oh dear, I have invited Maggie to stay with me for the full moon. Well, we shall just have to go to *Papa* Yorgos' together, I'm sure he won't mind.

22

The August heat really is slowing me down. I welcome the coolness of the evening. The campsite is very busy and very smelly. Thank goodness I have the shade of the office, but there is no air conditioning, in fact there is very little air, even though we are on the edge of the sea. I haven't much work; it is just a matter of being on hand for the odd tourist who wishes to buy a postcard or a bottle of pop.

I have a chair on the veranda, and a second hand magazine. It is amazing what you read in magazines: did you know that the average person falls asleep in seven minutes? Did you know that a cockroach can live for ten days without a head? Did you know that if you count the number of chirps that a tree cricket makes in 15 seconds then add 37, the sum will be very close to the outside temperature? One, two, three, four... anymore of this and I will be asl...

...Slow, go slower Kate, don't run you'll get there... Where? Where am I going? The sky is so blue. I am following a path, but I don't know where I am going. Trust Kate, trust. You have come a long way. Not much farther... Is

that you Grandad? I am sure I recognize your voice. Oh, it is you...

'Follow me Kate.'

... I am following Grandad, show me the way. Wait Grandad, wait for me, I am coming...

'Hey, any chance of a can of coke?'

That will teach me to count cricket chirps. I get the happy camper an ice-cold can from the fridge, and help myself to one as well. The little dream has brought back memories of my wonderful Grandad: prize chrysanthemums and horse-dung tomato beds, sardines on toast, learning to play chess, his lovely trilby hat. If I am on the same path as him I am sure it will lead me to somewhere very special. But, what am I saying, I don't want to go anywhere, not at the moment, my work here is definitely not over yet.

The guy takes his can of coke, and I am left alone again. I ring Maggie.

'Hi Maggie, are we still on for Saturday?'

'Aye, that we are, a've got me nightie packed.'

'Get a taxi from Neapolis otherwise you will have to climb the hill from the main road.'

'Ney worries, a'll be there about two.'

'OK, see you, byeee.'

Good, that's sorted. I will ask the lecherous Aleko for Saturday off - he owes me a favour for working overtime last week, when we had a camp barbecue.

Funny - that dream about my Grandad. Why should he pop into my thoughts now after all these years? I was only a little girl when he died. I remember looking into the sky and seeing a bright star which, for me, was my Grandad in heaven. It was a sort of comfort to know he was still there, watching me, protecting me. Maybe he is watching me now, protecting me still. Grandads are so wise. It is as though they pave the way for their descendants. Well, if the path was good enough for my Grandad it is surely good enough for me. Onward Kate: onward into the future.

• •

It is Saturday, mid-August, no wind, hot, clear blue skies. I have the day off, but there is no staying in bed. I want the house to be spotless for my visitor, so I am cleaning and polishing everything in sight. It is good to have visitors because they motivate you into the soap and water thing. August is not a time for such exhaustion and I am dripping perspiration in the heat; never mind, it is a good way to detox a bit. All spick and span, I take a quick shower, and it is time to go and meet Maggie. I reach the centre of Vrahassi just as she emerges from the taxi - her bold voluptuous self. She is carrying a medium sized carpet bag which looks quite heavy, and I guess that she has brought some of her crystals with her. Rocks are like pets, they are good company.

'Hi, you made it.'

'Ye did right to say get a taxi. A niver would a' made it up the hill.'

I don't want to tell her that to get to my hovel there is still more incline. We are out of breath and only half way up the hill. Thank goodness for old grannies hanging out in the shadows. They are sitting on a doorstep watching the world go by, waiting, waiting for the likes of me and Maggie to pass - the highlight of their day. We are grateful for the excuse to stop and chat. Within two minutes they have found out who Maggie is, where she is from, what is in her bag, what she will eat for dinner, cackle...cackle...cackle, and so on and so forth. I had better not mention the roof just now, let her get her breath back first.

Sitting under the shade of an old beach umbrella that I rescued from the rubbish dump at the campsite, we drink beer and yak, yak, yak, about all my adventure in Ierapetra. I still have not spoken to Maggie about *Papa* Yorgos but now I feel it is time. After all, we are going to spend the evening with him. Maggie doesn't know this yet but I think she will be excited when she hears about what I have to say. Well, here goes:

'Maggie I've got a bit of a surprise for you lined up for tonight...'

• •

The time is nearly five o'clock and Maggie and I are back down in the square in the middle of Vrahassi. I have informed her of every little detail, about Adonis and *Papa* Yorgos, and the link with Smee and his family from Ierapetra. Of course she isn't surprised. She is looking forward to our evening with the somewhat off-beat *Papa*.

Exactly on time, *Papa* Yorgos cruises into the square in his opulent looking saloon. It has beige leather upholstery. We get straight in. I sit in the front, Maggie in the back. *Papa* Yorgos is expecting Maggie as I rang him yesterday to see if it would be all right for her to come along. Once inside the car I realize that it is not a new one, although the dash has well-polished veneer. The front seat stretches right across like those I was familiar with when Jack and I first met. It is a very well preserved classic car, though I have no idea what make. Anyway it is a lovely shade of blue.

'This is our plan,' *Papa* Yorgos announces. 'We shall go to *Agios* where first I shall show you the work that has been done on my new house. Then we shall go to a restaurant that I know, where we shall be able to catch up on developments with regard to your dreams, Kate.'

'I have so much to tell you *Papa* Yorgos,' I blurt out excitedly.

'And I have so much to tell you, Kate.'

. . . .

The foundations to *Papa* Yorgos' house on the land by the sea at Agios Nikolaos have been laid, and wire structures built to hold the concrete columns. 'It is a beginning, Kate,' he says enthusiastically. 'By next year my house will be built - what do you think to it?'

'I think it will be great, *Papa* Yorgos.' What can I say, it is a building site in the very early stages and unlike *Papa* Yorgos I haven't a vision of the finished house.

'It is going to be splendid,' I say, trying to keep positive.

'I know, Kate, it is a long way off being finished, but the time will pass and the work will get done. Agios Nikolaos was not built in a day you know,' he says, tongue-in-cheek. But he is right, the town of Agios Nikolaos used to be nothing but a small fishing village, and now it is a beautiful Mediterranean resort where ocean going yachts moor, and there are enough jewellery shops to adorn a flotilla full of fabulous people.

'Well, better say hello to *Stone* while we are here.' I say.

Stone looks a bit lonely abandoned behind all the bricks and sand, and building site debris, but he stands, magnificent as ever, guardian of the plot. We introduce Maggie to him and she shakes her head.

'Now here's a granddaddy of them all. I can see ye're a bit carbuncled but ye're as warm as a stone can be.' She carries on talking to *Stone* as though he were an old man at the *kafeneo*. 'Well, I imagine ye've got a part to play in all that's going on, so I'm sure we'll be meeting again.' It is obvious that Maggie is very used to talking to stones. When she has had her say she turns to us. 'Come on then, let's be off to this food shop, I'm feeling a wee cavern in me tummy.' Maggie has a certain way of taking the lead and she marches us back to the car.

The restaurant turns out to be a souvlaki shop just out of town. It is run by one of *Papa* Yorgos' cousins, a paunchy sixty year old, with a cigarette sticking to his bottom lip as he breathes, through his mouth to take in the maximum amount of oxygen. He is unshaven, has big bags under his eyes, and stands no more than five feet tall. A roll-out canopy covers the outside of the shop, under which there are no more than four tables. We sit down on chairs that were ready for the tip last year, and *Papa* Yorgos orders souvlaki, chips, and salad, with a jug of wine to wash it down. When the souvlaki arrives there is a mound of it. More skewered meat than I have seen since the last campsite barbecue. *Papa* Yorgos wants to feed us well. This is not a tourist area, and I can understand why we have been brought here. It is quiet, and *Papa* Yorgos' cousin does not speak any English, in fact, his breathing is so bad it is a wonder that he can speak at all.

'To business, ladies,' *Papa* Yorgos starts in a very official tone. 'Did you do as I asked in my letter, Kate?' I produce my dossier of *everything* and open it at page one. Even though Maggie knows all about *everything* she is still interested to hear it again. While *Papa* Yorgos reads we eat, prompted by his occasional command, 'Eat, ladies.' I am waiting for a reaction, a comment: a look of disbelief, anything, but all he can say is "eat," and that is what we do. *Papa* Yorgos is now very serious. 'So ladies, we are all in this together, does anyone else know about the Crystal?' He is very stern.

'No, absolutely not, *Papa*, it is our secret, ours and that of your family in Ierapetra.' I am trying to sound reassuring, but I know that *Papa* Yorgos is very on edge about it all. Suddenly he turns his head to the sky,

'Look,' he says, 'the green moon is rising.' Now I understand fully why we are sitting where we are. From here we have a perfect view of the moon, as it appears over the silhouette of the Thripti Mountains like a big orange-red beacon in the blue-black backdrop of night. It is an awesome sight, and we are silent as we watch it climb the sky. It loses some of its redness as it slowly gets higher, and it shines down onto the earth, lighting the mountains and the land and the hearts of every romantic visitor who, at this moment, is beholding its beauty.

And so, under the influence of the full moon, *Papa* Yorgos discloses that he has spent the last few weeks at Mount Athos where, with the help of the Virgin Mary, he has been successful in acquiring the Emerald Crystal - on loan as it were.

'*Papa* Yorgos,' I utter in disbelief, 'don't tell me you've stolen it!'

'Borrowed,' he assures me, and he continues: 'At the monastery on Mount Athos I prayed long and hard, Kate. Did you know that on Mount Athos, the Virgin Mary promised St Peter that she would guarantee the salvation of the soul of any monk who stays there and struggles to fulfil his spiritual duties? I am struggling to fulfil my spiritual duties, but I believe in what I am doing and I believe that God has given us all different virtues. With the grace of God it is possible to transcend all problems. Man is a vessel for God's energy, and through God's energy we can share in all of God's qualities. The Crystal has been *borrowed* from the fathers who guard it on Mount Athos, with this in mind.'

I say nothing and for once, Maggie is silent too. Mount Athos is a bastion of the Orthodox Faith. Within its walls there are treasures beyond comprehension; religious relics, precious jewels, and ancient manuscripts. No woman is ever allowed to set foot in the sacred Monastery of Mount Athos.

'Now, are we together in this, ladies?' *Papa* Yorgos asks.

And so like some gang hatching a plot to rob a bank, we close in and listen to what he has to say.

'You know I have worked for a long time on the vibrations of harmony, Kate. I know that everything, and I mean everything, seen and unseen, has a vibration. You, yourself told me, that when you put your stones together in a certain way, they affected the miniature of *Stone,* and caused it to topple over. Nothing was known about the history of the Emerald until you came along with your fantastic story, which I have no doubt is true, Kate. The Emerald has great powers and I believe it can help me reach the vibration of *Stone*, and in this way, share in yet another quality of God. And with your help Maggie, for I can see now that we are meant to be the power of three, we will discover another law of the universe and be able to communicate with *Stone.*'

Maggie says nothing. Then holding her hand out to take *Papa* Yorgos' in hers, like some chieftain sealing a treaty, she states firmly, 'A'm ye're man,' and we all three shake on it.

Slightly stunned by what has been said, Maggie and I are bundled into a taxi, which is paid for by *Papa* Yorgos, and sent off back to Vrahassi. Our next reunion is to be in September on the night of the full moon – the hunter's moon when the stage will be set for *Papa* Yorgos' experiment to try to create the right sound which will put him in the same vibration as *Stone* and therefore be able to communicate with his lifelong companion. From my point, I hope to learn something of Rhamu's lost princess.

Of course, we sit up half the night talking about *Papa* Yorgos, and *Stone,* and the Crystal, and Rhamu-Tsuna and his Princess, and how on earth did we get into all of this? Sleep is good.

23

The old scooter that Aleko has provided me with to go to and from work has proved to be the most useful thing. It is easy to ride, and the open air journey down the mountain every day is such a fantastic experience. I focus on the V of the gorge as I wend round and down and round and down. It is not a fast journey, and I have to watch all the pot-holes, but to be in the same space as the nesting vultures, the tinkling goats and sheep, the ancient rocks, the holy monastery, and the very air of a sunny Cretan morning, fills me with a feeling that is so good. Breathe Kate. Breathe.

I have one month to ready myself before our full moon meeting. One month of rows of sun beds and big coloured umbrellas. It seems as though the whole world is taking a holiday. The campsite is full: hotels, apartments, swimming pools, bars, discos, restaurants, shops, car parks, beaches - all full of people enjoying themselves. The roads are busy with bicycles, scooters motorbikes, cars, camper vans, coaches and delivery trucks. The sea is busy with ferryboats, fishing boats, daytrip boats, caiques, swimmers, snorkelers, skiers and scuba divers. The air is busy with jet planes, helicopters, parascenders and bi-planes dragging flag-advertisements through the sky. Money is flowing, the resorts are thriving, a future is assured and there is a smile on the face of Sissi.

And so the summer passes - happy days, hot days, warm seas, blue skies music and friendship.

Calmer days arrive with the beginning of September. The blistering heat and blustery winds of August have given way to very pleasant temperatures, and my neighbours in Vrahassi are gathering their grapes to make wine. The old stone trough in my Maria's back yard is full of green and black grapes. Little black flies and wasps swarm around the ripe fruit, and I shrink back at the unhygienic conditions, telling myself that wine has been made like this for centuries. And, always ready for a new experience, I do not hesitate when Maria asks me to help with the treading of the grapes.

My shoes are off before they can say "Dionysus," and I am up the small rusty ladder and into the trough along with Manolis before I hear them cry out, 'Ochi!' I stop, oops! Mistake! I am ushered out and my feet are hosed down. Now what difference this makes I don't know, as Maria follows me into the trough in the pair of old wellies that she has been wearing all morning. Crumbling masonry and well pickled snails are trodden together with the grapes and the soft squelchy volume of mush feels like fruit-frogspawn between my toes. Once I have learned to ignore the flies, and trust to fate that the wasps will not sting me, I simply get on with the job.

A stream of ruby liquid starts to drain through a hole at one end of the trough wall. It filters through a branch of broom which has been stuck into the hole and drips onto a piece of muslin. The muslin soon disintegrates, and there are a few choice words which roughly translate as - oh dear, what a nuisance - before an old, pink plastic colander is brought from the kitchen. Bucketful by bucketful, the supposedly filtered grape juice is carried down the yard and deposited through a large tin funnel, into the side of a very antique barrel. A slop of heavy red liquid misses the funnel and swills onto the uneven stone steps, to soak away into the ground. When the barrel is full, the remaining grape mush is shovelled into a big plastic container and left to ferment for a couple of weeks before being used to make raki.

The raki-making, I have been told, is an event not to be missed, but I think I may just try to avoid it. I have seen the old still in Gregory's garden and know how potent raki can be. I go home, take a shower and head off down the mountain for another lazy day at work.

I have survived the intense heat of August, and I am enjoying Virgo sunshine and blue skies. Sanity returns. The main six weeks of summer holiday traffic is over, and things are beginning to quiet down. The great holiday soufflé has risen and is now deflating as it cools. Senior citizens replace the crazy young and all-night revelry becomes a twelve o'clock curfew. The population of the campsite has halved, restaurants and bars have less customers and I am almost redundant.

On my arrival this morning I am met by a glinting gold toothed Aleko. If I can manage to keep his hands off me for another month or so, keep the job ticking over, then the hovel in Vrahassi, hopefully, will be mine.

'Ah, *Katerina*, we have day off today,' he says. Hmm, what has he got up his sleeve now? He drives his old banger to the gate, stops it and rushes back to lock the office door.

'Get in *Katerina*, we visit friend today.' Aleko is dressed to go out; short sleeved cotton shirt instead of t-shirt and shiny, polyester trousers that look like they are the bottom half to a very old suit. At least he is not wearing his silly campsite hat. He is, however, still wearing his old flip flop sandals. Before he gets into the car he lights a big fat cigar.

'What's the occasion?' I ask, as I slide onto the shiny leather seat of the old Volvo.

'It's my friend's name day, Aristides.' That is all the information I get, so I take it as a mystery trip, not knowing where we are going, how far it is, or what to expect when we get there. '*Katerina*, I think you know my friend, Aristides.'

'No, I don't think so. Who is this Aristides? I'm sure I have never met him before. Where is he from, Aleko?' I ask.

'Do you remember the barbecue we had? Aristides was part of the company that arrived late.'

'Maybe I had left.'

'Maybe, anyway today we make fiesta at his house.'

We stop at a bakery to buy a box full of little cakes and a bottle of whisky and then turn off the main road and on to a tarmac drive that takes us up to, what I can only describe as, a palace. This huge house looms before us shouting, RICH, RICH, RICH.

'*Na*, here he is now,' says Aleko. Aristides appears through the foliage of the palace grounds to welcome us: a big, wide welcome; very open, very strong. I wish him '*Kronia Pola* – Many happy returns,' as we shake hands. Far below us I can see the coastline and the sprawling holiday resort of Hersonissos. The sea is a beautiful turquoise-blue, the sky is a perfect azure - and wine begins to flow.

Forget shepherds, forget pirates, forget Adonis and bring on Aristides. He is absolutely gorgeous: mid thirties, tall, bronzed muscles, dark, thick shoulder length hair, very intelligent looking, and very confident. His teeth are perfect, his smile... Oh, come on Kate, get it together. Why do you let men affect you like this? If this guy hasn't got a yacht, then he should have. And, he is nice. He is genuinely nice. He introduces us to the party and makes sure we get a drink. Aristides and I chat for a good ten minutes, mainly about my life on Crete. He cannot understand how I can live in Vrahassi with its reputation for crazy mountain people, falling down houses and the general uncouthness of its inhabitants. I defend the peasant farmers as being uneducated but kindly and we leave it at that. I wonder if he knows about the Mayor being put into prison.

'This is an afternoon party,' he tells me, 'because I work at night.' He can sense me wondering what he does, and puts me out of my misery. 'I am a musician,' he explains, 'I am a singer.' And then the penny drops. Of course, I have seen him before; he is a very famous singer: he is on all the big screens in the bars when they play his songs. Well, he is just as wonderful in real life as he is on the screen. My feet begin to tremble. Actually, my feet are not trembling - the floor is. The party holds its breath... it is an earthquake... Whoa, scary or what! The earth actually moved. I have to laugh at the timing of it. It is not the first quake I have felt: there have been tremors before. When the last one happened I was in bed. It was a weird sensation, like an air blast coming out of the ground. Anyway, this earth shudder sets the party talking.

Aristides passes on to other company, and I go off in search of some barbecued chicken. This is turning out to be a really fantastic day; one minute I am at work the next I am at a party. I circulate and get to talk to a man from the local radio who wants to interview me about my poems; I talk to a guy who grows carnations in big greenhouses, I talk to an archaeologist who goes along with me when I tell him that I think that the Palace at Malia was all part of the area of Milatos in antiquity, and that is why Milatos is the only name which has survived from those times. I talk with so many interesting people and when we leave I have several more addresses in my little black book, and several invites to events in the next few months.

'What a great day,' I say to Aleko, 'thanks for bringing me.' I am a teeny-weeny bit tipsy, but in a very pleasant way.

'We go straight back to Vrahassi, Kate, no working today.'

I accept the offer; it is seven already, and in any case there is nothing to do at the campsite. Before we reach the turnoff for the village Aleko pulls into the side of the road and goes for a pee in the bushes. He gets back into the car. Before starting the engine he looks at me. His hand lands on my knee. '*Katerina*, you good girl,' he digs his fingers into my thigh.

I know straight away what he wants. He is looking at me, tooth glinting, and I begin to feel revulsion. His hand creeps up my thigh.

'No, Aleko, don't spoil it.' I say, alarmed.

'Katerina, you know we make good.'

'Aleko, no,' I say again very firmly and place his hand back onto the steering wheel. Oh God, I hope I haven't blown it with the house. Surely going to bed with him cannot be a condition? I sigh with relief when he starts the engine and drives on. We part company in the centre of Vrahassi and nothing more is said. I suppose had it been the gorgeous Aristides, then I may have been tempted.

Back in the safety of my hovel I pour myself a stiff drink and retreat to the solitude of my roof terrace. God that was a different day! I make my thoughts turn as far away from Aleko as I can, and think about all the lovely people who I had met. The earthquake was a funny incident, but thinking about it seriously I begin to hope that *Stone* has not been affected in his exposed position on the cliff edge. I begin to imagine *Stone* as a lion about to leap. He is crouching, ready to spring, ready to attack. What if he wakes up and devours us all? Will *Papa* Yorgos discover the vibration of *Stone* - and what has it got to do with finding the Princess

Sisi? I muse over the possibilities with regard to *Stone* and find myself composing a verse.

LENDUS

The lion guards the gates of truth like the
Rock of Ages watching the east, for He
Knows the beast will one day come to stir his
Sleep: to shift his lien. And in the purple
Place his Queen sends messages to be felt
By symbiotic souls whose flames for his
Ideas light the way; they themselves an
Itch on the backside of a lion, but
Still an itch that proves him there, and when the
Fires, the flames, the fearsome beacon blinds the
Sight, then the golden sun, the lion, will
Consume the darkness and devour the night.

Well that has got me thinking. Is *Stone*, the lion, waiting for the return of the evil power that sent him hurtling into the abyss? Had Lendus, the Master, metamorphosed into *Stone* in order to preserve his life force? Had he been catapulted on a geyser of the earth's core into the high, airless atmosphere to plummet like a shooting star, where iron-laden, he had embedded safely into the loamy land? Had he sequestered himself from the world, torpid as rocks are, to live through the millennia until it was time? Is his Queen a High Priestess of the temple who, together with followers, kept candles burning as a medium of communication with their Master? Without the faith of followers there is no God. If no-one believes in Lendus, he will not exist. I believe in Lendus.

Does it follow then, that God can only exist if people believe in him? They do light candles and they do coexist with God. God feeds and nourishes our hungry spirits. He keeps our spirits alive. Without God man would not exist; without man, God would not exist, but if God is everything that is, then God does exist whether we believe in God or not. The question, then, is what, or who is God? And the answer - God is everything. Does it follow then, that when all humanity holds a torch for its belief in God, there will be no darkness? It is all a bit heavy, and I pour another glass of Metaxa. I am sure that everyone's idea of God is not the same. How can it be? Now, what was it that *Papa* Yorgos told to me to read? Ah yes, I remember, the teachings on the energies of God and the Divine Light, as explained by St Gregory Palamas. I wonder if this Gregory looked anything like the one I know. Come to think of it, these words could sum up my little Cretan friend very well, but we are really talking about God here. Have another drink, Kate!

> "He is both being and no-being;
> He is everywhere and nowhere;
> He has many names and he cannot be named;
> He is ever-moving and he is immovable;
> And, in a word, he is everything and nothing."

I take another gulp of my Metaxa. I am not prepared to accept the concept of God as being male; it just doesn't fit well today. I am confused. Is there an answer? If there is an answer it is only my idea of the answer, only part of the answer. Like a flea on the backside of a lion which will never be able to understand what a lion really is. I know that I'm rambling on, but my mind is all mixed up; there are so many questions inside my head. Am I ready to help *Papa* Yorgos with his experiment? Will I find the Princess Sisi? Kate, is any of this really happening?

24

It is the night of the hunter's moon. Maggie and I meet *Papa* Yorgos just before midnight at the site of his skeletal house on the edge of the cliff, overlooking Agios Nikolaos. A bonfire is burning near to *Stone,* and a small barbecue promises pork chops. We are to sit the moon through and await the dawn. Maggie tells us that this is the moon of the Virgin. It is even more wonderful than the August moon, and we can tell that it is pulling the tides of life. *Papa* Yorgos is very relaxed.

'Have you anything new, Kate?' He means dreams. I show him my poem about Lendus, and he muses on it. 'We shall see - we shall see.'

'There is just one thing *Papa* Yorgos, I still don't understand what you said about clouds bringing more than rain.'

'You will, Kate, You will.'

'Will you take the Crystal back, *Papa*?'

'Of course, Kate, it is only on loan you know.'

This is a strange night. Nobody knows what will happen at sunrise. We talk about life's journey, the people we have met, the roads we have travelled to bring us all together at this point. We talk about

Gaia, about Demeter, about Artemis about Isis, about Sophia, about the Virgin Mary, and about God. I have to wonder if Sisi is just a reflection of the truth. Is Isis, Sisi? Is Sisi, Isis? We look towards the heavens. Sirius is a giant, shining snowflake. As we gaze, a meteor shower blazes through the obsidian of night and, for the first time in my life, I see a comet trailing across the sky.

We are the power of three. Our all night vigil has brought us to daybreak. During the night, in the light of the moon we have prepared ourselves for a ceremony at sunrise. All is ready on the cliff edge. *Stone*, magnificent and sturdy as ever a war beast could be, has been surrounded by a circle of other semi-precious rocks. Amongst them is a giant amethyst geode, a smooth loaf-sized piece of lapis lazuli, and a pure white miniature Cleopatra's needle in quartz crystal. Blood red light outlines the horizon, pushing into the pewter of dawn. There is chill dew in the air. Maggie, cloaked in a Greek-island-blue kaftan, is standing behind her special rock crystal. I, in jeans and white t-shirt place my pink rose quartz on the ground. The outline of a pyramid base is formed inside the circle using large rocks from the cliff, all with holes in them. *Stone* looms up like a sinister tombstone at the apex of the pyramid.

– Wearing his black hat, black robes and a broad purple sash around his neck, Papa Yorgos steps forward carrying a parcel covered in black silk. He unveils the magnificent treasure, the Emerald Crystal, and places it in the centre of the triangle. I gaze at it, in trepidation of what it stands for, and the power that I know it contains. Is this

yet another dream? Will I wake up in my bed, safe in my Cretan hovel? It feels like a dream, but I know that is due to our meditations during the night. I am truly mesmerized by the Emerald Crystal, its beauty, its danger. I feel the weight of its influence all around me.

'It is time,' Papa Yorgos announces in a very serious ceremonial voice. The sun begins to rise over a pink expanse of Cretan Sea. We are the power of three. Papa Yorgos knows the exact pitch to start the chant and we follow his lead. Together we begin. 'Omm, Omm, Omm…' I am oblivious to all except my concentration on the sound that we are creating. I know that I must not be distracted; our unison is paramount. Unexpectedly, our note is picked up and is resounding through the air; a single, pure sound which seems to encourage us and give us energy. It is coming from four giant speakers that I now see positioned on top of the building rubble. We continue our chant, undisturbed; the music deep and resonant is affecting our minds.

Suddenly, as the sun rises in the sky, a flash of golden ray shoots through the hole at the top of Stone. It strikes the Emerald and instantly wakes up the dormant Crystal. Papa Yorgos signals to raise the pitch of our "Omm." The music from the speakers does the same. Stone begins to vibrate; it vibrates as purple, it trembles as blue, it shakes as green, it rocks as yellow, it fizzes and fuzzes from orange to a bright, glowing red until finally it blinds as a furnace of pure white-hot light. The sun's spear continues to stream through Stone's portal, penetrating the Emerald. The Emerald remains fast on the ground. It seems to be taking in the solar energy as though thirsty for light.

We three keep up our chant, accompanied by the amplified electronic note which slices the air. Papa Yorgos conducts, and we project our voices towards Stone. In our trance-state we hope to be able to communicate with the spirit within our carbuncled friend. We are blinded by the intense whiteness, and in the darkness we hold a round of 'Omm.' What pitch we have reached; I don't know, but it is a natural, unstrained tone which begins to make my head empty of everything but sound. We are the power of three but we are one. We hold fast our position until we know instinctively that it is time to step inside the circle. The rod of sunlight breaks as the sun rises above the portal. We join hands, the Emerald Crystal in the middle of us, and we feel its power: we feel the halo of light that is engulfing us. We are held in a force-field of song. There is music of angels, music of the rainbow: a polyphonic anthem of perfect pitch, unearthly pure, melodic and harmonic together, piano and fortissimo, there is no distinction between a single note and a symphony. It is impossible to know what is making the sound. It is infinitely intense. The sound is in our blood, it is in our bones, it is part of our skin, and we are all part of each other.

Then, the voices come. They are on the music; in the music. They are in the blue space between the blue sky and the blue sea and the blue that is in my head.

• •

'I AM THE ROCK OF AGES. I AM THE SOUL THAT YOU BELIEVE IN. I AM HE THAT BRINGS YOU TO MY SIDE. MY WORK HERE IS DONE.

I HAVE GUARDED THE SOUL OF SISI AND NOW I GIVE TO RHAMU-TSUNA HIS BRIDE. I, LENDUS, THANK YOU.'

'I AM THE ONE WHO HAS GRIEVED FOR A LOST LOVE. I GRIEVE NO MORE. I, RHAMU-TSUNA, THANK YOU.'

'I AM SHE WHO WAS LOST AND IS FOUND. I, THE SPIRIT OF SISI, THANK YOU.'

With one clicking sound and a sweeping "whoosh" through our minds, our eyes open.

The sun is well above the horizon already heating up the air. We are still holding our circle. The Emerald is still pulsating slightly at our feet. We look, one to the other, and are filled with overflowing emotion. Tears flow down our cheeks in uncontrollable reaction, and our bodies shake at what we have just witnessed. It is over, but we do not move; we are rooted. We breathe, breathe - breathe Kate, it is over. The music is silent.

But it is not over. The sky begins to darken; a cold wind begins to shriek from the sea and a tempest battle-blast ruptures the nebulous depression. Amid the thunder and lightning Papa Yorgos shouts, 'HOLD FAST... HOLD FAST.' But we cannot hold the circle and we are ripped apart by cruel wind-shrikes that beat down on us. Vitreous claws rip Papa Yorgos' black tunic as he tries to beat them off, vile iridescent storm-claws that flail viciously. I reach for a piece of olive wood and fling it desperately towards the unearthly foe. 'Rhamu,' I shout, 'If you are still there, help us – for God's sake help us.' I hear Maggie call out: 'Rhamu, if ye hear me, we need ye to save us all.' We are in the darkness of cloud that is gathering above us, menacing, threatening. Then, out of the cloud booms a voice, a voice so terrible that it shakes the ground beneath us.

'I AM SHE OF THE GREEN FACE. I AM SHE OF THE SNAKE. I AM SHE OF THE WILD CREATURES. I AM SHE OF THE THUNDERBOLT AND LIGHTNING. I AM SHE OF THE HUNT AND BATTLE. I AM SHE OF THE MOON.'

• •

It is Artemis, the dark side of light. The Crystal is still holding the black power; this is the Queen of Hades. My ears begin to hurt, my flesh is scorching and blackness begins to engulf my consciousness. Then heaven's water soaks the earth and brings me face down in the mud of the building site. I am rigid with a fear so terrifying, so sickening, so bowel-curdling that all I can do is embrace the clods of slip: even the earth is shaking with fear. My head is bursting with decibels that are so discordant that bile empties from my gut. I can smell cordite, gunpowder, sulphur – the putridness of hell. I feel myself writhe on my belly towards Papa Yorgos and Maggie in an attempt to join hands with them. They crawl towards me held back by the eye of the storm and the unremitting siren. Out of our minds with the sound, we hold our ears. The pain is killing me. I taste blood in my mouth. I can smell blood. I am looking at the face of death and I refuse to let it take me. In the torment of the moment, in the thrashing ice-biting tornado that is swirling about us, in the furious desperation of our plight, Papa Yorgos screams out: 'HOLY MOTHER, MARY, HAVE MERCY ON US.'

And the silence is instant.

Like a red hot javelin out of the furnace of Hephaestus, comes one single, searing, slicing blade of light that strikes the Emerald Crystal and turns it into a living aureole of silver and gold. The rain stops. The thunder clouds vanish. The enemy has left the battleground, and we breathe in life, as the sun climbs higher in the sky.

We circle the Emerald, gripping each other hysterically, not knowing whether our tears are of sadness or bliss, and the ketheric light that surrounds us is the light of Angels. The moment is brief and ecstatic. I am in this instant, pure spirit, experiencing pure love.

As the tingling vibration of my physical self gathers together, I hug Papa Yorgos and Maggie, reeling into the consciousness of my mind. We are still the Power of Three. But we are more than the Power of Three.

Adonis, who could not reach us until now, rushes up to help us. With him is his musical partner. They were the ones responsible for the speakers. They were the ones responsible for the amplification of our sound. And, looking more closely, I recognize the tall, dark, swarthy Cretan who begins to wrap a blanket tightly around me. He holds me together as my legs begin to give way. It is Aristides, the musician. He is in my dream.-

As Aristides carries me to safety, I see Adonis helping his father to get away from the scene. Maggie, meanwhile, in her voluminous attire, is standing on the cliff edge, arms outstretched to the rising sun and I hear her give thanks for the day. As I gaze into the smoky-brown eyes of the person who is comforting me, I see, for a split second, the reflection of a white steed, and hear its soft whinny.

Our little company stands, huddled together away from the cliff edge but on a small mount overlooking the sea. Conversation is out of place. We are each in our own heads, shocked, weakened by the long night; but eyes wide open. The storm has gone; the water is calm. Then, without warning, faint ripples appear on the surface of the sea and to our surprise, two dolphins leap, as if through a window of expanding time. Droplets of coloured water, like a bride's veil of miniature rainbows, cascade into the sea. The water glistens on their arched bodies like a thousand diamantes; a diaphanous curtain of liquid jewels. Time and time again they circle and leap and dive and dart, like acrobats full of joy and new life. Together they move as one through the fluidity of their world, and together they surface and call out, in the reality of ours. And, watching them, I know that the spirit of Rhamu-Tsuna has found the reincarnation of his princess. I know that he will take her, and cherish her, and love her. I know that they will be as one with the sun for as long as light sparkles, and that all our lives are bound in the memory of a fragile star.

25

Aristides and I have become very good friends. We have so much in common. Music, poetry, the love of the theatre, the writings of Nikos Kazantzakis, philosophical conversations, sailing, yes, sailing; it is a new one for me but Aristides has in fact got a boat, and he is teaching me how to sail. There is a whole new intellectual world outside Vrahassi, and I feel that where I was before was some other place, a place in the shadows. I no longer grieve my losses, but live with a lightness of spirit and a smile for everyone and everything. I feel reborn, and want to make the best, of this second chance. Of course, I am still in touch with Suzy, but gone are our mad outings since she moved back to England to nurse her old mum. Maggie unfortunately does not want to continue our friendship, she has told me that her purpose in my life is over and wants me to stay away from her. The loss of Maggie's friendship is difficult to accept, but I do accept it because I know that some people are meant to appear in your life for a short time and then move on. It was like that with me and Maggie. The Amazon, Kelly, has got together with Fuckin' Pete who is not the easiest of partners, but at least young Baz has a father figure. And *Papa* Yorgos, well, he is taking a rest somewhere quiet, no doubt somewhere mountainous, together with the sweet Adonis, who has decided to learn a little more of his father's teachings.

Since my experience on the night of the hunter's moon, when a large earthquake shook all the foundations of Agios Nikolaos and the whole area was engulfed in the eye of a tremendous storm, I have changed. Our meditation that night has made me truly wonder whether I am really in Crete or not. Somebody once said: "If it seems too good to be true, then it probably is." Maybe all of it, the whole thing, life, is just a dream. Am I the Kate that I think I am? Am I the Kate that you think I am? Are you in my dream? Am I in yours? Think very carefully Kate, what happens next may depend on it.

Today, I am sitting on my roof in the October sunshine, thinking about the future. Well - visualizing the future really. Very soon this wonderful roof will be mine, and I will have earned my home.

'*Yasou* Katy, I bring visitor.'

'Is that you Manolis?' I peer over the edge into the street, not believing my eyes. God! It's my Daddy! It's my Daddy at my gate. It's my Daddy at my gate in Vrahassi. I am rushing to open the gate. I throw my arms around him, and he squeezes me so tight that I can hardly breathe. 'Oh, Daddy, come in, come in, why didn't you let me know you were coming?' He can't speak, we are both crying - crying with the happiness of the moment. We just hold each other, kiss each other, and hold hands and dance around each other with the joy of being together again.

'OK, OK, - sit down, where are your bags? How long are you staying? Are you hungry? You must be hungry. A drink, a drink, I'll get us a drink. It should be champagne Daddy but is a beer all right?' My Daddy can't get a word in, but eventually I calm down and let him speak.

'I had to come and see what my little girl was up to in her wonderful Vrahassi. Your letters intrigued me Kate, and worried me a little, so I parked up the motor and got on a plane. It is some hideaway you have found yourself.'

'Look beyond the hovel, Daddy. Let's go and eat at the taverna in the square, you must be hungry.'

'It sounds good to me, and then I can tell you all about my adventures and maybe surprise you a little.'

'Surprise me Daddy; I think you will find that very little surprises me any more.' I say cynically.

This is a very strange moment, me in Vrahassi, my home of almost a year, with drinking partners all around me, with male admirers hovering, with all those neighbours who have seen me distressed, or else drunk, or else sick, or else deliriously happy, suddenly appearing with My Daddy. I get the introductions out of the way, and a table is prepared. It is not a table for two; it is a table for twenty two. It seems like everyone wants to join in the happiness of father and daughter being reunited. The age old custom of Cretan hospitality is thrust upon us, and a feast appears. Together with the feast comes, first Gregory, who inundates my Daddy with questions, none of which he can understand. Then

Manolis Taxi tries to interpret, without much success. In the end we just give up to the wine, and the music, and the wonderful company.

'Come on then, Daddy, what is the surprise you have for me?' I cajole. I link my arm into his like when I was a little girl and wanted something.

'Oh, I don't know whether this is the right time,' he says, teasing me.

'Of course it is Daddy. Please, please,' I urge.

'Then I have an announcement to make,' my Daddy says, ringing his glass with a spoon. Whatever is he going to say? I wonder, as he moves his chair back from the table. He slowly reaches into his jacket pocket, keeping up the suspense before producing, like a white rabbit out of a top hat, a small brown paper parcel.

'This, my very clever daughter, belongs to you,' he says, handing me the parcel and telling me to open it. I rip the paper from the back of what is obviously a new book. I dare not look, but instantly see the title. My first instinct is to kiss the cover. Holding it up for all to see, like a newly baptized child:

'It's my book,' I say quietly, almost unbelieving. 'It's the book that I have been writing,' I read the title, '"Tears from the Sun" - it is my book.' They are my tears.

Gregory's grubby hand is the first to take mine, 'Bravo,' he says, and the "bravo" echoes all around the room. My Daddy has certainly *surprised* me.

'A publisher friend of mine did a quick mock up for me to bring you, as a present. He says that he wants it in the bookshops for the spring, so I think you have another mission Kate. Now you have to go through the whole thing very carefully and make sure there are no mistakes.'

I can't believe that my work is going to be published, but here it is, in my hand. My head feels like it wants to blow a gasket, and I throw my arms around my Daddy, around Gregory, and around all his mates in a great sharing of the moment. Hearing the commotion, a group of black shirted shepherds strut into the taverna. As soon as he sees us, Manolis Shepherd, tall and proud, pushes his way to be near me, and holds a firm hand out to my Daddy. I know it is recognition of our friendship. More drinks land on the table. My Daddy could not have had a finer welcome to Vrahassi.

• •

Why is it that extreme happiness should be so cruelly balanced? Circumstances once again alter the direction of my life. All the joy of last night is sucked down the drain with yet more tears. This morning, early, before I have chance to be late for work, the gold-toothed Aleko arrives at my gate. He barely acknowledges my Daddy; he is so wrapped up in his own situation.

'Ah, *Katerina*,' he starts. 'I am so s-sorry,' he stutters.

'Sorry Aleko? Sorry for what?' For one moment I think that the world is about to end, he looks so glum.

'How to tell you, *Katerina*,' he goes on, the worry of the world on his sloping shoulders. 'It is time to pay, and I am not a rich man.' He takes hold of my hands, but cannot look me in the eye as he says:

'I... my... debts, *Katerina*... I have had to sell this house to pay my debts.'

I am silent for a moment, while his words sink in. Then I start to think how I have worked all those hot days for nothing. And then I begin to feel angry. The anger rises from deep down inside me. I swallow it at first, but it regurgitates and spews out all over Aleko.

'You lied to me, you bastard, you lied to me. You had me working for you for nothing. You fucking cunning bastard. All those false promises, and now you come and say you have no money. Well neither do I. Get out, you can have your crumbling hovel. You can have your old rusty doors.' I pick up the nearest thing to hand, one of my stones the size of a brown loaf, and hurl it at the kitchen window. 'And you can have it just the way I took it. THE HOUSE OF LEEKOS,' I scream in unison with the smashing glass, and at the top of my voice I yell, 'I know exactly what that means, and why Manolis smiled when he first brought me here. Leekos! WOLF! Get out!'

Daddy steps in to stop me wrecking anything else; Aleko steps out fearful that I will hit him.

'Stay, stay one month is OK,' he hastily adds and makes off down the street.

The promise of making the house over to me in exchange for work has come to nothing. Aleko has probably lost it in a game of cards. I look at Daddy and burst into tears. 'Oh, what the hell, Daddy, is this house that important?' As if to answer, a chunk of dusty masonry becomes dislodged and falls to the floor. Right at this moment my Daddy is more precious to me than anything in the world, and I let my tears turn to laughter - my hysterical moment is over. 'Oh, Daddy, I love you.' His hug grounds me, but underneath I am so very disappointed.

And that is when the aftershock of a bad morning brings my world crumbling down. It comes with my second visitor, the postman - a letter. I tear it open eagerly, but as soon as I begin to read I feel a sickness tighten my stomach. There is lightness in my head, and I have to sit down.

'Oh! No! No! I say, reading on in disbelief. 'It's horrible.' I don't want to see the words in front of me.

'What is it Kate?' Daddy looks on, unable to help my emotion, as the tears just pour from me.

'Two of my best friends have been killed in a car crash.'

The letter is from Smee, who informs me that both *Papa* Yorgos and Adonis have been killed in a car accident while travelling home from Mount Athos. Obviously they had been there to return the Emerald Crystal. The scars on my heart burst open. The only consolation is that my Daddy is here to hold me close.

'Oh Kate, my little girl, what tragedy life has thrown at you.' His shoulder is so good and firm and familiar. It soaks up my sadness and eases my hurt.

· ·

Lefteris – Smee, my pirate, is hardly recognizable in the line up of relatives outside the church of the Virgin Mary in Agios Nikolaos, which is swamped with a crowd of thousands. The queue to file past the stony bodies of *Papa* Yorgos and his son Adonis seems endless. I have shuffled slowly forwards for two hours to reach the sweet scented rose-petalled coffins, and as I kiss first one waxy forehead, then the other, I think of our secret, and promise to keep it. With me is Aristides, we are both aware that we could be in extreme danger if our connection with the Emerald Crystal is ever known. He squeezes my hand in support. I offer my condolences to Lefteris, and he kisses me on both cheeks. He is very solemn, very proud, and I pass on, knowing that we have both lost people very dear to us; knowing that we shared something very special, and knowing that there will always be closeness between us. There is no sign of Kalliope. Aristides gets me away from the scene as quickly as possible. We do not follow the procession to the graveyard; we go to a little bar on the harbour, drink cognac and toast our dear departed friends.

'To *Papa* Yorgos, my teacher, and to Adonis my friend; may you now know more of the secrets of the universe, and may your vibrations forever make it a better place.' Aristides' voice is shaky as he says the words, and his eyes are full of tears. We clink glasses and sit in silence, watching feather-shaped reflections of light dance over the Mediterranean. I have to accept that this is the way of the world. Pain and Sorrow; Joy and Love, there is always a balance.

26

I have decided to go back to England.

Saying goodbye to all my friends is not at all easy, but I do it, and I am ready to leave. Vrahassi is just the same as it was when I arrived almost a year ago, except for the rain. There is no rain today. The sun is shining, the air is still, and I am on my roof for the last time, looking across at the mountains, feeling the soft wind on my face, smelling the wild sage and the olive trees. Daddy is back in England and is waiting for me, to help me promote my book and settle into another new life. My shepherd is on his mountain, happy with his sheep. I blow him a kiss and say, 'Goodbye'. I say goodbye to my Cretan hovel. It was a temporary refuge, which, in a way, is best left behind in my memory, together with all that has happened during my stay in Vrahassi. I say goodbye to Maria - happy with her family around her. I say goodbye to the street. And, before I get into my taxi, I call at the *kafeneo* and I say goodbye to Gregory. Somehow, his farmer's finger nails have little significance today. We hug each other tightly - an unspoken love between us - people of different worlds.

'Come on then Manolis, let's go.' I say, to the gentle Cretan who has been my guardian.

'Stay Kate, I look after you.'

'No Manolis, I have someone to look after me,' I say, rolling the gold band on my left hand - part of me for so many years. My breath catches familiar remembrances of Jack, as I get into the taxi, smiling. Thank you, Vrahassi.

• •

It is a bright October evening, the light is slowly fizzling into dusk, and the sea has lost its blue to become that *wine dark* Homeric mass that is not to be trusted. The ferryboat *Festos* sways on the swell as though in time with the bows of a slow orchestral movement. Bouzoukis dither a soft *rembetiko* as I make my way up to the top deck from where I can see the lights of Heraklion begin to decorate the night sky. One last wave goodbye to my Knight, Aristides, who blows me a soft kiss, that I know, will follow me to England. I look to the moon, and tears begin to trickle down my cool cheeks. Breathe, Kate. I am not crying because I am leaving Crete. I am not crying for the friends that I am leaving behind. I am not crying for sorrow or grief. I am truly happy. I have found an inner peace that is working its way to the outer edge of my skin, like rays of white heat escaping from the sun. No, the tears that are streaming down my face as we slowly glide out of Heraklion harbour on the night tide are not the sad tears that I arrived with, they are not a mood of the moon; they have come from somewhere else, somewhere bright, somewhere very beautiful. I am sharing my tears today with two very special people, and I know they will always be close to me, Rhamu and Sisi, whose broken hearts helped to mend mine. Yes, these tears are warm tears: they are tears of knowledge, tears of wisdom.

- I am swimming beneath the ocean, as free as a dolphin, with a dolphin. I streak and turn and leap through the warm mosaic of a sun-flecked sea. All is blue and green and red and violet. I am kissed with gold and knighted with silver. Water flushes through my naked body and washes over my silky-sleek skin. I am aware only that I am aware. The yellow orb brings me to the shallows of aquamarine where I ride a turtle beneath the translucent pool of a shell-sandy bay. I bask in a halo of pure light: a phosphorescent fairy atop the rock of Amphitrite.-

There was never a time past that I did not exist, and there will never be a time future when I shall cease to be, for within me is the reality of my wonderful journey.

Notes:

Sissi was once a small fishing village but it is now a delightful holiday resort situated on the North coast of Crete, just east of Malia.

Knossos was once the nerve centre of Minoan Crete. The archaeological site of Knossos can be found just south of Heraklion.

The Monastery of Mount Athos is the Spiritual Centre of Orthodox Christian Monasticism. It is a treasury in which many artifacts of religious value are housed, and is situated on the peninsular of Halkidiki.

• •

About the Author

Jane Sharp was born a long time ago in Yorkshire. She lives in the Cretan village of Vrahassi together with her husband David, dog Zouki and all her neighbours. Her award winning poems have been published both in Crete and in England.